EVERYDAY GODS

DMS Lewis was born in Ayrshire in 1970 and now lives the life of an international electric gypsy. He has contributed to several anthologies of poetry and short stories including *When the Snow Falls, Autumn Leafs* and *New Scottish Writers*, and in 2005 was the winner of the LYM Scottish Poetry Award. Everyday Gods is his first novel.

BY THE SAME AUTHOR
Short Stories
Words of Wisdom and Other Tales

Poetry
Three Steps Along the Forgotten Path
One Hundred Haiku
Contact DMS Lewis: everydaygods@hotmail.co.uk

EVERYDAY GODS

D.M.S. LEWIS

AN ELECTRIC LOBSTER BOOK

First published in Great Britain
By LULU Publishing Ltd in 2010
First Edition 2010
ISBN 978-0-9559870-1-4
Copyright © DMS Lewis 2010

Printed and bound in Great Britain by
Lulu Press UK Ltd
26-28 Hammersmith Grove
London W6 7BA

For Kyle

Book 1

Prologue

Turn your face to heaven. Strain upwards, ever upwards trying hard to touch the moon and you are there. Then further beyond, leave the sun behind you gliding in the blackness of space towards distant galaxies. Look below now, far down below.

Come with me and fly with gossamer wings over dappled green-brown hills, winding blue rivers, low through valleys, high amongst stratus clouds. We skim across the great expanse of the loch, its' surface reflecting the dense pine forests and cruel November skies; until...

Stop!

On a bench over-looking the vast waters of Loch Lomond, sit two men. On the right, middle aged, unkempt, roughly dressed, sporting dark sunglasses and a white cane. A blind man? Seems a safe assumption. On the left, a much younger man; trendy, clean, smart, well groomed.

Look closer. Sorrowful expressions possessing their faces. Who are these men? Why are they here? Closer still. A tear falls from the blind man's eyes. He removes the dark glasses to wipe away his grief with the edge of a half-gloved hand. Quickly now...inside before he blinks...

Wherever I Lay My Hat

Jacob shuddered as he gave the receptionist his name; the last time he had been in a hospital he was having his hand stitched back together after a drunken accident. He hated hospitals at the best of times, but on a Friday night it was like world-war-three. The receptionist asked him politely to have a seat and someone would be along shortly to *'take him down'*. The waiting room was filled with what looked like the cast of a zombie movie, the odour of stale alcohol mixing with the warm aroma of piss and blood. Jacob decided against joining the walking – or rather the 'seated' wounded, and resigned himself to slumping on his left shoulder against the wall. He noticed an injured drunk, a blood stained bandage covering his right eye, smiling at him from the third row, and decided to take evasive action in case he attempted to instigate a verbal exchange. Jacob turned to face reception trying hard to melt into the wall. Behind him he heard the distinctive rumble and scrape of someone rising from their chair. This was swiftly followed by a shuffling of feet; whoever it was they were coming his way. Jacob pictured the drunk staggering towards him all broken smiles and toxic breath. Panic set in as the shuffling drew closer; there was nowhere to run to, his eyes darting frantically around looking for an escape route, all the while trying to keep his head still and forward, afraid of contact. Where the fuck were the toilets? The drinks machine? The hairs prickled on the back of Jacob's neck, there was someone standing right behind him now, he could hear them breathing. Jacob stared hard at the floor, sweat beginning to drip down his back.

'Mr Douglas?' A female voice, well spoken, English. He looked up to see a young black doctor addressing him, a look of professional sympathy on her face.

'Yes, that's me. Is it time Doctor?' Jacob answered apprehensively. The young Doctor replied with a nod and placed an affirming hand on his shoulder. 'We have your father ready Mr Douglas. If you would like to follow me please.' And with that she led him off down another neon-filled white corridor. Jacob followed the doctor into a small office. She asked him to take a seat.

'Mr Douglas, I know this must be a very distressing time for you and we will try and make this as easy as we possibly can. Now then, there are two ways we can do this, let me tell you what they are: Number one, behind you mounted on the wall is a monitor...'

Jacob twisted his body round in the seat; there was a small television attached half-way up the wall by a bracket. He turned back to face the doctor as she continued, '...there is a closed-circuit camera located in the room where your father is. Most people prefer this method, less...'

'Distressing?' interjected Jacob. The doctor shot him an austere glance.

'Quite, Mr Douglas; now... where was I? Ah yes, number two. So number two involves, as you might expect, viewing the body... excuse me... your father, 'in person' so to speak.' The doctor was obviously flustered and embarrassed by her *faux pas,* Jacob smiled to himself and spoke; there was no hesitation in his voice.

'I'd like to go and be with my dad please doctor.' The doctor called for a nurse who escorted Jacob to the room directly next door. The curtains around the bed were closed and the lights suitable low. An unusual quietness filled the room that made Jacob wonder if perhaps some sort of special soundproofing material had been built into the walls to contain the wails of the recently bereaved. Jacob heard the door of the room open and felt a hand squeeze gently on his upper arm The Doctor asked in a quiet voice if he was 'ready'; Jacob looked her in the eyes and lied silently with a nod of his head, then the doctor gestured for the nurse to pull back the curtains.

Jacob felt more surprised than shocked. It did not look like the man who used to take him and his brother fishing, the man who had taught him how to swim, how to ride a bike. His father looked like a waxy, grey caricature of himself. There was a suggestion of the person who used to be inside, but death had given his father a strange makeover and Jacob just could not work out what it was that made this face he knew so well, so different. He stared perplexed for a few minutes before it hit him with an uncontrollable smile; he looked… contented! In all the thirty-nine years that Jacob had shared this green earth with his father this was the first time he had seen him look truly happy. Jacob turned to the doctor.

'That look on his face, is that something that the medical staff do to soften the blow doctor?' 'Not at all Mr Douglas, this is exactly how your father looked when he arrived here at the hospital. In fact the paramedics who brought him in said when they got to the scene he had a huge smile on his face.' Jacob's gaze drifted back down to the bed.

'Where did he…I mean, where was he found?' A controlled eagerness infused the doctor's face. 'Well that is rather an interesting story Mr Douglas. According to the paramedics your father was actually found sitting at a bus stop staring at the sky, his arms outstretched, with, as one of the paramedics described it, *a smile on his face like he had just won the lottery*. A woman, who caught the bus into town from across the street, had noticed your father sitting like that around ten in the morning. She thought it was quite odd behaviour, but ignored it because *there are a lot of odd people around aren't there?* Her words Mr Douglas, not mine, I hasten to add. The lady in question returned from her shopping trip some three hours later, getting off at the stop she had saw your father at earlier in the day, and he was still sitting there in that same position. Thinking that there was something seriously wrong the lady went over to investigate and raised the alarm. Unfortunately though by the time the ambulance arrived on the scene your father had already been dead for several hours.' The thought of his father sitting dead at that bus stop annoying passers by and scaring the wits out of old women made Jacob smile.

'What's really strange about this whole situation doctor is that I cannot for the life of me remember my father ever setting foot on a bus, he hated public transport, even trains! So what was it that… I mean… the cause of death?' The doctor shuffled through some notes she was carrying,

'Everything points to acute coronary artery atheroma.' Jacob frowned.

'I do apologise Mr Douglas, it's been a long day. It would appear that your father died from a massive heart attack.'

'But you're not sure though?'

'As I said, medically, all the signs point to that conclusion and given your father's personal history, heavy drinker, smoker… he had already had a couple of minor attacks and there is also a history of heart disease in your family. Of course we will never know conclusively unless a post-mortem examination is performed, but that is normally only carried out if there are suspicious circumstances surrounding the death. As the attending physician I am satisfied that there are no such circumstances in the case of your father. However, if you are not satisfied, it is your right to request a post-mortem examination.' Jacob thought of his father lying on a metal bench being butchered.

'No doctor, he's dead now so what does it matter. Just let him be.' The doctor scribbled something in her notes.

'Okay Mr Douglas, I shall go and prepare the death certificate. Would you like to stay with him for a little longer?' Jacob nodded and pulled a chair up to the side of the bed. 'Your father's clothes and personal effects are in the locker beside the bed there, if you could please take them with you when you leave. Things have a habit of walking off here if you leave them in one place too long. I'll leave the completed certificate at reception for you to collect Mr Douglas. Take as long as you like though, there is no rush.'

Jacob turned to thank the doctor but the door was already closing slowly in her wake. He leaned and opened the bed-side locker, took out two bags, the first one large, PATIENT CLOTHING in red letters emblazoned on the front, constructed of too-thin plastic which pitted and burst under the pressure of finger tips; the second bag, small, made of brown paper, unmarked. He placed the oversize bag on the floor by his chair then emptied the contents of the smaller bag out onto the bed by his father's left hand.

'So is this what it all boils down to then dad? A gold watch, a wedding ring, a wallet, sixty-seven pence in loose change, twenty Benson and Hedges and a silver Zippo? Is this all that's left of the man you were?' Something moved on the bed causing Jacob to start and quickly look up. 'Dad?' His father gave a long, slow melodious fart. It startled Jacob for a moment, causing him to stand up. He thought about buzzing the nurse, but remembered reading about this somewhere, how the body expelled the various gases produced by the progression of decomposition. It was all just part of the process of death. There were even accounts of corpses sitting up and farting as their tendons and ligaments contracted. 'Always have to have the last word don't you?' Jacob picked up the wallet and unclipped it. There were three twenty-pound notes and a five inside.

He pulled out the driving licence, his father looking his normal grumpy self on the face of it. 'Now that's what I remember you looking like.' Jacob said turning the licence toward his father. He quickly flicked through the various credit, bank and business cards whilst thinking of the one lonely cash-point card in his own wallet. In a zipped pocket he found three photographs and a folded up piece of note-paper; one of the photos was of Jacob and younger brother Simon, on either side of their mother. Jacob reckoned he would be about five or six when that picture was taken, which would make Simon three or four years old. It had been taken in front of a small whitewashed cottage they had stayed in during one of the family holidays 'up north'. They all looked so happy, the sun on their faces eyes bright with the future. Jacob flipped the photo over; scribbled on the back in his father's own unmistakable and forbidding hand, it read, "Rosemary and the boys, summer 1974." He slid the photograph into the breast pocket of his shirt, exposing the next picture, an ancient black and white photograph of his mother as a very elegant young woman. She was wearing a chic satin dress with a daring cleavage-revealing neckline and slightly flared skirt, her hair, shiny and black, tied up in the style of the time. His mother's eyes were dark and beautiful, full of expectation, her whole life ahead of her with the man she loved. Jacob felt a twist of surrogate regret and quickly moved the picture underneath.

The third and final photograph faded almost sepia and frayed at the edges. It showed a younger version of his father beside a very pretty, fresh-faced young woman standing in front of what looked like an oak tree. The girl could have been anything from sixteen to twenty years of age, Jacob didn't recognise her. 'Who's the young lady then old man?' He studied the photograph. 'Who are you pretty girl... a relative... an old friend? Maybe simply a pretty face dad met and wanted to remember?' He turned the picture over; there was some faded writing on the back... a date. Jacob squinted hard to make out the inscription.

'By the old tree (1969) remember? S x.'

'So you definitely knew her then old man... but 1969? You were a *happily* married man by then; but, then again that never stopped you, did it ...' Jacob studied his dead father's face; that expression, like he was saying *wouldn't you like to know! 1969?*' Jacob did some quick mental arithmetic. 'You'd be about thirty-four or thirty-five in 1969... she looks a bit young for you though?' Jacob had witnessed the explosions between his parents through the years, detonated by the continual infidelities of his father. The aftermath had never been pretty. He had lost count of the number of times during his childhood that his father had been forced to sleep in the office until the emotional fallout had cleared. His mother had always relented and taken her husband back and Jacob had never understood why. If that was love then he would never understand it. His mother's devotion to the preservation of the institution of marriage had shattered her nerves and resulted in several hospitalisations, but every time she returned to the matrimonial household to continue her obsession. It was no surprise given her delicate disposition and her psychological fragility that his mother was the first to go. However, it was still a shock when he answered the telephone on that September morning to be told by his dad that mum had *'jumped the queue'*. The photograph in hand came to his attention once again, and another revelation struck; what if she was an illegitimate daughter? His father would have been really young when she was born, but it wasn't totally impossible. Some more mental arithmetic followed. 'Yep it's possible… if she was around sixteen or seventeen. So I might have a half-sister you old rogue?' Jacob considered the tattered photograph again; her laughing eyes, the half-smile. 'But only you can tell me *S*. I wonder where you are right now?'

Jacob's father's tattered bunnet tumbled out and onto the polished white floor. Brown and grey chequered on top with a dark green band, his dad had had owned it for as long as Jacob could remember and made many cameo appearances in shared memories. Jacob bent down and lifted it to his face; it smelled just like him, tobacco, brylcream and hard work. Jacob was momentarily transported back to his childhood, sitting by the fire at his father's feet, just after work… just before dinner. His dad would smoke a cigarette then fall asleep in his armchair with Jacob curled up on the floor underneath his legs, safe and warm.

The folded piece of notepaper revealed itself in Jacob's palm. He had completely forgotten about it in his reverie. It unfolded into what looked like a letter, again in his father's handwriting, but addressed to his mother. Jacob thought about folding it back up, considering it perhaps too personal to disturb, like exhuming a long dead relative. However, his eyes had already begun to read and Jacob was powerless to resist.

My Dearest Rose,

The leaves on the trees are gold and red and a million other colours besides outside. This was always your favourite time of year my darling, and yesterday would have been our wedding anniversary. I thought about you all day. I miss you so much it hurts and I don't think that this pain will ever go away? I dreamed about you again last night. But, again when I woke up it was just me alone in our bed. I am doing all right though, I'm keeping myself fed and watered and clean and tidy. You would be proud of me Rose. I am not as angry as I used to be. Your picture still has pride of place on the mantle piece in the living room. I miss you. I want you to know that I am sorry if I ever hurt you, and that you were always my best friend. Remember that last day in the hospital, when I told you that you could go that I wasn't scared of being alone anymore? I know you knew I was lying. I just can't believe how much I miss you.

Yours Forever

Adam

The asphyxiation of grief and regret closed around Jacob like a cold, wet blanket. He wiped away the blinding tears and staggered towards the door.

*

The middle of the day is always a strange time to enter the Dolphin Bar. The sunlight, what there is of it on any particular Partick afternoon, is diffused through its' coloured windows, illuminating the pub's interior and the patrons therein a soft blue-green. Unusual, but not unpleasant, considered Jacob; a bit like having a dram in an aquarium. Jacob was transported back to a theory of colour lecture at art school that talked about the varying sensitivity of different receptor cells, or cones, in the retina to different wavelengths of light. Red cones perceive greenish yellow light whereas green cones are most sensitive to green light. He wondered if anyone else in the room had ever considered this information?

The Dolphin had been the closest his dad had come to a local pub. A place where he was always known as '*big man*' rather than the boss; just another punter. He always seemed to be well enough liked by everyone, just didn't frequent the place often enough to be considered '*one of the boys*'.

Jacob scanned the room for familiar faces as he made his way to the bar, noticing for the first time since he had walked out of the hospital that he still had his dad's bunnet firmly in his hand.

'Pint of lager please.'

The barmaid nodded acquiescence and began to pour. Keeping one hand on the bar as an anchor Jacob turned and again surveyed the faces. An intense four-way game was in full flight at the domino table, the clack of the tiles splitting the general hubbub of the bar. One member of the quartet paused momentarily and lifted his gaze towards Jacob. Recognition sparked between the two and had Jacob frantically searching his memory bank of mug shots.

Sandy McCully used to be the foreman at the Partick factory back in the 1980's. A nice big fella, as far as Jacob could remember. He waved his free hand, still clutching the bunnet.

'Ah, wee Jakey!

Bellowed Sandy across the bar. 'I thought it wiz you! C'mon ower and join us.'

Jacob nodded a little too enthusiastically in reply.

'Two-eighty-five pal.' The barmaid cut in with her treacle tones. Jacob fished a battered fiver from his trouser pocket and handed it over. He pocketed the change unconsciously and took a sip of his pint to avoid spillage on his commute to the domino table.

'Hi... Sandy?'

'Aye son, it's me alright. Still the same big eejit! Sit doon son, join the body eh the kirk.' Sandy patted the empty square of bench next to him. 'Is it right enough about yir faither Jake?' Jacob swallowed hard.

'Aye Sandy. I was just up at the hospital, seeing him like. You know, identifying the bod… I mean my dad.'

'That's a sair yin son. Glad ah didny huv tae dae that for ma ain faither. Wid've took a wee while right enough though, seeing he wiz blaun tae bits et the Ardeer munitions factory! Mind you, I wiz aye gid et jigsaws whin ah wiz a boy!' Sandy let out a huge guffaw and slapped Jacob on the back. A stinging impression remained long after Sandy's large red work-hardened paw had retreated to the table and surrounded his half-full pint of the black stuff.

'Aye good one Sandy.'

'Well, ye've got tae huv a laugh son. Whit's the alternative? And I'm sure it's whit yer faither wid prefer us tae dae, he liked a gid laugh yer auld man. And he liked the the wimmen as well. Shag a fag-burn in a fur coat that yin! Nae offence son.' Jacob felt as though Sandy had just punched him in the stomach.

'None taken Sandy. I think we all knew what he was like.'

'Aye but your mother wiz always special tae um though Jake. Ah know that might sound a bit daft son, but yir faither wid nivir hear a bad word said against her. He gubbed mair than wan boy ower that yin.' Jacob though of his mother's face smiling but unable to mask the sadness in her eyes. She had known all about the affairs but had held it together for the sake of her boys.

A strong rhythmic vibration around the top of his right leg made Jacob jump. He pulled the ringing mobile phone from his trouser pocket. Unknown caller. Jacob thought about rejecting the call but decided it better to answer in case it was something to do with his dad.

'I'd better take this Sandy.' Said Jacob standing and making for the door.

'Aye, nae problem son, you take your time.'

As he emerged into the blinding afternoon sun, Jacob pressed the green button.

'Hello?'

'Hello, Mr Douglas?' a female voice, distinctive… familiar.

'Yes this is Mr Douglas. Who am I speaking to?'

'It is Doctor Olali, we met at the hospital earlier today?'

'Oh yes of course doctor, I thought I recognised your voice. What can I do for you?'

' Mr Douglas you left the hospital without the death certificate, you may need it for funeral arrangements and insurance purposes and such like. Would it be possible for you to drop by and pick it up?' Jacob's mouth felt dry, his eyes still adjusting to the sudden increase in light intensity. Chest tightening, head dizzying…

'Yes… yes of course. I'll come right away.'

'Just when you have time Mr Douglas. There is no rush.' But Jacob missed this last statement, the phone already on the downward journey to the darkness of his pocket.

*

As Jacob made his way back towards the waiting room he could not help feeling that the funeral procession had already begun before the ink was dry on the death certificate. It was his father who was now being prepared for the grave, but Jacob felt eternity weighing heavy on his shoulders. He shuffled along the sterile corridor like a condemned man on his way to the gallows. Was this guilt that he was feeling?

'Maybe I didn't love him enough?' He pondered silently. *'But how do you repay a person who is responsible for your existence?'* Jacob had always tried so hard to make his father proud of him; but now everything he was and had become seemed dwarfed by his memory. No, it was not guilt that Jacob was feeling it was deep, cutting grief. He had lost a huge part of his life, the man he had modelled himself on, the person who had defined what it was to be a man. Jacob had drawn the very essence of his identity from his father: As a child he had followed him around everywhere, copied everything down to the way he combed his hair. To Jacob his father seemed ten feet tall; he knew everything; he was the greatest human being who had ever lived. Jacob had been a 'normal' teenager and

rebelled against everything his father stood for; but he soon realised that without him he would have had nothing to rebel against. It was only as a grown man, with his own worries, pressures and debts (emotional and financial) that he had for the first time truly come to understand and appreciate what it was like inside his fathers head. Jacob thought now of all the wasted years, the regrets; all the things he wished that he had never said or done and all the things that he wished he had. Sadness engulfed him, he struggled for air. *'There is just never enough time, never enough time…never enough time.'*

A short way along the corridor he spotted a drinks machine secreted in an alcove to the right, and staggered towards it. Jacob fumbled out enough change and bought himself a cup full of a hot, brown liquid that barely passed for coffee. Half in a dream he staggered the last twenty feet or so to the waiting room, located an isolated seat in the far right hand corner and sat down to await the call from reception. Jacob breathed a soundless prayer for no-one to sit next to him. As he swirled the coffee around in its white plastic cup, watching the steam spiral up and evaporate into the white air, a woman in a wheelchair was guided into the waiting room by a nurse and parked directly opposite him. The wheelchair had one of the footrests elevated, and the woman's heavily bandaged left leg rested upon it. Jacob looked up through his eyebrows without moving his head. The woman was looking out through the window to her right. Her face strangely familiar to Jacob and he found himself staring trying to work out where he had seen her before, and before he could look away the woman turned her attention away from the window and caught Jacob's gaze. He felt his face flush red and tried to make out that he was studying the infectious diseases poster on the wall behind her, but he could still see her looking over at him from the corner of his eye.

'Excuse me...' She was talking to him. Jacob tried to make out he didn't hear, afraid she was about to reprimand him for gawking at her. 'Excuse me...' She wasn't going to give up. Jacob prepared himself to accept a public embarrassment, it wasn't the first time, he supposed, and it probably wouldn't be the last. He lowered his eyes from the poster and feigned surprise at her call.

'Who, me?' The woman smiled at him. Maybe she didn't think he was a creep?

'Yes, you. I don't suppose you could do me a favour could you?' Jacob returned the smile, relieved that she did not scream visual rape.

'Sure...no problem...' He replied, standing up and walking over,

'...what can I do to help?' The woman dug deep in her handbag and rummaged around. For a moment Jacob thought he had been tricked, the woman was about to pull out a can of pepper spray and hit him square in the eyes. *'Ah, the old double bluff should have known better than to trust a...'* The woman withdrew her hand and up a pile of loose change to Jacob in her open palm.

'I'm really gasping for a cup of tea, could you go to the machine and get me one? I can't really go myself, as you can see. I'd really appreciate it.' Jacob breathed a sigh of relief and smiled easily at her,

'No problem at all, and let me get it I was going to get myself another anyway,' he lied. The woman urged Jacob to take some money, but he put his hands up in surrender and refused. 'My father always taught me never to take money from a lady.'

The woman relented and poured the loose change back into the central zipped compartment of her handbag,

'Well if you're sure…milk and two, thank you very much.'

'Oh don't thank me so soon…' Jacob replied, '…you haven't tasted the tea yet!' Jacob smiled over at her as he waited for the machine to dispense the drinks, convinced that he recognised her from somewhere, but he just couldn't work out where. The drinks machine grinded and coughed out liquid just slightly cooler than molten iron into two flimsy plastic cups which Jacob lifted tentatively by the rims and tiptoed back towards the injured woman. 'Here we go…' he said almost apologetically, carefully handing the woman one of the steaming plastic cups '…be careful now, it's really hot.' Jacob shook the spilled tea off his hand and sat down next to her.

'I'm sorry if I was staring earlier…' Jacob continued '…but I was sure that I knew you from somewhere, I was just trying to work out where.'

'Have you ever seen Crimewatch?' Jacob nearly dropped his coffee.

'Eh?' The woman laughed and took a sip of tea, her face screwing up in a repulsed grimace.

'I did try to warn you.' Said Jacob; the woman shook her head in disgust and rested the tea on the arm of her wheelchair.

'The big glass bank up the high-street.' Jacob frowned, a bit confused by the woman's statement.

'Excuse me?' She fixed him with a smile,

'That's where you probably know me from. I've worked there for just over two years now.' A tide of relief washed over him; Jacob had been afraid that the woman had been a drunken one-night- stand, or worse still, that he had made a pass at her and been rejected.

'That would be it! I've actually been in that bank quite a lot recently for work.' He could see that the woman was hooked.

'Work... so what is it that you do exactly?' Jacob took a sip of his coffee, the bitterness causing his face to contort into a scowl.

'I'm a painter.'

'What? Like people's houses and stuff?' Enquired the woman. Jacob smiled without difficulty, he was really warming to this girl.

'No, I'm not that type of painter. I do a lot of commercial stuff, illustrations for magazines and books that kind of thing, but my real passion is portrait painting.'

'Wow...sounds like a really interesting job! I didn't think that too many people would be into getting their portrait painted now though, what with digital cameras and all that.' Jacob shrugged apologetically,

'Unfortunately that's probably true. I get very few commissions, mainly corporate stuff, you know, like the bank.' The woman grinned mischievously, leaned in closer to Jacob and mock-whispered to him,

'So tell me about the bank job then; who is it you're 'working' on?' Jacob mirrored her surreptitious movements and lowered his voice,

'You mean who *was* I working on – finished that job last week, come to think of it, I haven't actually been paid for it either; will have to chase that slippery agent of mine. Justin his name is, never in touch unless it's in his best interest, know what I mean?' The woman looked at Jacob a bit confused.

'Justin? Is that the name of the person you're painting at the bank? Never heard of him.'

'No, Justin's my agent...allegedly. The person I've just finished painting at the bank...well I could tell you their name, but then I'd have to kill you. Client confidentiality and all that you understand.' The woman turned, looked him in the eye and smiled. Jacob reciprocated, and continued. 'Let me just say that it's the 'big cheese'. The woman tapped the side of her nose in a gesture of covert understanding.

'Ah... I know exactly who you mean, but he's based at corporate headquarters, why's he using our branch? Are you painting him in the nude?' Jacob threw the rest of his coffee into the bin by the side of his chair, the hot brown liquid splashing up but not quite making it over the rim.

'Not at all, I always paint with my clothes on!' He watched, a little surprised, but pleasantly so, as she laughed. Jacob had always had difficulty communicating with the opposite sex, but found talking with this woman so incredibly easy... she even laughed at his stupid jokes! 'But seriously though, the design of the building, the huge glass windows provide wonderful natural light and there's an amazing view of the city from the boardroom on the top floor...' Jacob was transfixed, unable to tear his eyes away from her.

'So a brilliant place to hang out on a Friday night then?' The woman added. Jacob frowned, confused shaking his head slightly.

'What do you mean?'

'On a Friday night you could watch all the drama unfolding as the pubs and clubs spilled out; be better than the soaps.' The reference became clear to Jacob.

'Oh yeah, I'll bet it would be. So what's your story then?' He asked pointing to the woman's bandaged leg. She winced in recollection and rubbed her shin.

'This was all one huge, fat mistake. I still can't believe that it's happened. If I'd just waited, asked for help in the first place I wouldn't be sitting here right now...' Jacob felt an imaginary blow to the solar plexus. The woman continued, 'This is all my own doing, my own stupid fault...' Jacob gave her a consoling look.

'You don't have to tell me, if it's too painful... oh shit, sorry... probably a bad choice of words, given the circumstances.'

'No it's fine...' she replied, '...I want to tell you, get it off my chest.'

'And what a lovely chest it is,' thought Jacob trying hard to maintain eye contact. The woman took a sip of her tea,

'Yeauch! Can you toss that in the bin for me,' she said leaning forward and passing the half-filled cup to Jacob. The woman eased herself back in her wheelchair and wriggled into a comfortable position then began her story. 'Well, few weeks ago I split up with the guy I was seeing...' Jacob felt immediately encouraged, wanted to ask if she was still single, but resisted the urge for fear of appearing too needy. The woman continued, 'It was nothing serious, at least not as far as I was concerned. We were work colleagues to begin with, went out a few times, became friends and it just developed from there. Developed a bit too fast for my liking, if you know what I mean...' Jacob did not know what she meant, but smiled attentively and nodded recognition anyway. '...Before I knew what was happening he was leaving more and more of his things at my flat, even buying things, household things like a toaster or bloody scatter cushions! Jacob considered this last statement, and reflected how nice it would be to have someone thoughtful enough to buy nice things for you, but decided to hold his tongue. 'He was moving in bit by bit and I didn't like it. So we had a talk, or rather I talked and he listened... well for a little while at least before he stormed out, which actually suited me fine. I didn't have to bother with any pathetic *can we still be friends* type speeches. So there I was, a strong single woman, trying to show the world how I could stand on my own two feet, trying to demonstrate how independent I could be. Bloody aquarium!' The surreal statement and the venom it was delivered with both surprised and amused Jacob.

'What? What do you mean 'aquarium'?' He asked more than a little bemused. Her scowl softened into a smile.

'I'm sorry, I should have explained, the *aquarium* was another one of his *gifts*.' She said punctuating the word 'gift' with two imaginary inverted commas drawn in the air with both index fingers - a practice which usually evoked a desire in Jacob to beat the 'punctuator' around the face and head with a blunt instrument, but one which on this particular occasion, evoked desires of a far more sensuous flavour. 'I'm sorry; I must be boring you...' Jacob snapped back from his reverie, 'No... not at all... I was listening... *aquarium*... yes, please, go on.' The woman seemed almost relieved. She composed herself and continued,

'Well, he had always taken care of the bloody thing, cleaned the filters, all that kind of crap, but with him out of the picture the thing just got grubbier and grubbier. The wee fishes were having trouble breathing. They kept coming up to the surface for little gulps of air. Poor things, wasn't their fault. So I began emptying out the tank; first with a plastic basin and when I got near the bottom, I switched to a small saucepan. But eventually even the saucepan was too big to get at the last few dregs.'

'What about the fish?' asked a fake-concerned Jacob.

'Oh they were fine, I had re-located them before the ill-fated clean-up operation begun. They were swimming around quite happily in the kitchen sink. So, anyway, I thought that if I could lift the thing that I'd be able to carry it through to the bathroom and empty it into the bath, maybe even give it a bit of a shower. So I managed to manoeuvre the tank up enough to slip one hand underneath, and I wrapped my other arm around the side, then I started to lift. I didn't realise how heavy the bloody thing was going to be! I managed to stagger out from the living-room and started along the hall in the direction of the bathroom. But about half-way along, just outside my bedroom, I felt it start to slip. I tried to get a better grip, but my hands were still wet from emptying the bloody thing in the first place, so I walked as fast as I could which only made the aquarium slip even more. I lost it about twenty seconds later...' She threw both her hands up dramatically into the air. '...The aquarium fell to the floor and shattered into a thousand pieces. I didn't feel anything at first, in fact, it was only when I had the sensation of water still pouring onto my feet, I noticed. When I looked down blood was gushing from my shin. The edge of the aquarium had caught me on its' way down. The next thing I remember is waking up on the hall floor in a pool of my own blood.' Jacob winced at the thought of the glass slicing into her tender flesh.

'Ouch! How long had you been laying there?'

'I have no idea, but I was freezing cold and when I tried to get up I couldn't because my leg had gone completely numb. I don't know whether I had been laying on it and it had gone to sleep, or whether it was shock or what, but the bloody thing was a dead weight! It took me forever to drag myself around the shattered glass to the telephone, which I couldn't reach anyway because it was up on a bloody shelf! But I managed to somehow hoist myself up on one hand and make grab for the flex and pull the phone down onto the floor. So there I am lying on my hall floor, leaking blood all over the place, barely managing to maintain consciousness, and do you know the only number I could remember?' Jacob shook his head. 'My ex-fucking-boyfriend's! His heart sank. Maybe she still loved him? 'Sorry, you must excuse my language. I just get mad every time I think of that selfish, no-use arsehole of a man...' Jacob's inner smile returned. '...I didn't even have the sense to dial 999, the 'ex' dialled it for me from his flat. I mean, why couldn't I have had the brains to do that for myself?'

'You were in shock... not thinking straight.' Jacob offered in consolation. A flicker of appreciation softened her eyes for a moment.

'He arrived just before the ambulance, even offered to come to the hospital with me, said he wanted to *make sure that I was taken care of.* Wanted to gloat more like! I told him 'thanks, but no thanks'. And when he said that he was not going to take no for an answer, I asked him if he would accept 'go fuck yourself'. Again I apologise for my language.'

'No need...' replied Jacob with a smile, '...I appreciate an accurate report, and it was a very good answer, especially given the circumstances. So your leg, is it bad?'

'The glass cut through the muscle almost to the bone. Twenty-seven stitches. The Doctor said I'll have scar around six inches long, but because it's on the inside of my shin they said that the only time it would ever be really noticeable would be if I had a suntan. But even then I should be able to cover it up with make-up.' Jacob attempted a consolatory smile,

'Well that's good... I suppose. Are you able to walk on it?'

'Doctor advised me to rest up for a few days to let the wound nit together, but he did say that it was a *good clean cut*, and that it should heal up nicely if all goes well. Said I should be back to normal in no time at all.' Jacob had a thought; it was risky, but what the hell, nothing ventured...

'So, is your ex picking you up then?' The woman spun round quickly in her wheelchair as if mortally offended.

'That will be bloody right! Absolutely not a snowballs chance of that happening while I'm still breathing! No, I'll be making my own way back home tonight thank-you very much!'

'Bingo!' Jacob touched the tabletop next to him for luck - laminated imitation wood, but it would have to do.

'I'm actually going back into town pretty soon if you'd like a lift... I promise you I'm not a psycho or anything. Rest assured, you are completely safe with me!' He held his breath, waited for her to answer... hoping...

'It's very nice of you to offer, but...' There was that word, 'but', not quite a no, but as good as. '...I've already booked the taxi. It should be here any minute now.' Jacob really wanted to see this woman again; there was something different, something *special* about her. He wasn't normally in the habit of asking women out, not when he was sober anyway, but this one was different... maybe she was the one? Perhaps this was his chance? Maybe his last chance; he had to say something...

'Taxi for Alison Spencer!' A voice shouted from the waiting room entrance.

'Well that's me...' said the woman, if he was going to say something it had to be now. If he waited any longer she would be gone.

'Alison.'

'What?' she replied fumbling in her bag.

'Your name... Alison. Well, anyway, I'm Jacob and I'm very pleased to meet you.' He said, reaching out to her. But Alison was busy scribbling something onto a piece of paper. Jacob felt abandoned; his open hand withering like an autumn leaf.

'Jacob, I hope you don't think this too presumptuous or anything. I mean, I don't normally do this sort of thing, but it's been good talking to you and, I don't believe I'm going to say this, I was wondering, if you're not too busy, if you'd like to continue this *thing* some other time? That is if you'd like to see me again?' Jacob took the piece of paper from her, a little too quickly perhaps.

'Yes that would be great, when you're feeling up to it of course.' He pointed to her damaged leg, trying hard not sound too desperate.

'Oh I'm not going to let this thing slow me down. I got some really amazing painkillers from the doctor anyway. How about tomorrow, you free?' Jacob almost jumped on the poor woman.

'Nothing I can't move, cancel or ignore!' He replied a bit stunned.

'Well just give me a call anytime, we could meet in town for a coffee or something.' Jacob tried to suppress the enormous smile that was trying to burst out.

'Carpe deum old boy... How are you fixed for tomorrow afternoon? Granny Gibson's Café in the high street about two-thirty?'

'Sounds good to me.' The taxi driver found Alison and begun wheeling her toward the door.

'That's a date then?' Jacob called to the back of Alison's head.

'I'll see you tomorrow Jacob, and don't be late!' Alison replied over her left shoulder as she was escorted towards the exit. Jacob watched as she receded, worrying that he may have come on too strong and scared her off. Maybe she wouldn't turn up tomorrow?

'Oh Alison!' Jacob shouted after her, not really knowing what he was going to say. The taxi driver halted the wheelchair by the exit and swivelled the chair round so as Alison faced towards him. Jacob scrabbled and searched the recesses of his brain for something to say. 'I hope your fish are okay.' Alison gave a rather perplexed smiled, a wave of the hand and she was gone. Jacob sat with a stupid grin on his face, scarcely able to believe what had just happened. A beautiful, funny, intelligent woman liked him. Liked him so much that *she* had actually asked *him* out! *'What a great night this is.'* He chuckled to himself.

'Mr Douglas?' Said a firm and solemn voice from somewhere above him. Jacob, unable to drop the broad smile from his lips, looked up.

'Yes, that's me.' It was the young black doctor from earlier; she looked more than a bit surprised at Jacob's overly cheerful expression.

'I have the completed death certificate for you… if you would just like to come over to the desk and sign for it please.'

He missed the simple things in life most, like reading a good book or a newspaper, but got around this with the assistance of Radio 4. However, not even the lilting eloquence of Neil MacGregor could capture and convey the exquisite beauty of the setting sun in autumn.

FOR MY NEXT TRICK I'LL NEED A VOLUNTEER

Jacob had never been good at relationships. It wasn't meeting women or even the whole chatting up process, although god knows he was hopeless at that. His technique was generally just to ask some inane questions and hope they found him interesting. It was maintaining a relationship, keeping a woman that was Jacob's problem. But this time was going to be different, this time he felt it was for real, this time he would make it impossible for her to leave him.

Jacob tried desperately to control his nerves as he drove along the grey-damp Glasgow streets. He had not been out with a woman in any shape or form for such a long time. He tried to convince himself that work had taken up so much of his life recently that there had been no room for anything or anyone else. The truth was that he was fed up of attracting the wrong type of women. Jacob's most recent disaster had involved a beautiful if rather talkative woman who had imparted her entire life story within the first five minuets of them meeting. He didn't mind her loquacity too much, but as Jacob got to know her better it became apparent that *her* story was the only one she was interested in hearing. This narcissism pervaded every facet of her character, Jacob found it abhorrent. When they embraced all he could think of was the stench of perm lotion and cheap perfume, and when they kissed she always used her rough tongue.

Jacob was getting near to the café now, his eyes darted round looking for somewhere to park the car. A quick glance at the dashboard clock told him it was 2.10pm. As he cruised past the café Jacob attempted to crane his neck round and see in. Was she there already, waiting for him? There were too many heads bouncing around inside to distinguish and the café passed by too quickly. A black BMW pulled out from a side road ahead and Jacob had to break quickly to avoid slamming into the side of it.

'Bastard!' he yelled after the car as it sped off in a mist of kicked up rainwater, before manoeuvring his own beat-up 1990 V.W. Passat into the space vacated by the B.M.W. Jacob pulled off his tatty spectacles and threw them on the dashboard. Leaning over into the back seat he lifted a large blue and white striped golfing umbrella. One of the spokes had ripped itself from the material and tangled with the seatbelt. Jacob struggled ineffectively to separate the two, bending the spoke to near breaking point in the process. 'Fucker!' He spat tossing the umbrella back onto the seat in exasperation. Another quick check of the dashboard clock told Jacob it was 2:17pm. 'Get a fucking move on boy, this woman might not wait on you!' Jacob reprimanded his reflection in the rear-view mirror. 'That's if she's turned up in the first place!'

The rain had eased off a bit now and Jacob decided to risk leaving the golf umbrella on the backseat of the car, considering that it always seemed to get in the way, poke people, trip him up… You're too fucking big!' He shouted, pointing at the wrecked umbrella. A concerned looking old woman tried hard not to peer in as she passed. Jacob gave her his best innocent smile as she quickly looked away. 'It's not that far to the café from here. Just a short walk...' He reasoned under his breath and exited the car.

A blast of cold air slapped Jacob hard in the face as he stood up into the afternoon street. He turned his collar against the drizzle and tried to avoid the puddles as he made his way along the pavement, remembering how damp his socks had been last night when he had arrived home from the hospital. *Leaky shoes*, was the verdict, but there had been no time to buy another pair and Jacob's only other 'shoes' were a pair of green Wellington boots and some open toed 'Jesus' type sandals, neither of which he considered to be appropriate foot-ware for a romantic liaison. A florist was spotted a florist on the opposite side of the road. *'Flowers?'* He pondered briefly, quickly dismissing the thought for fear that such a gesture may appear over-eager, maybe even slightly desperate... both of which Jacob indeed was! *'No flowers are for second dates.'*

Another time check, this time on the battered old Tissot fastened to his left wrist, an inheritance from his grandfather; 2:24pm. He quickened his pace, weaving in and out of the Saturday shoppers. The café had seemed closer when he was in the car and Jacob wondered if he'd passed it and thought about turning back. But at the eleventh hour, it appeared in front of him like a vivid oasis. A final time revealed that he had succeeded, 2:29pm. *'Perfect timing.'* Thought Jacob smugly and strode towards the entrance, his foot splashing deep into a large puddle inches from safety. As the bell on the café door pinged cheerfully and his feet sloshed in, Jacob made a mental note, *'Must buy new shoes!'*

Inside was bustling and noisy. Jacob made for the back to get a better view, but was headed off half-way along by two elderly women shuffling menacingly towards him. He tried desperately to get out of their way but there was little room for manoeuvre. The best Jacob could do was turn side-on and try to make himself as tall and as thin as possible. His attempts at evasion proved ultimately futile, the first old woman crushing his waterlogged toes under the wheels of her heavy, tartan shopping trolley as she trundled past. Bubbles squelched up through Jacobs sodden shoes as he winced, took a sharp reflexive in-breath through bared teeth. He closed his eyes and braced for another pummelling as the second granny lumbered ominously in his direction. A tug from behind sent Jacob falling back off his tip-toes. He reached out for something to steady himself and felt a soft warm hand grab his and pull him down into a chair. Jacob quickly withdrew his battered feet to safety and spun round to see a laughing Alison sitting opposite.

'That was very entertaining! Do you always make such grand entrances Mr Douglas?' Jacob straightened his jacket and smoothed back his hair with the palm of his right hand.

'Only when I'm really trying to impress someone. So you arrived before me then?' Alison handed Jacob a menu.

'Got to on a Saturday afternoon, it's chock-a-block from about twelve thirty with hungry shoppers. This thing came in handy though…' she pointed to her injured leg, '…soon as I hobbled in on my crutches everyone was jumping up trying to give me their seats! First time ever I haven't had to wait for a table in this place.'

'I can't believe you came.' Said Jacob, immediately regretting his heartfelt proclamation, fearing that Alison would find it somewhat piteous; but she accepted the remark with the reverence of a complement.

'Of course I came, why wouldn't I?' Jacob was surprised, but pleasantly so, by her thoughtfulness. He relaxed, looked her in the eyes, smiled.

'Well, you hardly know me.' Alison returned his smile.

'I'd say that's just all the more reason to be here. And, anyway, I feel as if I know you already.' Jacob was just about to add excitedly how he felt exactly the same way when a rather rotund waitress appeared and asked if they were ready to order.

'Coffee and sticky buns?' Enquired Alison; Jacob nodded in reply. The waitress scribbled down their order and waddled off. 'So tell me about yourself then.' Alison continued. Jacob pulled his chair up closer to the table.

'Well, where to start? My full name is Jacob Jonathon Douglas, most people call me Jake.' Alison considered this for a second.

'Well I'm not most people, I think I prefer *Jacob*.' Their eyes connected. I'm five-feet-ten…

…actually five feet nine…

…a bit out of shape at the moment…

…at least a stone overweight…

…thirty-seven years old…

…thirty-nine…

…dark brown hair, slightly greying…

…'Natural Brown Number 10', £4.99 from Boots…

…Blue-grey eyes…

…nearer to grey than blue…

…and I've just given up smoking…

…on weekdays.'

The waitress arrived back surprisingly quickly Jacob considered, plonked their order unceremoniously on the table between them and waddled off again, all without saying a word. They both looked slightly bemusedly at each other and shared a secret smile. Jacob blew the froth on the top of his coffee and took a sip.

'So now Alison, it's your turn.' Alison smiled and stirred two teaspoonfuls of heavy brown sugar into her coffee.

'Well my full name is Alison Catherine Spencer, I'm five-feet-six, average weight, thirty-five years old…' she gave Jacob a steely glance, daring him to contradict her; but Jacob's father had taught him well, under no circumstances should you ever ask nor question a woman's age or weight. It was one of those *religion and politics* type of things. Jacob gazed back at Alison with casual acceptance. She continued, ' Blond hair... slightly natural, blue eyes and, unfortunately, I'm still trying to give up smoking.' She sighed apologetically, 'That's about it really.' Alison took another sip of coffee without breaking her gaze at Jacob. 'I never asked why you were at the hospital last night, nothing wrong I hope? You haven't got any hideously infectious diseases I should know about do you?' Jacob smiled back mournfully.

'No, nothing you can catch.' he took a deep breath. 'It was my father I was up there seeing.' Alison's expression changed instantly to one of genuine concern.

'Oh please forgive me Jacob... I didn't realise. How's he doing? Is he okay? Nothing serious I hope?' It felt strange, Jacob wanted to laugh. What was going on? He swallowed hard.

'It's about as serious as it gets I'm afraid. He's dead. I was up at the hospital identifying the body.' Alison's expression was a mix of shock and disbelief.

'I... I am so sorry... If I had only known I wouldn't have gone on about my self so much last night. Some crazy woman wittering on about her own stupid, trivial existence and all the time you were sitting there having to deal with this... this huge thing.' Jacob raised his hands to pacify her.

'No, no, listen to me...please Alison... meeting you last night, listening to you talk about your life, well... it was just what I needed. You really helped to take my mind off everything.' Alison was turning her coffee cup around in it's saucer, clearly agitated.

'Why didn't you tell me last night?' Jacob sat back in his chair and fixed her with a questioning look.

'Would you honestly have turned up today if I had?' Alison returned his look with one of mild uncertainty.

'Honestly?' She replied as she fidgeted now with the sugar bowl. Jacob nodded. She looked up at the ceiling briefly, before catching Jacob's gaze once again. 'I suppose the honest answer is, I don't know. Oh god Jacob, I'm such a horrible person.' Jacob reached across the table and placed his hand tenderly over Alison's.

'No you're not! I'd probably feel the same if the shoe was on the other foot. And if anybody should feel bad it's me for not being straight with you from the off. But the thing is... I really wanted to see you again and I thought that if I told you everything it might scare you away.' The same thought was going through Jacob's mind at that very moment. He looked hard at Alison trying to read her mind. Was she getting ready to make her excuses and fly? Jacob had to act fast, think of something to say, something that would make things better, something that would make her stay. 'But I'm fine... really. My dad was pretty old and he enjoyed his life. A bit too much at times, if you know what I mean. Life goes on and all that, and I know we've only known each other literally hours, but I really like you, I feel like we've got a connection or something. I can't explain it, I've never felt anything like this before.' He paused, looked into her eyes, tried to determine her reaction. Had he came on too heavy? Said too much? Alison looked upset, but he could see softness, empathy, there was still a chance. 'I don't mean to get all heavy on you and scare you away, but...' Alison butted in,

'But nothing... I'm not going anywhere.' Jacob felt his stomach somersault. It was like having that first schoolboy crush come true! She pulled one of her hands out from under his and Jacob's heart immediately began to sink, but quickly rose again with hope as her hand fell featherlike coming to rest gently on top of his and squeezed it firmly. Her voice came softer now, 'So when's the funeral?' It suddenly hit Jacob that he had not even contemplated the funeral yet! He had no idea *when* it would be, although he did know *where* it would be, as his father had made both his boys promise that they would make sure he was buried in the 'old country'.

'Either Wednesday or Thursday I would expect...' Jacob lied, '...everything still has to be finalised though, lots to organise.' Jacob hoped that Alison would be satisfied with his vague response. However, he noticed her brows crease with curiosity and decided to play his joker. 'My dad was Irish you see, he made me and my brother Simon promise to see to it that he was planted '*back in home soil*', so to speak.' Alison nodded in appreciation, apparently content with this explanation. But in those few moments it had all became oh-so-real to Jacob. He was already imagining the nightmare of organisation, the phone calls, the invitations, having to arrange for his father's body to be transported and having to accompany it to make sure that the bloody thing arrived on time and in one piece! Jacob felt the vein in his temple starting to throb. It was only a matter of seconds before the cold sweats begun.

'Wouldn't it be quicker and much less hassle to go by plane?' Asked Alison. Her voice snapped Jacob from his desperate inner turmoil.

'I'm sorry... did you say plane?' Alison nodded in reply. 'Not an option I'm afraid, dad has a fear of flying.' Alison looked puzzled.

'But he's dead though?' Realising his gaff, Jacob smiled, relaxed his shoulders.

'Yes, of course he is... sorry Alison. He *had* a fear of flying, but he also made us promise to take him by boat because of his phobia. We should just bury the old swine at sea and save us all a load of grief! Even from beyond the grave my old man can still manage to fart right in my face!' Alison tried hopelessly to suppress a giggle.

'I'm sorry. She managed to cough out. Jacob smiled back.

'No, no, it's fine...really. I'm just a bit freaked out by the whole thing; all of a sudden it seems so real! The relatives in Ireland will be in their element though; nothing they like more than a good funeral. In fact I'll bet that they're busy stock-piling booze and sandwiches for the wake as we speak!' Alison smiled warmly, delicately touching Jacob's cheek with the back of her hand.

'If you need any help, or even just someone to have a good moan to just give me a call... anytime.' Jacob felt touched, oddly aroused and guilty all at the same time.

Looking deep into her eyes, he took her hand in his, brought it to his lips and pressed them gently on the milky-white skin, all the while wondering if she felt *it* too.

'Thank you...' said Jacob swallowing hard to avoid an embarrassing emotional outpouring, '...that really means a lot to me.' He looked at Alison's hand soft and pale in his, lightly stroked the graceful curve from her thumb down to the knuckle of her index finger, and repeated. As he looked up, Alison was smiling, content, relaxed. Jacob returned her smile. 'I just want it all to be over, you know?' Alison turned her hand over on the table and hinted to Jacob to continue his caress on her upturned palm.

'I speak from bitter experience I'm sorry to say. I lost my mother, how long has it been now? Be a year past in July.' Jacob adopted a look of quiet concern.

'Oh, I am sorry to hear that Alison.'

'What a game of cards that was!' She replied, mischief colouring her voice. Jacob's expression of concern instantaneously switched to one of bewilderment.

'Eh?' Alison patted his hand reassuringly.

'I'm only joking; and there's no need to be sorry either, she was a cantankerous old bat at the best of times! In the end it was a blessing.'

'How do you mean? Was she suffering?' Replied Jacob, the air of concern returning. Alison, seemed to consider her words for a second before answering and Jacob wondered if she perhaps she didn't trust him, that maybe she was

50

having second thoughts. Alison shot Jacob an almost imperceptible smile, more like a nervous tick, a speedy curling upwards at the corner of her mouth. Blink and you'd miss it.

'No, mother wasn't suffering. But I was! I was galloping towards middle age, working in a poky little branch of the bank in the back of beyond. I was single, still living at home and having to look after my dear old housebound, incontinent mother. I had no bloody life! As soon as the old dear popped her clogs I got the house straight on the market, requested a transfer to a branch in the city and, well, here I am. A free woman at last!' Jacob was strangely surprised by this revelation.

'So you don't miss your mother at all then?'

'Don't be silly... replied Alison, '...I miss her like mad. There isn't a day goes by that I don't think of her at least a hundred times. She drove me completely crazy but she was still my mum and I loved her with all my heart.'

'Yes, dad was a bit like that too...' added Jacob '...he treated mum like shit most of the time, drinking, running around with other women.... But you could tell, deep down that they were both nuts about each other. There was nothing either of them could do that wouldn't be forgiven by the other. Mum was no angel either though. I remember my Granny Sarah telling me a story about her that I would never have believed had it come from someone else...' Jacob's voice trailed off,

'…I'm going on too much about myself aren't I? I'm boring you.' Alison raised her hands in mock defence.

'No of course you're not. Please, tell me the story.' Stimulated by her apparent sincerity Jacob continued.

'Well, it was way back in the *olden days* when I was at art school. It was the summer holidays and I had headed over to Ireland for a bit of a cheap holiday staying with the relatives, doing some backpacking, you know the kind of thing. Anyway, I was sitting in the kitchen with my old granny, smoking her fags and having a cup of tea… just the normal same old, same old. I remember I was telling her of my intention to go to London sometime in the next week with a couple of mates. We were going down as part of a CND rally, but the three of us were really meeting up with some friends down there to go partying. I was saying to her how excited I was as I had never been to the *big smoke* before, but as I was speaking I noticed her giving me this funny look. I'd seen that look before when she was talking to my dad; a *knowing* look, like she really wanted to tell me something, but wasn't sure if she should. So I just asked her straight if there was something on her mind? She told me I actually *had* been to London before, but that I was so young at the time I probably wouldn't remember.' Alison looked puzzled.

'I'm sorry Jacob but I don't understand?'

'Well, mum had taken me and my brother off to her sisters' house near Kilburn. Didn't even leave my dad a note to explain why she'd left or where she'd gone. He couldn't understand what was going on, as far as he could remember, he hadn't done anything wrong. Dad tore the house apart looking for a clue as to what the hell was going on. In the kitchen rubbish bin he found pieces of torn paper that looked like a letter. He fished them out and pieced the letter together like a jigsaw. Turned out it was from a loan shark demanding immediate re-payment of the five hundred quid he'd leant her. That was a hell-of a lot of money back then you know. Dad was desperate; he had to find his wife and children, sort this whole mess out. He called at mum's parents' house, but they said that they hadn't seen or heard from her for over a week and that they were equally puzzled by her disappearance. Next up, he visited mum's older sister, Sharon. Aunty Sharon was an old friend of my dads' - they'd known each other for years before he and mum got together, she was even married to my dad's best friend for a while. Aunty Sharon didn't get on particularly well with her parents and decided that dad had the right to know everything so... she told him. The money that my dear old mum had borrowed from the loan-shark wasn't for her, it was for her parents who couldn't get a loan by themselves because they were both blacklisted. The dear old bastards had promised mum that if she took the loan out in her name, they'd pay it back to her in weekly instalments, which of course they never did. The loan-shark sent the heavies round to deliver the demand, put the frighteners on mum, who then, understandably, panicked and went straight round to her parents to confront them and ask what they intended to do about the situation. Unsurprisingly, both pleaded poverty and then advised mum to get on the next bus to London where she was to stay with her other younger sister Margery.

The plan was for mum to lay low for a spell whilst they sorted everything out with the loan-shark and my father. The old fuckers, excuse my language, promised to call mum as soon as everything had calmed down so as she could come home.' Alison appeared genuinely concerned.

'So what did your father do?'

'Well, I know if it had been me I'd have gone straight back to the in-laws house and, let's just say, *expressed* my abject annoyance. But dad, being *dad*, simply got into his car and drove all night and into the next morning, down to London to bring his family back home. In the end he had to give up his job, a good job, to pay off the debt. Took voluntary redundancy from the factory that had employed him straight from school, where he'd managed to work his way up from tea-boy to junior management before his twenty-first birthday. Dad promised not to throw mum out onto the street without a penny as long as she promised never to see or speak to her parents ever again.' Jacob looked across the table from a painful past he had no personal memory of. In front of him was a future yet to be tasted.

'Holy shit...' Alison cleared her throat and begun again. '...I mean ... your poor old dad. How did he ever manage to bounce back from that? Did he manage to find another job okay?' Jacob smiled.

'Well, yes and no I guess you could say. I mean, he was completely devastated by having to take his redundancy, as I said before, dad had started off in that factory making the tea and sweeping the shop floor, but he had stuck at it, learned everything he could about the business, worked his way up to management. The thought of starting from scratch all over again simply horrified him. So he decided to go it alone, start his own business. He begun with a little stall at the *Barras* knocking out knitwear, you know, woolly jumpers, scarves, cardigans that kind of thing. He put in the hours though and the stall done really well. He eventually had to open up another stall at the new indoor market in the city centre and even take on staff to run it for him. Things were going really well, but the really big breakthrough came when he decided to cut out the middleman, and bought a couple of second-hand knitting machines. He and mum started making the stock themselves. It all kind of snowballed from there. Within a year he was opening his first factory, then another, and another. Dad had four factories going at one point, employing over three hundred staff. The business just sort of took over his life, he was a total workaholic, never at home...' Jacob's eyes softened as he tried to focus his father's face in his mind. 'It's funny the way you don't realise what the hell is going on around you when you're a child, and the way you don't really understand why you only see your dad when it's dark.'

'So are any of the factories still on the go?' Enquired Alison. Jacob sighed.

'Unfortunately not; the last one closed down in the early nineties, too many cheap Asian imports flooding the market. Priced my dad right out of the game. His last place was running at a loss for years. He only kept it open out of loyalty to his staff, couldn't bear the thought of that last handful of employees who had stuck with him from the very beginning, having nothing.' Alison leaned forward.

'Oh Jacob, you poor thing, I shouldn't have let you drag up all these painful memories.' She brushed his cheek with her hand again. Jacob was convinced; he could definitely sense something between them… an electricity almost.

'No, no... it's actually been really good to let it all out, it's me who should be saying sorry to you for going on so much about myself.' Alison put her index finger to Jacob's mouth to quiet him.

'Shush now, I think that you've been through quite enough for one lunchtime. Now, let's go and do something nice, try and take your mind off things for a while.' Jacob made a weak attempt to protest.

'But the funeral… there are things to arrange, phone-calls…' Alison simply shook her head.

'I'm sure everything can wait for one more day, it's not as if your father's going anywhere is it?' Immediately realising the insensitivity of her remark Alison recoiled in embarrassment. 'Jacob I am so sorry. It just slipped out; I didn't mean to offend you...' But Jacob brushed the remark off like spilled sugar.

'Don't be daft Alison, you're perfectly right, I've wallowed in enough misery for one day. So what do you fancy doing for the rest of the afternoon? We could go see a film, or get something to eat, or go for a drink, or...'

'I know a great little pub within hobbling distance, it's got a well stocked jukebox and the food isn't bad either.' Alison interjected.

'What about my car? Will it be okay on the main road here?' Jacob noticed a definite glow in Alison's eyes.

'Probably not, but my flat is just round the corner, we'll drive round, drop it off and you can pick it up later.' The glow transferred across the table and absorbed Jacob.

'You make it impossible to refuse.'

*

They didn't stay out for very long; Alison's leg became increasingly painful as the day wore on and she eventually had to give in and ask Jacob to help her home. As soon as they had arrived inside her cosy first-floor flat overlooking the Botanical Gardens, Alison had asked Jacob to open a bottle of wine, before disappearing into the bathroom at the end of the long narrow hall-way and swallowing a handful of painkillers. The combination of these and the wine subsequently imbibed had a distinctly tranquillising effect, and Jacob found himself being used as a pillow a very short time later, her hair spilling over his lap in golden waves.

He was not exactly sure how long they had been in this position. His eyes fixated on the beautiful, exciting new creature that lay purring in his lap. Jacob breathed in deeply, Alison's sweet perfume intoxicating and arousing. He felt himself grow hard.

'What if she woke up right now?' he thought to himself, *'...and felt this throbbing lump under her cheek? Would she jump up, scream rape, call me a pervert, throw me out and call the police?'* He wondered if she might still actually be awake, just pretending to be asleep, that maybe this was really a test to find out what kind of man he was? Alison's breath was warm and heavy on his open hand. *'Maybe she wants me too unzip my fly and... No!'*

Jacob eased his hands under Alison's head and carefully slid out from under her. Covering her with the deep red chenille throw-rug that draped over the battered brown leather chesterfield, Jacob retreated backward towards the door as quietly as the naked wooden floorboards would allow.

In the hallway he paused by a small side table upon which the phone rested and a knot twisted in his chest as he imagined Alison lying bleeding on the floor unable to call for help. Amongst the earthquake-like devastation on the table's surface the corner of a notepad reached up appealing for liberation. Jacob pulled the notepad free and scribbled Alison a note:

Had a very nice time today, will call you tomorrow.

Hope you're feeling better.

Jacob XXX

*

Outside the early morning air was crisp with autumn. Jacob made for his car which was parked in the alleyway next to Alison's building. At the door, he patted his jacket in vein search of the car key, remembering how he had handed it over to Alison after his third pint of lager.

'Fuck!' He thought about going back and chapping the door, but could not bear the thought of waking Alison from her dreaming. 'Pick it up tomorrow – probably still a bit too pished anyway.' He concluded philosophically.

The orange street lamps plinked out one by one as Jacob made his way along Great Western Road towards the park. Heavy prison-blanket-grey cloud hung low in the Glasgow sky, the sun burning its edges a thousand shades of red as it attempted to raise the dawn curtain. He made Kelvin Bridge and ducked down the stairs to cross the footbridge into the park. A groan came from somewhere under the bridge behind.

'Fuckin' winos!' Concluded Jacob, but decided to quicken his pace anyway, 'Can't be too fucking careful at this time of day.'

Jacob walked in the shadows alongside the river, checking back every now and then, but whoever had made that noise wasn't following. He cut across the grass to reach the next bridge and climbed the steps to the street two at a time. At the top Jacob glanced quickly back, still no sign of any one following, then hooked a sharp left down towards Woodlands.

He was nearly home, but instead of walking the last few feet into the close of his tenement, Jacob shot across the already busying road and entered the park through the ornate iron gates on the other side.

As he walked Jacob revisited and examined microscopically every detail of the previous day and evening; every furtive glance, every intonation, every syllable of every word. The way her brows creased delicately in the centre when she made a serious point, the tiny crescents that appeared at the corners of her mouth just outside the lip-line when she smiled. *'Alison you overwhelm me.'*

The path grew steep as he climbed towards Park Circus. Jacob felt as if he had known her forever.

'Old souls maybe once together in some long ago dark time?' Then something else remembered blackened his sky. Alison had spoken of her ex-boyfriend. She had only split with him very recently, what if she was on the rebound? *'What if*

she's just using you to make herself feel better, an ego boost? But she seems so genuine, so together.'

Jacob was almost at the top of the hill and was breathing heavily, his shirt sticking cold to his back. The Great War memorial loomed dark in front of him. He wiped the sweat from his eyes and struggled up the last few feet of the footpath.

'Oh Alison, my beautiful angel, my redeemer, why would you crush this exquisite flower?' As Jacob stood on the summit and looked out over the park and beyond, the stubborn Scottish gloom was at last penetrated by the ruthless sun, a single ray bursting through and illuminating the apex of the university tower like some great gothic rocket. *'He can't have her; I'm her special one now. His time is over, he had his chance.'* A relentless golden wave washed over the city from the east engulfing everything in its path. Jacob drank in the dramatic panorama, threw his hands in the air and offered up a prayer to the cold morning. 'Please, let it be me!'

Going to the toilet for a pee could prove a bit of a lottery, a bit like bombing by trial and error.

After several nasty instances of *splashback* and wet socks, he decided that it would be safer and, indeed, more hygienic to take a seat, whatever the occasion…

The Mermaid

He climbed to the top of the dark shining-wet rocks and surveyed the island. Jacob had no idea where he was, how he had been transported here or, indeed, why. He climbed back down to the beach where the sand was strewn with debris, broken glass glittering all around him like a million tiny jewels. An angry sun burned in the azure sky making his pores bleed, he needed to find shelter fast and made for the apparent sanctuary of some nearby flowing dunes. Cresting the first ridge he slid down the other side to the entrance of an avenue of statues, heads turned and eyes looking out to sea. They were statues of mermaids and it sounded as though they were crying.

'Why are you all so sad?' asked Jacob as he walked uneasily between them. The statues did not answer. He decided to get closer and approached one of the statues; her head was turned away and Jacob walked round to the side to look her in the face. It was her. 'Alison?' He said brushing her cheek tenderly with the back of his hand. She turned her eyes toward his and in the same breath the wind reduced her to fluid black dust. The dust flowed like a river carrying Jacob along through the alien island landscape. He managed to grab onto the twisted branch of a long-dead apple tree, and pull himself free of the increasing river. A distant rumble soon grew to thunder as the black dust was sucked up through a tornado into a huge ominous looking storm-cloud. Jacob watched in quiet awe as the cloud swelled red and angry. Far off, almost inaudible through the roar, a voice was calling his name. Amidst the enormous spiralling arm of the tornado Jacob saw Alison, hands beckoning him forward. He ran as fast and hard as he could, pausing intermittently to survey the panorama, but she was gone.

Night descended rapidly, blue-black. Wandering in the darkness in no particular direction, Jacob came across a street of tidy white houses, the curtains chinking with yellow shadowed faces as he passed. The smell of salt-water hung like a veil on a sea breeze. At the top of the street a cobbled road turned left into the wind, sweeping down to a familiar harbour, the hypnotic ebb and flow of the tide drawing Jacob closer. By the ancient tidal walls, faithful sentries who resolutely defended the town and its' inhabitants for generations, stood a group of fishermen staring down into the sea. They pointed and gesticulated excitedly at something in the water. Jacob ran up beside them and stared deep into the ocean. A strange blue light illuminated the water. Something just under the waves, blue-dark, fish-like, elegant, flowing... it face broke the surface and glowing electric blue, she rose free of the sea.

'My mermaid!' Shouted Jacob as Alison's tail whipped out in glorious thunder. Unfurling magnificent feathered wings, she ascended heavenwards in a brilliant golden light. Alarm spread like wild fire amongst the fishermen. One of them pulled a gun from under his yellow waterproof jacket and took aim. Jacob sprang forward to try and stop him, but he was too late. A bullet detonated skyward. Jacob looked on hopelessly as the shot found its' target and Alison's pale breast was stained crimson red. Her head hung limp and the golden light began to dim. Overcome with utter disbelief and pain, Jacob fell to his knees and wept. A noise like a thousand bee stings startled him from mourning and he looked up to see his mermaid now transformed to a burning red angel hovering intensely in the low sky, her eyes fixed and unforgiving on the group of fishermen. Slow lightning blazed from her hands, lifting the fishermen into the air... and they were gone. The angry-red subsided and Alison smiled golden and resumed her ascent. A feather fell from his angels' wing as she soared heavenward away from him. It drifted slowly down and landed gently on Jacob's upturned face. Its warmth enveloped him and he closed his eyes and smiled. Jacob stood there for an eternity filled with divine love. When at last he opened his eyes, his angel had gone and all was darkness except for the lights of the night sky. He strained upwards trying hard to touch the moon until he was there; then far and beyond. He left the sun behind and glided in the blackness towards the stars and became one of them, looking down upon the Earth. But still Jacob could not find the angel who had left him behind.

*

He awoke with the dream still dripping from his fingertips… The fluorescent green readout of the digital alarm confused Jacob for a moment before gradually drifting into focus. It read 10:55AM. He tried to close his eyes and fall back to dreaming, but for some unknown reason his brain thought it was time to rise and was for none of it. After much tossing and turning, rearranging the duvet, straightening his pyjama top, pulling the legs pf his pyjama bottoms down from thigh to ankles and out from the crack of his arse, Jacob decided to put 'Plan B' into action swinging his legs stiffly out from under the duvet before dragging the rest of his body upright. Perched and crabby on the edge of his bed he remembered the dream.

'Fuck knows?' he concluded after brief contemplation then rumbled in the drawer of his bed-side-cabinet for the packet of cigarettes and lighter he kept for *emergencies* such as this. 'Well we're all allowed a little lapse every now and then, are we not?' He reasoned as he lit up one of the cigarettes and inhaled deeply. The smoke felt warm and familiar… comforting. Jacob relaxed and fell into a convulsion of uncontrollable coughing, beating his chest into submission, before taking another drag on his cigarette and stubbing it out. 'That's better,' he barked and lay back down on top of the bedclothes. There was an uncomfortable lump in the duvet just below his left shoulder. He attempted to pat it flat, but the lump refused to subside, so he stuck a hand under to investigate and pulled out

66

yesterdays' jeans. Alison's scent still clung to the thighs and crotch where she had rested her head the previous night. Jacob remembered how he had placed them on the pillow opposite so he could smell her as he drifted into sleep. He lifted them to his face, closed his eyes and smelled deeply. It was faint, but she still lingered, and he imagined Alison slipping silently into his bedroom, sliding naked into bed beside him...

The shrill tone of the telephone ring cut into Jacob's fantasy. He threw the jeans down on the bed and marched grumpily into the chilly hallway to answer it.

'Hello?'

'Hi Jacob, it's me.' Spoke the voice of Alison; Jacob felt his heart jump in his chest.

'But, I left you a note, didn't you get it? I was going to call you.'

'Yes, I found the note Jacob, but I just felt really bad for falling asleep on you like that... wasn't very sociable of me was it? I think it must have been the painkillers... well that and the booze. It says on the bottle not to drink or operate heavy machinery when you've taken them. We didn't steal a JCB or anything did we?' Jacob laughed easily; that was another thing he loved about Alison, her bizarre sense of humour, she had the same abstract way of viewing the world as Jacob's younger brother Simon, the only difference being that his brothers' strange tales more often than not turned out to be factual accounts!

67

'I can honestly say that no heavy machinery was nicked nor operated... at least not before I left. Whatever you got up to after that is between you and your god.'

'What time did you leave at?'

'Not sure, around four-thirty I think.'

'Why didn't you just crash here?'

'Why didn't I just crash there? You stupid fucker! You could be there with her now if you had! Never mind, play it cool, don't mess it up... I wasn't sure how you'd react, you know?'

'What do you mean, react? React to what?'

'Well... waking up on top of a strange man for one thing.' Jacob heard Alison sigh at the other side of the line and thought that somehow he had blown his chances.

'Honestly Jacob! In the first place, you are not a strange man, you are a very charming and handsome man.'

'Handsome... she thinks I'm fucking handsome! You absolute fucking Beauty!!!'

'And, secondly,' she continued, 'I think that it would be rather nice to wake up with you in the morning.'

'Ya dancer, she wants to sleep with me!' Jacob tried to hide the elation in his voice as he replied with mock formality.

'That is very kind of you to say Miss Spencer, thank you very much. I'll bear that in mind the next time.'

'So there's definitely going to be a next time then?' Jacob tried to appear laid back.

'Oh I think it's fairly safe to say that you can count on it Miss Spencer.'

'And when is this 'next time' going to be Mr Douglas?' Enquired Alison, quite mater-of-fact.

'Fuck being cool, I need to see you as soon as humanly possible!' Jacob decided to take a chance, lay his proverbial cards on the table.

'The sooner, the better as far as I'm concerned Miss Spencer. In fact, I have to come over and pick my car up later on, so maybe we could grab a bite to eat or something. How about lunch?' There was a brief pause during which Jacob worried that maybe he'd come on a bit too strong too soon...

'How about breakfast?' ...Or maybe not strong enough!

'Your place or mine?'

'Bit clichéd Jacob, don't you think? But it'll do fine for me. How do you like your eggs?'

'Fried until nearly burned on the outside but with the yolk still runny on the inside.'

'You're very particular, some might even say fussy.'

'Well I know what I like if that's what you mean.' Jacob answered trying desperately to mask the excitement in his voice and failing miserably.

'So I'll see you in about half-an-hour then Jacob?'

'Oh I think that I can do better than that… be there in fifteen minutes.'

'Excellent, I'll be ready… and waiting for you…Mr Douglas…' She put the phone down before he had a chance to say goodbye and Jacob was left listening to the empty static purr of a vacant line.

The handset bounced out of its cradle and onto the floor as Jacob flung it down. Back in his bedroom he rummaged amongst the piles of clothes strewn over the floor for something clean and decent to wear, settling on a pair of grey cords and a washed out blue t-shirt. They didn't smell too fusty and the creasing was minimal compared to the rest of his clothes. Jacob clumped barefoot down the hallway breaking into a hop as he attempted to pull on a sock in full flight, an attempt which proved ultimately unsuccessful resulting in a head on collision with the front door. No time for concussion. From a more sensible and secure position sitting on the hall floor against the wall, Jacob safely attached to his person socks and a pair of heavy black leather boots. As he got to his feet Jacob's still felt his napper a little woozy from the earlier disagreement with the door and tried to shake it off. 'Fuckin' teeth!' Jacob exclaimed as he pulled on his overcoat. 'Can't go round with breath like a badgers arse!' he continued stuffing a set of keys into his coat pocket before ducking into the bathroom. Thinking that there was not enough time to brush with any degree of thoroughness, Jacob squeezed the toothpaste straight out of the tube into his gob and sucked cold water from the tap, swishing around the mixture in place of mouthwash. However, in his hurry to exit the building, Jacob made the mistake of swallowing instead of spitting. 'Yeauch! Well at least if I fart in front of her it'll smell nice and minty!' And with that, Jacob set off running, tripping over a stray bootlace en-route and head-butting the front door again.

He never went out much anymore, instead relying on others (friends relatives…) to help him pay the bills or get some shopping. It wasn't that he was scared of going out, he just didn't see the point. The view was the same wherever he was and inside was warmer.

ANGEL

They skipped breakfast and made love until lunchtime instead. Alison did not even say hello when Jacob arrived at her door; she just flung her arms around his neck right there on the doorstep and pulled his mouth to hers. They kissed deeply and long, and when their lips parted without embarrassment she spoke for the first time,

'The bedroom's through here...'

*

They fucked like wild animals. Alison was screaming and scratching and tossing her hair, writhing her hips, grinding and groaning. Jacob shouted at the top of his voice as he exploded inside her then collapsed, almost passing out. He could not remember ever having had such an intense sexual experience.

'I don't know what you just did or how you did it...but just keep on doing it, please!' Jacob soon felt himself grow erect again and began rubbing himself against the side of Alison's thigh, caressing her neck with his lips.

'Again so soon? Who's a hungry boy then?' Was all she had said as he they rolled together again.

*

Second time round was pretty quick, but no less passionate. Afterwards they both lay exhausted and sweating on top of the bedclothes. Jacob listened to the soft wheeze of Alison's breathing, watched the gentle rise and fall of her soft breast. He leaned down and pulled the duvet up off the floor and spread it over them all the while never taking eyes off his angel for more than a swift heart-beat. Tucking the quilt tightly around her so that only her face poked out as if from some immense white parka, Jacob sat and studied every inch of that face; each tiny wrinkle, laughter lines around the corners of her eyes, the mole on her cheek below the left eye, the faint freckles peppering her pretty nose sweeping down onto her face were they faded into the blush of her cheeks. He brushed the back of his hand along Alison's chin feeling the delicate vibration of her lips as she kissed and smiled in sleep.

'Your ethereal radiance is invisible to strange eyes, but I see it my angel.' Jacob whispered on a breath as he kissed both her sleeping eyes.

The lovers awoke around one-thirty pm. Jacob leaped out of bed, threw together a mess of lunch and served it to his woman in bed. Alison ate quickly and was up and dressed before Jacob could suggest making love again.

'Sorry babe, but I have to make tracks got an appointment in town at two-thirty that I really can't miss.' Immediately suspicious, Jacob imagined her rushing out of the arms of one lover straight into those of another.

'Not another man is it?' He quipped trying desperately to disguise his true feelings.

'Yes of course it is my dear; there just aren't enough hours in the day to keep you all satisfied!' Alison giggled in reply. Jacob felt hurt, betrayed almost.

'I could give you a lift if you like?' But she was already pulling on her coat and hobbling towards the bedroom door.

'No don't be silly babe, just relax, stay as long as you like. I'll be back around five, if you're still here maybe we could pick up where we left off?' Jacob tried hard to look nonchalant, but in truth he was close to begging her not to go, or at least take him with her.

'Yeah, okay, no problem... sounds cool. I'll just hang out for a while, there're a couple of things I should be doing, but I suppose they can wait.' Alison blew him a kiss from the doorway.

'Great! I'll see you when I get back then! We could have some dinner together. Now I really have to run babe… well hobble as quickly as I can anyway!'

'Okay, I'll see you later then.' Inside Jacob was screaming as the door banged behind her and clicked shut.

*

It had been almost five minutes since he had last looked at his watch. Jacob dragged his carcass out of bed and studied his reflection in the mirror of Alison's dressing table. He rubbed the three day old auburn-grey stubble on his chin and checked his watch again - two-fifteen.

'Shit! She won't be here for hours yet.' He could not free the memory of that morning from his mind; everything had happened so fast. 'I hardly know this woman.' And yet, already he could not imagine life without her. Padding through to the living room, Jacob fruitlessly searched the mantelpiece for cigarettes. A second reflection observed him from the large mirror on the wall above the fire-place. 'What you looking at?' He tried in the small drawer on the table beside the couch where he came across a rolling tobacco tin. 'Bingo!' Inside, the tin contained a little bundle of rolling tobacco and some cigarette papers, a disposable lighter – no surprises there – but also a small lump of a brown substance that looked suspiciously like… 'Marijuana?' Jacob picked it out, put it to his nose and sniffed. It was undeniably, 'A tiny chunk of hashish! Alison you little raver!'

Jacob got to work building a joint; the piece of hash so small that he kept burning his fingers in the process. A few minutes, and several blisters later, he had finished. It could never claim to be the finest example of a spliff, a little bit crumpled, a little bit worn at the seams, but Jacob loved it... He quickly lit the thing up and puffed greedily and long. The smoke was sharp and harsh; it burned Jacob's throat and made him cough as he tried to take another inhalation. Sparks flew from the end like a roman candle, sending flaming hot rocks of marijuana hurtling downward onto his bare cock and balls. The *rocks* scalded like burning needles in his flesh. Jacob immediately threw the joint into the ashtray and ran screaming to the bathroom, leaped into the bath and snapped on the shower. The coldness caused a sharp intake of breath and an involuntary scream. Jacob could not work out what was worse, the stinging sensation of blistered flesh or the excruciating ache as his bollocks shot up trying to find his stomach.

As the pain at last began to subside to a pulsating ache, Jacob shut off the shower and stepped up, over and out of the bath. He grabbed a towel from the radiator and rubbed his hair and body vigorously, before gently dabbing at his wounded genitals. 'Ohya! Ya fucker! Jeezus!' Jacob searched the medicine cabinet above the toilet for something to soothe his tender penis. It was filled with tampons, makeup, toothpaste, perfume... but nothing specifically formulated to relieve the pain of a singed willy. He lifted Alison's red kimono-style dressing gown from a hook on the back of the bathroom door, adorned himself with it and exited in the direction of the kitchen to continue his quest for some sort of coolant.

There was no first aid kit to be found anywhere in the kitchen and his scorched dick was beginning to throb again... and not in a good way! He had to improvise. A bag of frozen peas procured from Alison's small top freezer proved far too cold. Next on the list for consideration was a tub of strawberry ice-cream, but this option was quickly rejected for fear of frostbite. He threw the small freezer door closed and opened the large door of the fridge underneath. The light wasn't working so Jacob had to hunker down to see what was inside. A lump of cheddar cheese, milk, processed cheese slices, orange juice, cottage cheese, butter, cheese spread... 'Shit girl, but you sure do love your bloody cheese!' Lurking in the far dark bottom left-hand corner Jacob spotted a tub of plain organic yogurt. He remembered reading somewhere that it was good for thrush or something. 'Well if it's good enough for thrush then...' He said hurriedly ripping off the lid before unceremoniously plopping in his pulsating scarlet member. 'Ahhhhh!!!' The relief was almost instantaneous.

Jacob carried the pot, willy still ensconced therein, through to the living room and retook his seat, clasping the yogurt tightly between his thighs. There was still a good bit of the joint left in the ashtray, but instead of jumping in feet first and firing it up, Jacob considered the situation carefully for a moment and decided to lift a magazine from the coffee table and place it cautiously over his lap for

78

protection before reigniting the spliff.

A couple of healthy lung-fulls of smoke later when he was feeling a bit sick and thinking seriously about putting the joint to bed, a flaming meteor flew from its' end. Caught in the earths gravitational pull it plummeted downward and landed on the magazine where it proceeded to burn its way through the face of some scantily clad *celeb'* on the front cover. Fate had stepped in and decided the action for him. Jacob stubbed the joint out a little too enthusiastically in the ashtray then dripped spit on the magazine, swirling the saliva around as if panning for gold until the glowing ember hissed into extinction. Jacob stood up and threw the soiled magazine into the waste paper basket to the right of the fireplace and looked at himself and the room reflected; the clock on the mantelpiece underneath the mirror read two forty-five. 'Looks like it's going to be a long day boy!'

*

Lifting the telephone with all the delicacy of a bricklayer, Jacob punched in the first few digits of Alison's mobile number. His right index finger extended and hovered above the key-pad gripped by an invisible force that would not allow him to complete the call. 'Fuck it! Don't want her to think that I'm the type of desperate wanker who can't bear to be on his own. Should really be calling Si about the funeral anyway.' He reasoned and wandered off in search of his jacket which was last seen hiding crumpled behind an armchair. Pulling his wallet from the inside pocket, Jacob thumbed through the various cards and pieces of paper inside looking for his brother's latest mobile phone number - the tattered photograph found amongst his fathers' things providing a momentary distraction. It seemed to Jacob as though Simon changed his mobile phone number about as often as he changed his underpants! But there it was, Si's latest eleven digit incarnation scribbled in red pen on the torn corner of a beer mat. Jacob returned to the telephone and punched the number in…it was ringing. The dialling tone repeated several times without reply and Jacob was about to hang up just as Simon answered. There was a definite air of suspicion apparent in his brusque voice.

'Hello?'

'Hi Simon, It's Jake.' Simon's voice relaxed,

'Hi Jake, didn't recognise the number, what's up bro?'

'Well apart from our dead father decomposing on a mortuary slab whilst we fanny around pretending all is well with the world, everything else is pretty much tickety-fucking-boo.'

'Are you feeling okay Jake? You sound a little wound up?'

'Sorry Simon, it's nothing really, just had a bit of an accident earlier, I'm still a bit tender to tell you the truth.'

'Tender? I'm scared to ask bro.'

'Well don't then. Honestly, you really don't want to know the gory details; suffice it to say that my cock had an argument with something very, very hot.'

'Ouch! You poor bastard!'

'Yes, thanks for your concern, Now listen Simon, have you had made any plans about the funeral?'

'Plans…what do you mean?'

'You know, getting time off work, how to get there, somewhere to stay, that kind of thing?'

'To tell you the truth Jake I haven't really given it much thought. Probably just grab a flight, or maybe get the ferry from Troon and then stay overnight with Auntie Esther and Uncle Andrew near Lisburn. I stayed with him last year when I was over for our Gary's wedding. As for getting time off, I don't think the woman at the dole office will mind too much if I don't go in for a couple of days.'

'Gary's wedding? Oh yeah, I remember, last July wasn't it? I couldn't make it because I was tied up with some project or other. Can't seem to remember what it was though.' There was a slight pause on the other end of the line.

'Big brother, are you tripping? Don't you remember? You were in hospital with food poisoning Jake. Don't you remember? It was me that took you there in a taxi.' A sudden flashback; Jacob had managed to delete the event from his memory for over a year, but here it was again, rising to the surface like a corpse bloated with death gases. It had not been food that had poisoned him, and it had certainly been no accident. A nervous throb nagged at his left eye as images from that night flickered like the replay of an old black and white movie... the she-devil slipping out of the door leaving the tragic hero to self-destruct in a quicksand of whiskey and pills.

That fateful night love had died for Jacob, and he remembered the feelings of crushing disappointment at being discovered by his brother collapsed and incoherent on the studio floor. He couldn't even do that properly. But now there was Alison, his angel, his salvation.

'Jake? You still there?'

'Yeah, just about Simon.' Jacob pushed the memory back to the bottom and regained his composure. 'I was just thinking that I never really got round to thanking you for all you did for me that night, you really saved my skin Si. I owe you one.'

'No problem, you'd have done the same for me. So, dad's funeral, has a date been finalised yet?'

'Nope, haven't even spoken to the undertaker yet, but I plan to get onto it first thing tomorrow morning.'

'It just doesn't seem real somehow, you know what I mean ?'

'Yeah, I know exactly what you mean. I suppose when everything's organised it'll all start to sink in. I'll give you a call with the details as soon as I now them myself. Did you say that you're back on the dole?'

'Yeah, that last job at the call-centre didn't really work out.'

'Oh yeah, what was it this time? Go in drunk again?'

'How dare you insinuate such a thing bro! Got caught shagging my supervisor in the stationary cupboard. Thought a written warning at most, but apparently it's a sackable offence!'

'The world's just not a fair place is it Si?'

'You can say that again bro. It was boring as fuck though, and this way I get to sign on right away.'

'I can never understand how you can be so casual about stuff like that Si, I'd be stressed out not knowing where my next pound is coming from.'

'You know me bro, life's too short and all that shite. As long as I've got enough money for a couple of pints, my beans are Heinz and my toilet paper is Andrex Quilted Velvet, then I'm a happy bunny.'

'So I'll book us a couple of seats on the ferry from Troon then. We have to take the old man by boat, remember?'

'Yeah, his fear of flying, forgot about that one! But anyway, that sounds cool Jake. I'll pay you back as soon as I can.'

'Yeah right, and the rest!'

'No, I promise bro, I'm due a housing benefit cheque on Tuesday, I'll give you the money then.'

'Listen Si, don't worry about it, really.' Jacob caught sight of the dead joint in the ashtray and the empty tobacco tin lying beside it on the table. 'There is one really huge favour you could do for me though.'

'Name it Jakey boy!'

'Well, I was wondering if you would be able to get your hands on a bit of hash for me. I'm not looking for a freebie or anything like that, I'll give you the money to buy it for me.'

'What the hell! Has my sensible, middle-class older brother turned into a raving pot-head?'

'Come on Si, I went to art school, remember? Smoking hash was on the bloody curriculum! Stop mucking about, it's no big deal. I just need to unwind you know? Fed up with the drink as well. Call it nostalgia if you like. So can you get me some or not?'

'Are you sure about this bro? I don't want to be the one who corrupts you; the one who sends you down the slippery slope to hard drugs and prostitution!' Jacob frowned frustrated at the other end of the line.

'Well if it's too much trouble for you I'll try someone else!' He snapped.

'Simmer down there big man, keep your knickers on, I'm only having a laugh, just winding you up a bit. Sure I can score you some weed, no sweat. Now then, down to business, how much of *da ganja* are you actually looking for?'

'Oh? I'm not sure exactly? Enough for a good few smokes. How much would that be…a few grams, I guess?'

'I'll see what I can do bro, but no promises, okay?' This was one of two expressions Jacob had heard too many times before and which generally meant *fuck you*. He needed something more, a definite answer.

'Listen Simon, seriously, call me at this number in about an hour if you can't get any, I don't want to be hanging on all night.'

'Oh right Jake, so you can call your *main dealer* and score from him? Now listen to me bro, be cool, I'll sort it, just kick back and chill out man.'

'Simon, that's not what I meant. It's just… I'm at someone's house… a woman. She'll be back about five and I want to be here waiting for her...*alone*'

'Ah now it all becomes clear! Don't want to be disturbed. I get it Jake, clear as fucking crystal mate! What's the address?'

'Flat six, Thirty-three Woodlands Road, top left-hand buzzer. But why do you need to know the address?'

'I'll drop it off for you bro.'

'You sure ? It's a bit out of your way isn't it?'

'Normally yes, but I'm meeting some people in the west end later on tonight, so it's sort of on my way.'

'Well, if you're positive, that would be excellent.' Jacob had a sudden flash of inspiration, one of those romantic gestures that would be sure to charm the pants off his woman.

'Oh, and Si, could I ask you just one other wee favour please?'

'Depends what it is bro. Shoot.'

'This might sound a little strange, but do you have a copy of the Elvis Costello album 'My Aim is True'?'

'Hmmm? Don't think so Jake.'

'Fuck! Greatest hits?'

'Nope. Sorry Jake.'

'Do you know any one who does have copies of either of those two albums?'

'Not offhand, but listen, I'll be heading off up the town shortly so if you're really desperate I'll see what I can do.'

'I'm not exactly, what you'd call, *desperate* Si, but I would really appreciate the favour mate.'

'No problem bro…what was the name of it again? My Aimy's Foo?'

'No, 'My Aim is True' you dunderhead!'

'Okay…and it's by Elvis?'

'Aye, Costello thought, not Presley!'

'I know Jake, I'm only pulling your plonker mate! Dinny fash yersel! I'll speak to you later Jake.'

'Aye, see ye later Si...ya fanny!'

'No problem bro. I won't let you down.'

And there was the second expression! It was now three o'clock.

*

The allotted time came and went and there was still no sign of Simon. It was almost four thirty-five and Jacob was getting desperate. Alison would be coming home very soon and he didn't want his brother here when she arrived. He needed to be with her...alone.

'Little shit!' Jacob shouted at the clock. The sound of footsteps echoed up the stairs, was it Simon? What of it was Alison? Jacob panicked and rapidly tip-toed in the direction of the front door to spy out of the peep-hole. Standing there peering out, fish-eyed at the empty hallway, he had no idea what he was going to do if it was Alison. Jacob prayed for his brother's arrival as the footsteps drew nearer. A shadow appeared on the wall opposite and grew larger and darker accompanied by the loud rasp of a chesty cough - a male cough. Jacob stood down from the peep-hole, took a firm grip of the door handle and prepared to throw it open and lambaste his brother for cutting it so fine. Voices, he heard voices from the hallway and leaned in closer to the door. It was only one voice, male low and gruff accompanied by, panting? The voice came again, closer this time.

'C'mon you or you'll no get any tea the night.'

Confused, Jacob let go of the door handle and pressed his eye hard to the peep-hole. A scuffling, heavily over-coated, flat-capped grey-beard bent almost double with the weight of time, was slowly disappearing up the hallway, dragging in his wake a knackered looking border collie at the end of a makeshift rope-lead. The old dog stopped and looked round, its ears pricked up.

'How the fuck did it know I was watching?' Jacob thought and held his breath. The old man gave the lead a sharp yank.

'C'mon tae fuck Rover, the fitba's on at five!'

The dog gave a half-hearted yelp and reluctantly obeyed. Three sharp knuckle-raps on the door the other side of his face caused Jacob to jump back almost four feet and land on his arse.

'That you I hear in there Jake? What's all the racket? You shagging already ya dirty cunt?' The letter-box squeaked open revealing Simon's peering eyes. 'Did you get tired waiting, have to sit down bro? Well I suppose you are getting on a bit now, need to take things easy.' Jacob got to his feet as quickly as he could, adjusted his, or rather Alison's, dressing gown, and opened the door. Simon flung his arms open in salutation, his long army parka spreading like two giant, green fur-lined wings to reveal a white *'Devo – Mongoloid'* t-shirt, ripped denim jeans (looked like ancient Levi 501's) and on his feet, a pair of tattered red Converse baseball boots. Jacob looked less than impressed.

'Well as you can tell I am not as you so delicately put it *shagging*, I'm stuck in here waiting for you. Where the hell have you been?' Simon stepped over the thresh-hold carrying the smell of pubs and the outside world in to the flat, his hands raised in conciliatory manner.

'Calm down big brother, keep your, what is that, a kimono? Whatever it is, keep it on. I'll be in and out before you know it. And no punch-lines about actresses and bishops please! Listen Jake, I am really sorry about the delay, but I ran into an old mate of mine that I hadn't seen for years, so, naturally, I had to go for a pint with him. Why were you sitting on the floor by the way?' Jacob's initial thought was to grab the nearest heavy object and beat his brother about the face and head until unconscious. But Simon's last statement had caught him somewhat off-guard. The onus was now on Jacob to explain the situation.

'Well...' He stumbled clumsily through the library of excuses stored in his brain, but none seemed to fit the circumstances, '... The reason I was sitting on the floor is...' he had to improvise, '...the floor is... this bit of the floor here by the door specifically, is eh... is nice and cold... the accident I told you about on the phone earlier, remember?' He could see that Simon was having difficulty with short-term memory, this was normal for him, you just had to give him a moment to fish it out. A smile of recollection surfaced and spread slowly over his face.

'Oh yeah!' Simon pointed a thin finger in the direction of his brother's crotch, 'And how is the *little general* now then?'

'Never mind my *little general,* and we'll have less of the *little* thank you very much.' Simon rummaged in the left-hand pocket of his parka, pulling out a small brown lump wrapped in Clingfilm.

'I've got your illegal substances here bro.' He said holding it aloft and giving it a shake. Jacob shot out his right hand grabbing his brother's lapel and pulled him into the flat, slamming the door behind in one motion with his left.

'For fuck sake Simon, a little more discretion please! I don't want Alison's neighbours phoning the fucking polis on us.'

'So that's her name then…Alison?'

'What? Yes her name *is* Alison and she'll be back any minute now, so we need to make this quick. How much do I owe you?'

'Well, seeing it's you Jake, we'll call it an even fifteen quid.' Simon replied, casually dropping the lump of hash into a pocket of the kimono.

'Okay, wait here, I just need to get my wallet from the bedroom.'

'No problem big brother, I'll just hang out and admire the view of the coat-stand.' Jacob hurried off to find his wallet trying to estimate all the while just how much his brother was ripping him off. He rescued the wallet from his jacket once again which had by now somehow managed to get itself trapped under the wardrobe! Inside the cash flaps were three ten-pound notes - no loose change.

'Have you got a fiver on you Simon, I've only got two tenners?' Jacob knew what the reply was going to be and wondered why he had even bothered asking.

'Sorry bro, I haven't been to the bank yet. I'll give you back the fiver when we get the ferry.' Jacob knew that there was more hope of his dad taking him for a pint than ever getting his fiver back, but what choice did he have? He took two of the notes from his wallet and tossed it onto the dressing table. Back in the hallway Simon was busy trying on one of Alison's collection of woolly hats that lived on top of the coat-stand.

'What d'ya think Jake? Pink's not really my colour though eh?'

'Put it back Simon, I don't want Alison catching nits or something.'

'That's harsh Jake, I have a bath once a year, whether I need one or not!' said Simon replacing the hat.

'Here you go...' said Jacob handing over the cash, '...and I will get my change back Si, won't I?' Simon took the money with a smirk.

'Oh, nearly forgot bro...' Said Simon pulling a CD from his inside pocket, '...that Costello song you wanted is on this old compilation CD; completely forgot I had it. You can keep a hold of it if you like, I never listen to it.' Jacob accepted the CD, perhaps a bit too eagerly.

'Thanks a lot Si, one I owe you mate.'

'Oh, it's like Christmas has come early for you Jake! Got another little surprise here for you...' Simon said sticking two fingers into the small 'watch' pocket of his jeans. He slid out a small square of paper wrapped in silver foil and dropped it into Jacob's hand. '...Courtesy of Mr Alexander Martin.' Jacob looked at the

91

small silver package then at his brother.

'Alexander who?'

'Alex Martin... big Ally? Tall skinny guy? Long curly blonde hair? Completely off his head?' Simon had a habit of doing this, starting to tell you one thing then going off on a tangent and it secretly drove Jacob nuts. He was about to tell his brother to bugger off in no uncertain terms when the thought occurred that Simon' services might be required in the not to distant future should he have to score again soon. In any case, Jacob had a vague idea who his brother was talking about this time and so decided to humour him.

'I think I remember him... was he the guy that blew himself up on Bath Street?'

'The very man! He did that when he was working on the roads with the council, drilled into an electricity cable, his hair's never been the same since. Man that dude was so fucking lucky that time. Got sacked from his job for it as well, which I thought was a bit harsh.' Jacob now knew exactly who his Simon was talking about; Alex Martin was a six-foot-four-inch nutcase who used to drink in his local pub. He had a run in with the psycho one night after accusations of cheating at the domino table were aired. Jacob had managed to slip out the side door before the big man had gone ballistic and chucked a bar stool through the gantry.

'The last I heard of him he had been found burying himself in the sand on Dumbarton beach... said the street lights were after him or something?'

'Oh yeah, I remember, the big man had swallowed about a hundred-and-fifty magic mushrooms that particular afternoon. Ended up remanded in the Bar 'L' for that one.'

'So what's the big psycho up to now then...' enquired Jacob, '...on the dole, rehab, jail, Carstairs?'

'None of the above bro, he's actually just finished his Ph.D. in experimental particle physics.' Jake's jaw almost hit the floor.

'You must be fucking joking!'

'No way Jake, straight up! The boy has hidden depths. He said it was something about measuring background radiation in the universe... trying to work out the exact moment when everything exploded into existence. He's scored this really cool number with the ministry of defence down south developing short-range nuclear missiles. Starts on Monday, so it's his sort of farewell do tonight over at the Aragon Bar. I'm heading down there now, but we'll be there pretty much all night if you fancy a couple of pints.' But Jacob didn't even need to think about his answer.

'Might give it a miss tonight Si, got other plans, if you now what I mean.'

'I know exactly what you mean bro, couple of joints to loosen her knickers up a bit, get her in the mood... eh... eh? I'll leave you to *it* then, and I'm sure you know what *I* mean...' As Simon turned the handle and opened the door, Jacob again had the urge to assault him with a blunt object, but just managed to resist the temptation.

'Hey Simon, before you go… what is it then?' Jacob called after his brother nodding referentially to the small silver package resting in the palm of his upturned hand. A large grin opened on Simon's face.

'Ah yes, that oh brother of mine, is one lovely little tab of LSD. Cracking bit of kit apparently, double dipped strawberry, just for you.' Jacob folded back a loose flap of foil to reveal the half image of what did indeed appear to be a strawberry.

'Well thanks, I guess? I haven't touched that stuff since I was a student.' However, the truth was that Jacob had never touched *that stuff* at all, not even as a student. He had pissed his time away at art school in the bar punctuated with the occasional joint in the toilets which was usually followed by the occasional 'whitey'.

'Oh keep it anyway, in case of emergencies…' Simon replied from the hallway, '…and you'll let me know about the funeral, yeah?'

'Sure, as soon as I know something you'll know something.'

'Sound as a pound Jake. Seems like a long time before the old boy will finally be planted though doesn't it? I mean, he croaked on Friday for Christ sake, will he not be getting a little smelly by the time we finally manage to get him to Ireland?'

'No dear brother, he won't be *getting a little smelly,* as you so delicately put it, because as far as I am aware, he's still inside a big fridge in the hospital morgue.'

94

'All sounds a bit weird to me Jake, keeping a hold of the old man for so long and everything? I thought he'd have been shipped off to the funeral directors or somewhere by now?' In truth Jacob probably agreed with Simon, but there was no way he was going to admit to having the same opinion as his brother.

'I'm not one hundred per cent sure what's happening exactly, if I'm being totally honest Simon, they didn't tell me much at the hospital. But I'll call them first thing tomorrow morning and try and get some answers. I'm sure there's a perfectly rational explanation.' Simon shrugged in reply.

'Perhaps the old bugger's not dead after all, eh bro? Just all a big joke, an elaborate hoax.'

'Nope, he was definitely stone-cold deed when I saw him at the hospital.'

'Yeah, but how do you know it was him? It could just have been some random corpse made up to look like him or something.'

'He farted at me Simon.'

'Ah well, no mistake then, it was definitely him then! Anyway Jake, love to stay and chat, but I've really got to shoot off. Enjoy the smoke, and give me a buzz if you need any more.'

'Yeah, thanks a lot. See you later Si.'

'See ya bro.' Jacob threw the door shut and pulled the hash from his kimono pocket. He brought it to his nose and sniffed deeply. It smelled good. 'Time to get busy rolling a number boy!' He chirped and checked his watch - four-fifty-two.

*

Alison arrived home a little after five-fifteen, Jacob met her at the door and kissed her tenderly, passionately, before any words were exchanged or jackets discarded.

'Nice dressing gown Mr D...' She frowned and sniffed the air. '...Is that what I think it is?' They walked along the hallway and entered the living room, Jacob hesitating, to answer attempting to gauge her reaction. He wasn't sure; maybe the tin had been left by an old boyfriend?

'Should have thought first you twat!' Jacob decided to play it safe. 'Yeah, it's... eh... cannabis. My little brother Si was here, you just missed him in fact. He smokes quite a bit and, well...' Alison cut in before Jacob could finish.

'Did he happen to leave any behind? I could murder a good smoke! Oh sorry Jake, maybe you don't approve?' But all he was feeling was a deep sense of relief.

'Not at all, I approve wholeheartedly! He actually gave me a little bit for myself. I don't really smoke that often these days, but sometimes the notion just takes me, you know?' Jacob poured out two large glasses of the red wine he had opened in readiness ten minutes earlier, shortly after cueing up the *special* track from the CD Simon had dropped off on Alison's stereo. He handed a glass of wine to Alison who had sat herself down on the sofa. 'And I've got another little surprise for you babe.'

''Mmmm, lovely, I love surprises…well nice ones anyway.' She said accepting the glass and taking a sip. 'So come on then, what is it?' She continued. Jacob moved behind the sofa towards the stereo.

'Just an old tune I found that I thought you might appreciate.' Replied Jacob, his finger poised over the play button.

'As long as it's not that awful Elvis Costello song *Alison*! My ex used to play it to me all the time. I can't stand that bloody tune! The mere sound of it makes me physically sick!' Jacob's heart sank. He pressed eject then dropkicked the CD under the sofa and started to panic.

'Eh…I'm sure I put it down here somewhere.' He was breathing heavily pretending, to look for something. A proverbial light-bulb flashed somewhere above Jacob's head. 'Oh bugger! You now what's happened don't you?' He began, introducing his master plan. Alison shrugged her shoulders. 'My dozy brother was dropping off that *message* earlier, right? Well, I bet he's lifted the bag with the CD in it by mistake on his way out. Dozy gitt!' Jacob held his breath, fake smiled as best he could, looked at her, tried not to crack and give the game away. Alison casually took another sip of wine. *'She's not buying this bullshit…think of a plan b quickly Jake!'* Alison broke her silence.

'That's a shame, but never mind babe. So what was the tune anyway?' But Jacob hadn't thought this far ahead. He started to panic again.

'Think fast you fuckwitt! Think romantic, sexy, cool...big Marv! 'Feel All My Love Inside' by Marvin Gaye...it's a song from the album 'Love Songs and Bedroom Ballads'...a classic.' Alison paused. *'She's never bloody heard of it...she hates Marv...how can she hate Marvin Gaye?'*

'I don't think I've ever heard of that album'

'Shit! She does hate Marvin Gaye! What are you woman, made of ice?'

'But I do really love Marvin Gaye though, such a sexy voice. I'd love to hear it sometime... when you retrieve it from your brother of course.'

'Result! She's human after all!' 'I'll get it right back from him as soon as I can babe.' Jacob sat down next to Alison and she responded, moving in close, slipping her hands inside the kimono, rubbing his chest and gently scratching her nails. She looked deep into Jacob's dilating eyes and spoke in a voice like smoke blown through honey.

'Well then big boy, you roll us a fat one and I'll go and warm up the bed.' Alison flicked out her moist, pink tongue and licked Jacob's lips. 'Don't take to long...' she continued, brushing his crotch as she slipped past him towards the bedroom.

It was the fastest joint Jacob had ever rolled! When he entered the bedroom, Alison was already under the duvet wearing nothing but a wicked smile. He placed the joint, lighter and ashtray on the table beside her.

'You don't hang around do you?'

'Not when there's something tasty on the menu.' Alison smiled and lit the joint, placing the ashtray carefully underneath to catch any flaming debris. Jacob wished he'd thought of that earlier.

He had always considered himself a hypocrite when it came to tobacco, having never really liked the look of a woman smoking. But the way that Alison held the joint so suggestively between her lips, lazily sucking in the smoke. He had never seen anything so sexy. She passed him the joint.

'Bit dangerous isn't it?' Jacob looked perplexed.

'Normal cigarettes are just as bad for your health.' He ventured. Alison's face broke into a smile - that was another thing about her he loved, the way she would smile with her whole face, not just her mouth or her eyes; Jacob swore that when she smiled even her hair looked happy!

'No silly, I meant smoking in bed!' Jacob forced a laugh, but secretly felt like a total idiot. He quickly attempted to move the conversation on.

'This is actually the first time that I've really smoked a joint since my student days.' he lied, 'What about you?' Alison studied the ceiling for a second then back at Jacob.

'I've had the occasional smoke at parties and that, but I haven't smoked on a regular basis since I left school and started work.' Jacob was a bit taken aback, he hadn't even heard of cannabis until he was at least eighteen years of age; and here was his sweet, innocent girlfriend telling him that she had been smoking dope *regularly* as a school girl!

'At school? You have hidden depths indeed Miss Spencer… if that indeed is your real name?' He passed the joint back to her.

'Yep, there's a lot you don't know about me Mr Douglas. More than a few skeletons rattling around in my closet!' Jacob paused, waited for further information, but nothing was revealed.

'So tell me one more of your dark secrets then.' Alison sucked on the joint, exhaled slowly.

'All in good time lover, all in good time.'

Jacob wondered what could be so bad that she felt unable to tell him. Was he not the most important person in her life now? Surely she could tell him anything, everything? He wanted to take her by the shoulders, shake her ask her why, but managed to ride the wave.

'Better to play it cool anyway. There's more than one way to skin a Cat' Jake.'

'How about I tell you something about my past and then you tell me something about yours?'

'My past isn't really that interesting.' replied Alison passing him the joint, 'But if it makes you happy my dear. You go first then.' Jacob again felt the anger swell - why was she avoiding sharing herself like this? He felt cheated and betrayed, but was not about to let Alison win. He would play it her way, open up and show how easy it could be. Then surely she would have to talk?

'Okay then... now, let me think? Ah yes! Well here goes. I was at this party over on the south side, somewhere around Shawlands. It was mostly full of hippy art school types. Anyway, I used to be known as a bit of a star at the old joint rolling back then you know.' Jacob looked at Alison in mock arrogance - she reciprocated, ironically impressed. 'So at this party two of us, me and a friend of mine called Larry, known to his close associates as *Larry the Lung* due to his propensity for smoking dope, went around getting bits of hash, rolling tobacco and fags from anyone who could spare, encouraging donors with the promise of a smoke from the resulting joint. So we ended up with two huge piles of dope and tobacco sitting on the kitchen table, and then got to work putting together a monster joint. We must have gone through about ten packets of roll-up papers putting the skins together. The thing looked like a kite! Then, just as we were about to start rolling the joint up, Larry pulled this wee plastic bag from his pocket full of white powder, said it would make this party and him a legend.' Alison frowned.

'What was it, speed... coke?' Jacob shot Alison a resigned look and shook his head. 'I wish it had been either of those, but sadly no. When Larry the lung did something he did it properly. The bag was full of heroin... grade 'A' smack. He poured the whole lot in when no-one was looking. I tried to stop him, but he just kept saying that it would be a laugh.' Jacob stopped and took a long drag on the joint and waited. Eventually, Alison gave in.

'So what the bloody hell happened then Jacob?' He pretended to be lost in thought. A moment passed and Alison grew more impatient. 'So come on, for heavens sake tell me Jacob, don't keep me in suspenders babe!'

'Chance would be a fine thing!' He said offering Alison the joint. She took it, her eyes remaining fixed on his. Jacob gave a long sigh.

'Well, it wasn't pretty I can tell you that. Three people ended up in hospital, one girl almost died.' Alison looked shocked.

'Oh my god! She was okay in the end though, wasn't she?' Jacob now had her right where he wanted, hanging on his every word. He loitered yet again, building the tension.

'Once she came out of the coma she was fine…well physically anyway. Psychologically she was completely fucked up, totally paranoid, couldn't trust anyone, and who would blame her? Imagine your best friend almost killing you.' Alison shot him a puzzled glance.

'Who's best friend? Yours? Larry's?' Jacob's eyes were lost for a moment, but he quickly retraced the thread of memory back to the present.

'Not my best friend, I hardly knew the girl. No, no she was Larry's friend.' Alison seemed momentarily satisfied.

'So what happened to the girl then? What's she up to these days?' Jacob sat up feeling a little uncomfortable with what he considered to be too many questions.

His eyes caught the image of his reflected self in the mirror on Alison's wardrobe door.

'No idea. Like I said, I never really knew her anyway. Lost touch will that crowd years ago.'

'And Larry?' Jacob turned his attentions back to Alison.

'Larry? I saw Larry a couple of weeks after the party, but, well, things were never the same, no trust left. If you can do something like that and not even feel in the slightest bit guilty, well… Anyway, enough about me, you're up next I believe. So spill the beans Miss Spencer!' Alison attempted to take a puff at the joint, but it was so charred by now that it kept burning her fingers and lips. She stubbed out the glowing doubt in the ashtray, throwing it a look of satisfied disgust as she did so. 'That was like trying to smoke a hot brick!' Jacob smiled.

'Yeah, well it had started to burn my fingers as well so I thought I'd better get rid of it before I had an accident.' He added with a hint of mischief in his voice.

Jacob waited impatiently for Alison to begin her story, but she just sat there smiling inanely. He shrugged, raised his brow, 'So?' She stared blankly back, a vacant sign posted in her eyes for a second before she remembered.

'Oh yes, sorry babe, I was off floating in the stratosphere somewhere. In actual fact it's not really that good a story anyway.' Jacob forced a smile.

'It had better be fan-bloody-tastic after you bared your soul to her… It doesn't matter how shit you think it is Miss Spencer, a deal's a deal. I shared my past

with you now you have keep your side of the bargain.' Alison fixed and plumped her pillows before sitting back to begin her tale.

'Well, it happened when I was at college, me and my best friend, who for reasons soon to be made apparent shall remain nameless, had just picked up our grant cheques - that was back in the good old days when you still got student grants! I don't know how the poor buggers get by on these student loan things these days. I mean imagine coming out of uni' or college and having to start off your working life with twenty grand of debt...' Jacob tried to mask his impatience. '...Sorry, was getting on my soap box there? I do apologise... now, where was I?'

'You and your friend had just picked up your grant cheques... in the *good old days*.' Jacob prompted sarcastically.

'Oh yes... well the first thing we did after depositing the said cheques in the bank and, of course, drawing some money on them, is hit the student union for a few *light refreshments*. Cider and blackcurrant was what we all used to drink back then - horrible stuff, I don't know how I managed to keep it down to be honest! But I do remember that it made your vomit a wonderful shade of purple though. You see, all term long there had been this running joke in our particular clique that when we received the final instalment of our grants, we were all going to bugger off straight to the nearest airport and buy a ticket to somewhere warm with a nice beach. So me and my mate are sitting there swilling back the booze and thinking out loud where we would like to go. A few more of our crowd filtered in and joined us and before we knew it we were right in the middle of a full on afternoon session with no way out! All of us ended up back at someone's flat partying - the wine and beer was flowing and the joints were flying around. What happened next exactly, I'm not sure, events of that afternoon are all a bit of a blur. But the last thing I do remember is the both of us, me and my friend, that is, heading out to the off licence for more booze, but I'm not entirely sure if we actually made it or not.' Jacob felt a bit cheated.

'Is that it? You got smashed and can't remember what happened? Shit woman, I've lost count of the number of times I've done that!' Alison raised her hand and stopped Jacob dead mid-diatribe.

'Excuse me Mr Douglas, but I hadn't quite finished.' Jacob raised his hands in defence and bowed apologetically.

'I do beg your pardon Miss Spencer. Please accept my humble apologies and pray, continue with your tale of drunken depravity.' Alison reciprocated with a small but elegant nod of appreciation.

'Well the next morning, as, I'm sure you can imagine I woke up in a rather *delicate* state. I was afraid to make the slightest move, even my hair hurt! My mouth tasted as if some kind of small animal had been using it as a toilet during the night, and my throat was as dry as the proverbial Arab's sandal! I needed to get myself a drink of water fast, so I very gingerly peeled back the quilt and rolled out of bed as slowly and carefully as possible. When the room had stopped spinning I had a look round and noticed that things were not as they should be; I didn't recognise the room at all, had no idea where I was. Things around me began to ring alarm bells, tell-tale signs - a kettle with individual coffee sachets and tea bags, those little white cartons of milk and brown cartons of cream; fresh white towels neatly piled on a chair by the door, a 'Do Not Disturb' sign hanging from the handle. I was in a bloody hotel room! Then I heard snoring coming from the other side of the room and looked over to see my friend asleep in another single bed. And so, naturally, I thought that we'd actually gone and done it, you know, blew our grants on a couple of air tickets. I shouted at her to wake up, which she wasn't too amused about. She shouted something like *fuck you* and turned over. But when I explained our situation she came to very quickly. We both just sat there in a daze for about ten minutes trying to piece together the events of the previous evening, where the hell exactly were we and how the fuck we'd got there?' Jacob sat up intrigued and excited at the illicit adventures of this woman.

'So the two of you had got *bloottered* and blown your grant on a cheap holiday then?' Alison screwed up her face.

'Well sort of...' She raised her eyebrows, shook her head, '...not exactly.' Jacob frowned.

'What do you mean?'

Well, we did make it as far as Glasgow Airport, but we were so pished that none of the airlines would entertain us, so we booked into the Travel Inn at the airport for the night.' Jacob laughed but couldn't help feeling a little disappointed. He rubbed Alison's shoulder then lay back on the pillows and put both hands behind his head. 'Well I suppose you tried babe. And you nearly got there, didn't you? Maybe we could go away together sometime?' Alison leant in and brushed his cheek with her warm lips.

'Or maybe we could just stay in bed for a week or two?' Jacob took her by the shoulders pulling her on top of him and kissing her mouth hard and open. Alison felt Jacob's cock stiffen against her stomach and broke off the kiss. Reaching backward, her naked golden skin stretching taut and shining like polished wood, she clicked off the bedside lamp.

They were enveloped by a forest of darkness. Jacob reached out his hand into the velvet black searching for Alison. She took his hand and kissed its' upturned palm before guiding it onto her breast. Jacob could just distinguish Alison's silhouetted form as she moved towards him; he felt strangely displaced, floating in a vacuum, unaware of time or anything physical outside of that particular space inhabited only by him and his woman. She washed over him in tidal animation and he was completely and absolutely submerged within her. Bodies transformed, became a flowing metamorphic form, both part of and cloaked in the blue-blackness of night. Jacob felt his soul merge with Alison's, the sensation drawing every breath from his body.

As their essence divided Jacob was thrown backwards through eternity into even darker waters. Soft rain falling onto trembling flesh wrenched him from the dream zone. The bed felt empty and lonely - Jacob panicked and sat up quickly.

'It's okay babe, I'm right here.' Spoke Alison from his right. He looked towards her voice. She was stood by the window smoking a cigarette, the moonlight painting her naked body a strange Chiascuro. Jacob had never seen anything so beautiful.

'Am I dreaming?' She turned her head in his direction.

'Nope, I'm as real as they come Jacob.' Alison focused her attention back on the window and used her finger to write her name in the condensation that covered its surface.

'Come back to bed...' Pleaded Jacob, '...I miss you.' Alison giggled.

'How can you miss me you silly bugger, I'm right here?' Jacob sighed and took a breath, tried to explain.

'Alison, I miss you when you go to the toilet, when you fall asleep beside me...' He hesitated, unsure whether the time was right, thinking that it might be far too soon, fearing the tearing pain of rejection.

'There's no way you can cope with that J.J.... not again.' But there was no way he could deny the intensity of these feelings either. This was it! Alison had to be

the one. '…I love you Alison.' Jacob's heart rushed all the blood in his body to his brain then stopped beating. Alison stood there in silence. Jacob strained, but could not make out her face in the gloom. Was she smiling, shocked, angry, repulsed? He watched anxiously as his woman, if she was indeed still his woman after this revelation, stubbed out her cigarette and closed the bedroom window. She seemed to take an eternity to walk the five or so steps over to the bed where she sat down facing away from him. A moment passed. Jacob closed his eyes and prepared himself for the killer blow. The sound of Alison moving herself around on the bed, twisting her slender torso towards him she broke the darkness. A soft hand brushed Jacob's cheek and he opened his eyes in time to see Alison lean and place a kiss him softly upon his lips.

'I love you too Jacob…'

*

Jacob felt himself fall again. Music off in the distance; voices flitted into his head and out again before he could distinguish what they were telling him. He strained to hear, concentrated, the voices were barely audible. Were they calling his name? He listened harder. Someone was telling him how wonderful Alison was, but not in a friendly way. There was something cruel and ugly in this voice. Jacob spun around searching the room. No-one, he was still alone. Turning his head to the right Jacob saw a shapeless blue blob being absorbed by his pillow. The colour resonated and intensified as it bled into the material, he could feel a peculiar musical vibration and was drawn towards it. The blob glowed with a familiar light that burned brightest as the last remnants blinked into infinity. The voice came again.

'So you think that she's the one then Jacob?' He recognised the voice, could not match it to an owner. 'But you'll probably screw this one up like all the rest wont you?' Something in the tone, so familiar; who the hell was it hiding in the shadows? 'You are so predictable, so transparent...so pathetic!' The darkness closed in around Jacob like cold black tar. He tried to run, but the darkness was concentrated, impenetrable. It weighed so heavy and crushing on his chest. Jacob had to fight for breath. Light cracked through an opening door and he made a lunge for it, falling towards and through onto a bare wooden landing. A naked light-bulb swung pendulous, flickering yellow overhead. These walls were familiar to Jacob. He rose to his feet and checked the view from the window. Dull orange street lamps cast heavy and sad over the grey September roads and pavements, oscillating and merging in the desolate gloom to form a vast velvet ocean. It bred an uneasy feeling in Jacob's soul and he turned away, walking briskly toward another opening door. Inside many dark, faceless bodies swayed in a half-light to wailing backwards-music. Jacob spotted his brother Simon standing by the back wall, drink in one hand woman on the other, and found his way to him through the crowd.

'Hi Jake, welcome to my wedding! I'm glad you could make it bro.' Simon handed Jacob a glass of Champagne. 'Would you like to kiss the bride?' Continued Simon gesturing to the woman on his arm. She was adorned in a loose-fitting mould-green dress with bits of what appeared to be some kind of sea-weed clinging to her in various positions. Jacob scrutinised her face; it was covered in flaking patches of brown and yellow skin, her hair hanging in matted tresses, snagged with twigs and leaves that dripped wet on the cold stone floor. Sickened and repulsed, he closed his eyes rigid-taut and was back in Alison's bed, warm and familiar.

'Thank fuck for that; what a fucking nightmare!' He breathed relieved. A shadow moving at his feet caused adrenaline to pump up his heart rate and goose-bumps. There was a figure sitting at the end of the bed. 'Alison?'

'What would you do if someone broke into your room while you were sleeping and started to beat you Jacob?' It was a female voice.

'What? Alison, how did you…' But he already sensed that something was not right.

'What would you do Jacob?' That voice?

'Who are you?' Jacob shouted and tried to sit up; but before he could move she was upon him, punching and slapping, kneeling on the bedclothes either side of Jacob's arms, trapping him down.

'What will you do Jacob? What can you do?' The woman spat at him. Jacob struggled under the bedclothes, thrashed and strained every sinew of his body trying to force her off. 'What are you going to do little man?' He twisted violently and managed to off-balance the woman toppling her over to the side. Jacob leapt from the bed.

'Who the fuck are you? What did I do to deserve this?' The woman screamed and flew at him again. Jacob felt a dull crack followed by sharp pain as her forehead connected with the bridge of his nose and the floor rushed quickly up to meet him. Almost instantaneously the woman straddled his body once again, pinning his arms with her knees.

'What would you do Jacob?' As she leaned forward her face was illuminated by the blue moonlight and Jacob saw her for the first time. It was the woman from the party, the woman Simon had introduced as his new bride.

'You? But why? She answered by bringing her clenched fists crashing down onto Jacob's face raining blow after blow.

'It would be self-defence, wouldn't it? That's what they'd say.' Jacob managed to work one of his hands free. He grabbed the woman's arm and pulled her over onto the ground. 'That's right, Jacob... it would only be self-defence, wouldn't it?' That voice, it was the same voice he had heard calling him in the bedroom earlier. 'Show me what you would do Jacob. Come on show me what you would do. Show me, come on little man, show me; show me! Fucking show me!' He just had to make her stop! Jacob manoeuvred himself on top of her using his body weight to pin her down. 'Show me you useless little fuck!'

'I'll fucking show you all right bitch!' Shouted Jacob, and punched her hard in the face, making a red mess of her nose.

'Is that the best you can do? You're nothing you cunt!'

Jacob punched her over and over shouting,

'Why? Why? Why...' But she kept on talking, even began to laugh at him. Jacob bit at her face tearing off great lumps of flesh and spitting them out. But her shrill, crow-rasp laughter growing louder still.

'Come on little man, you can do better than that! Ha, ha, ha, ha...' She spat. He dug his thumbs deep into the woman's eyes and felt her brain squelch under his nails. He ripped the eyeballs from her head then watched in horror as two new staring electric blue eyes formed in her empty sockets. All the while the voice continued, 'Is that the best you can do? Is that the worst you can think of?' He felt as though his head might explode and tried to run. But the woman grabbed his foot and sunk her yellowed teeth deep into the back of his ankle. Jacob felt something snap and fell screaming to the floor, pain electrifying every cell of his body. The woman spoke again, but this time her voice was stained blue with melancholy. 'But Jacob you said you loved me. You promised that you would never hurt me. You did love me Jacob, didn't you?'

113

He sat bolt upright, heart racing, struggling for breath. Somewhere far outside the city a ship sounded its' lonely horn. Jacob checked the bottom of the bed for unwanted shadows before fumbling on the bedside table for a cigarette.

'Holy shit! I had better cut down on the caffeine!' He whispered trying to make light of his nightmare – it didn't work, he was still shaking. Perching on the edge of the bed Jacob lit up and inhaled deeply. A comforting warmth radiated from Alison who had slept through his nightmare. Jacob put his free hand on her shoulder and gave a brief and silent prayer of thanks. *'You are the only thing that is real my angel.'* Alison purred on in contented oblivion, the sound of her breathing like far off waves crashing over rocks. Jacob sucked on his cigarette, the bitter-sweet smoke consoling and constant. He clicked on the small transistor radio Alison kept by her bed and it lit up to Johnny Cash singing about *hurt*. The sombre tune made Jacob think of his childhood, the summer visits to his grandparent's farm in Ireland. His grandfather always seemed to have Johnny Cash playing somewhere in the background.

Things seemed much simpler back then, as long as you had enough money to last you the weekend and your stash of porn magazines were safe then there was nothing much to worry about. School was a breeze, nothing but constant fooling about and figuring out new ways to see girls naked. Jacob often wondered what all his old class-mates would be up to now, but could never be bothered finding out. He stubbed out his cigarette and slid back under the duvet.

'Probably all married with shitty jobs, mortgages, two-point-two children...'
Surrounded by the comforting warmth of his lover, Jacob relaxed and flashes from
the past illuminated his mind; faces barely recognised, the noise of small running
feet, many unbroken shouting voices, the smell of varnish in the school gym hall,
harsh disinfectant in the toilets. Then he remembered Tam.

Jacob had always felt really sorry for Tam because he wore a prosthetic leg – the
result of some kind of birth defect. Nobody seemed to know what caused it, his
mother had taken no strange new medications during pregnancy, she was one of
the very few who didn't smoke or drink. It was just one of those things – one of
natures trick shots. But Tam coped really well, he never complained, just got on
with it and, in actual fact, he had been better at sport than most of the other boys.
'Maybe because of his disability he tried that bit harder than the everyone else?
Fuck knows?' In truth Tam was really competitive wee bastard who would do just
about anything to win! When it came to the crunch – a noise quite often
associated with Tam's tackles - his false leg was completely forgotten about and
his opponents did everything they could to stop him; pulling his hair, punching
him in the, taking wild swipes at his prosthetic limb trying to knock it off. *'I*
suppose that's why the poor bugger never actually won anything.' But then
Jacob remembered that this wasn't strictly true; when they were both eleven years
old, Jacob and Tam had been members of a school team entered into the annual

inter-district five-a-side football tournament. Jacob's eyes shot open as the memory surfaced and replayed.

The team had progressed to the semi-finals with some panache, sweeping aside all comers and conceding only three goals in the process. However, the semi-final was a slightly tougher affair going to extra time before eventually being resolved by a hotly disputed penalty. Everyone was saying what a great achievement it was for a team which included a guy with a false leg, to reach the final. But no-one ever thought that they would have the audacity to go on and win the bloody tournament!

In the final Jacob and Tam's team was down two nil by half time, but came back strongly after the break to level the score and eventually take the match into extra time. Both sides proceeded cautiously, afraid to give anything away and penalties quickly began to look like the inevitable outcome. The final whistle sounded with honours even and the teams retreated to either end of the hall to decide on the order of penalty takers.

The first man for the opposing team stepped up and stroked the ball home with sartorial elegance; the onus was on Jacob and Tam's team to do the business. First up was wee Billy - he was only in the side because his older brother Brian was a really good goalkeeper, and had threatened not to play unless his brother got a game. Wee Billy blasted the ball over the bar, but that was what everyone expected anyway. Everyone felt more sorry for the wee man rather than angry with him. The next two penalties for each team were despatched with clinical efficiency, and it looked as though wee Billy's miss was going to be the difference between the two sides. But then something special happened; it was big brother Brian to the rescue with a magnificent one handed save from what seemed like an unstoppable spot kick by the oppositions big number four. Then Jacob himself had stepped up to slot the ball home and level the game at three penalties a piece. The atmosphere was electric as the opposition's captain placed the ball down to take his kick. He wiped the sweat from his eyes and readied himself. A short two step run up before the ball was sent crashing off the corner of the upright. It was real Roy of the Rovers stuff now and Tam was on the last penalty with a chance to score the tournament-winning goal!

A silence descended over the crowd. Everyone knew that Tam had the ability, but he had never before been asked to handle pressure such as this. He wiped the sweat from his brow with his shirt-sleeve and walked slowly towards the penalty spot. The crowd collectively held their breath as Tam placed the ball down carefully and had a long look towards the goal before turning to prepare for his run up. The referee gave one short blast on his whistle and Tam sprung forward and let fly with a venomous right-footed drive, hitting the ball with such ferocity that it tore away the straps fastening the prosthetic leg to his hip. Tam's leg flew along side the ball - the goalkeeper hesitated, unsure which one to save and both ripped into the roof of the net!

The *'phweep'* of the referee's whistle signalled a goal. The losing team protested the decision claiming that Tams' leg flying off had confused their goalkeeper and provided the opposition with an unfair advantage. But the ref' ignored their remonstrations and stood by his decision. *'Seems a bit ironic... viewing a false leg as an 'unfair advantage'.'* Thought Jacob as he drifted into a, thankfully, dreamless sleep.

His fingertips traced a path along the acned wood-chip surface of the wall, to the heavy curtains behind which was concealed a large bay window. He found the middle, and then threw the curtains aside, metal rings scraping along the pole. As the sun cascaded warmth over his upturned face, he imagined its' overpowering luminescence.

I Don't Like Mondays

Loud noises and bright flashing lights startled Jacob from sleeping. He tried to shake the confusion from his head then rubbed the nighttime crust from his eyes. The clock read nine-fifty-five A.M. emptiness filled the bed beside him, Alison had gone and only the imprint of her head and the faint aroma of her perfume remained frozen on the pillow. A note on the bedside table came into focus.

Good morning lover man...

Had to go in to work - boring I know. Hang around for as long as you like, I should be home around four.

Alison X

P.S. I Love you...

Loud wailing sirens forced their way through the glass in the window, and red and blue flashing lights slashed the dull Scottish daylight that was trying desperately to illuminate Alison's bedroom. Jacob struggled free from the warm cavern of the duvet, unfurling his body into the cold autumn morning to investigate.

'What the fuck is going on out there?' He thought out loud, stuttering baby steps towards the window. Peering through a crack in the curtains he observed that two cars had collided at the junction on the corner. The bigger of the two cars, looked like a white Mercedes, had smashed into the side of the smaller car (a Corsa or a Micra or something similar, Jacob could not quite discern the make and model due to the damage it had sustained) pushing it onto the pavement and into a phone-box. He strained to see exactly what was happening amongst all the mayhem; two paramedics were frantically buzzing around a figure, looked like a man, who lay prostrate on the pavement, whilst the crew of a fire-truck were employing some kind of hydraulic cutting device to slice the roof off the smaller car, or rather, what was left of it. Jacob rubbed the stubble on his chin, stretched his arms upwards yawning. With a scratch of his arse he closed the curtains and made his way back towards the bed, pausing to grab the cigarettes and lighter that lay beside Alison's note. Jacob took up the note and contemplated the beauty of her handwriting. He had not really considered the content as yet, but it now dawned on him, 'She's gone into work?' Today was a bank holiday and Alison worked in a bloody bank! There was no way she could possibly be working today, so where the hell was she? And more to the point thought Jacob,

'Why did she have to lie to me?'

Jacob took a cigarette from his packet and lit it up, rewinding his memories of the past few days, searching for a sign. Did she have another man on the go? She could even have a husband hidden away for all Jacob knew! He sat down on the edge of the bed, a study in confusion and consternation, smoking his cigarette sharply and quickly. He placed it half-smoked, still burning in the ashtray and sprung to his feet, moving quickly around Alison's flat looking for something…anything! A photograph, a man's razor in the bathroom, an extra toothbrush, a large raincoat on the hall stand, in a cupboard…a wardrobe He searched for anything vaguely masculine, but could find no incriminating evidence. The mask of angst slipped from Jacob's face, 'Could be some kind of staff training, I suppose…' he reasoned, '…I'm sure there's a perfectly innocent and rational explanation for it…' he went on, trying to convince and console himself.

Jacob re-entered the bedroom and resumed his perch on the edge of the bed, lifting the smouldering cigarette and sucking hard. The cold air of the room bit hard and Jacob hugged himself and rubbed his arms vigorously. Shoulders hunched he padded quickly across the naked floor to the still open window. In the street below the fire crew had managed to remove the roof of the smaller car exposing the top half of the driver's body protruding from the mangled interior. He was a youngish looking man although his face was obscured by a torrent of blood gushing from the multiple lacerations on his face and head. Probably late twenties, maybe early thirties Jacob guessed. Various professionals hovered, desperately trying to keep the young man alive as they attempted to free him from the wreckage, his agonised cries barely audible above the *stramash* of engines, voices, car horns and the general symphony of a Glasgow morning. Jacob flicked the near dead cigarette out onto the pavement below and watched it bounce once, trailing a cloud of orange sparks before extinguishing in the gutter. Stretching up Jacob pulled the window down and closed. As he whipped the curtains together the paramedics gave up and pulled a blanket over the face of the older man on the pavement.

Safely back under the duvet, Jacob tried to shut out the morning. But the bed felt too big for one person and he was quickly overwhelmed by feelings of isolation and loneliness. 'She won't be long...' he thought in a vein attempt to console himself.

He turned and tossed for a while, staring at the ceiling, at every wall, the ceiling again... Until finally utter boredom and a fear that the intense friction would cause the bedclothes to catch on fire, drove Jacob out of bed and onto the living room couch. He considered rolling a joint. 'No, better keep the little hash I have left for pre and post coital joints later!' The television was flicked on instead in an attempt at distraction. It was the usual mix of bank holiday shite – old western films, horse racing... 'Boring as fuck!' Jacob mused philosophically as he shut off the TV and deflated into his seat. Staring out over the rain soaked city, the sky, a blanket of light grey, reflected Jacob's mood.

10:35AM

123

Shortly after his fifth cup of afternoon coffee, the theme tune from The Magic Roundabout rung out from his mobile phone. Unable to distinguish exactly where the ring-tone was coming from, he took a gamble that it might be hanging out with his jacket in the hallway. The gamble paid off... for once.

'Alison?' He pleaded rushing the phone to his face.

'Mr Douglas? Answered a sombre sounding male voice from the other side of the line.

'Yes, speaking.' he sank back into his depression, 'And exactly who am I speaking to?'

'Ah yes Mr Douglas, I am so sorry. This is Mr Raymond from the Co-operative Funeral Directors. I am ringing regarding your father's service.'

'But it's a bank holiday?'

'Well, forgive me for being so blunt Mr Douglas, but people do not postpone their passing because of bank holidays. We have to provide a twenty-four hour seven days a week, three-hundred and sixty-five days a year service to the public.'

'Three-hundred and sixty-six if it's a leap year.'

'Quite so, Mr Douglas.' Jacob strolled through to the living room, plonked himself down on the couch and reached for his cigarettes.

'I've been meaning to contact you to, you-know, to make arrangements; collect the body and all that kind of stuff.' He lit a cigarette.

'There is no need Mr Douglas, in fact that's the very reason for my call. You see everything has already been taken care of. ' Jacob was puzzled.

'What do you mean exactly?'

'Well Mr Douglas, your father left very detailed and strict instructions. A driver has been appointed to oversee the transportation of your father, all the way to *his final resting place*. We have also organised catering for the wake and the after service reception. The service itself will be conducted in your father's local Parish church in Ireland, beginning at eleven-thirty a.m. Everything has been arranged Mr Douglas, there is nothing at all for you to worry about.' Jacob almost dropped his cigarette in surprise. The funeral director continued. 'You should receive a full time-table in the post first thing tomorrow morning. It would have been today, but what with the bank holiday.' Jacob sat there in open mouthed silence, completely taken aback. He became aware of the funeral director still speaking at him. And snapped back into preset time. 'Hello? Are you still there Mr Douglas?'

'Yes... eh, sorry...I'm just a bit eh...you know...taken by surprise. So what do I have to do then?' The funeral director cleared his throat as if trying to get Jacob's attention.

'Well apart from turning up I can't really think of anything offhand. Oh! I do beg your pardon Mr Douglas, there is one thing I did forget to mention; in your

125

father's instructions he requested that you say a few words at the service.' Jacob felt his stomach almost drop out of his arse. If there was one thing that terrified him more than anything else it was having to speak in public, and his father had known this only too well.

'Yes that should be fine...' he lied and felt the vein in his left temple begin to throb and his chest tighten.

'If you have no more questions Mr Douglas I'll let you get on, I'm sure like myself you are a very busy man.' Jacob took a drag on his cigarette.

'Yes, rushed off my feet actually. Thanks for calling and letting me know.'

All part of the service Mr Douglas, and allow me to offer my sincerest condolences on the passing of your dear father.' Jacob stopped himself from swearing.

'Thank you very much Mr Raymond, my father was a... *unique* individual.' he spat through gritted teeth and ended the call with the push of a button.

Once again his father had managed to undermine him, this time from beyond the grave! 'For a dead man you're really beginning to piss me off!' He shouted at the sleeping telephone. At least I get to book my own ferry ticket; you'll let me pay for that myself you tight old bastard.' Jacob grabbed up Alison's telephone and dialled the number for directory enquiries. After three rings a woman's voice answered and asked him which number he required. 'Yes, can you give me the number of the ferry terminal in Troon, that's in south Ayrshire? It's P and O

Ferries I think.' The woman replied that it would just take a moment, which was followed by a clicking ticking noise that sounded as if she'd hung up.

'Hello? Is there anybody…' an automated voice cut him off in mid-sentence.

'The number you require is 0-1-2-9-2-3-1-0-1-0-0. I repeat, the number you require is…' Jacob quickly typed the number into his mobile then pushed the cradle-button and hung up on the automaton, before punching the number right back into Alison's land-line. It was ringing. *'Better book a ticket for Simon as well.'* Jacob thought as he waited for the other end to pick up. It was still ringing.

'Come on, come on… Oh for fu…' Again he was cut off mid-sentence

'Good afternoon P and O Ferries Troon, Martin speaking, how can I help you?'

'Hello there Martin.' replied Jacob rather startled, 'I'd like to book two tickets to Belfast please.'

'Foot passenger tickets sir?'

'Yes foot passengers, no car.'

'And will they be return tickets sir?'

'Yes that's right, two return tickets to Belfast please.'

'Certainly sir; and when will you be sailing?'

'Oh shit!' Jacob thought, realising that he hadn't thought to ask the undertaker when the funeral was; and the timetable wouldn't be arriving until tomorrow!

'Can you give me a second to double check my diary please?'

'No problem sir.'

Jacob had to think, and fast. He pictured his father sitting in the armchair opposite watching his poor son panic; laughing away and telling him he would never amount to anything.

'Right, you old swine, you pegged it on Friday, the undertaker said the driver will be accompanying, yes definitely said will be so hasn't gone yet. The information is coming tomorrow so they know when it is and they'd have to give us plenty of notice, a couple or three days at least so that would take us to Friday... So the funeral could be Friday? Hello?'

'Yes sir.'

'Sorry to keep you waiting.'

'That's quite all right sir. Now then, when would you like to sail?'

'Friday... no, no Wednesday, I mean Wednesday.'

'Are you perfectly sure sir?'

'Yes, definitely Wednesday, late morning preferably.'

There was a slight pause as the sales assistant searched for availability.

'We have a crossing at 11AM sir'

'That would be fine.'

'Boarding begins at 10AM and we ask that foot passengers be aboard no later than 10:45AM sir.'

'No problem.'

'Okay; lets just total that up for you sir. And that comes to seventy-six pounds exactly. And how would you like to pay?'

'Credit card please… Visa if that's okay?'

'Visa is absolutely fine sir, debit or credit?'

'Eh, credit please.'

'Certainly; could I have your card number please sir?'

'Okay… I really must apologise yet again, but could you hold on just one second while I get my wallet? The wife must have moved it off my study desk. I am so sorry.'

'Absolutely no problem at all sir, please take your time, there's no rush.'

Jacob skidded off down the hallway, the mocking laughter of his father echoing after him. He pulled the wallet free from the inside pocket of his jacket and headed back to the phone to pay the ferryman.

'Your tickets will be available for collection at the booking office front desk from five o'clock this evening sir.'

'Is it okay to collect them on the morning just before we sail?'

'Sure, that's no problem sir, we just ask that you arrive about half-a-hour earlier in case there's a bit of a queue. We don't want you to miss your crossing now do we sir?'

'No *we* certainly do not.'

'And if you could both bring some form of photographic identification with you sir that would be great.'

'Like a passport or a driving licence?'

'Yes, anything along those lines would be acceptable sir.' Jacob couldn't remember where his passport was, and only had the old paper driving licence. He had been meaning to get around to sending for a new photo-card type licence, but… This could be a problem.

'Okay, that should be no problem at all.'

'We would normally send your tickets through the post, but what with it being bank holiday Monday there is no guarantee that they would arrive on time.'

'That's no problem, as I said, I'll pick them up on the day.'

'Right you are sir. Well goodbye and thank you for choosing to sail with P and O ferries. I hope you have a pleasant journey.' But Jacob had already slammed the phone down.

'Fucking bank holidays!'

12:25PM

Jacob thought about calling Simon to let him know that the ferry tickets had been booked. But considered that his brother might attempt to engage him in conversation and decided to send a text message instead.

`Frry @ 11am Wed – gt 2 b thre 4 10 – pck u up @ 9am – plse b rdy!!! J.'`

Jacob knew that he would have to call his Uncle Andrew in Ireland to let the relatives know when he and Simon would be arriving. He stared at the phone for a bit then lit a cigarette and went to make yet another cup of coffee.

12:37PM.

*

A cat was sheltering from the unremitting rain in the bin-sheds at the bottom of the shared back garden. Jacob finished the dregs of his coffee and rinsed his mug under the hot tap.

'Ach I suppose so...' he uttered with fatalistic resignation and headed for the phone. The handset seemed to have increased in weight by several kilograms as Jacob laboured to lift it to his face. One hand slowly dialled the number whilst the other almost put the telephone down on three separate occasions. But in spite of himself Jacob fought on, pushing through. He persevered and, at last, it was ringing. He breathed long and deeply mimicking, the relaxation techniques he had been taught in therapy: Slowly in through the nostrils, count till three, slowly out through the mouth. The phone was still ringing. 'Where the hell is everybody today?' Jacob was contemplating with horror having to endure the whole agonising telephoning procedure again later, when the answer-phone kicked in. An almost euphoric feeling of relief washed over him as a rather mechanical sounding recording of his Uncle Andrew's voice apologised for not being able to come to the phone and enquired politely if he would like to leave a message after the tone. Jacob duly and happily obliged, imparting the details of his and his brother's impending arrival on the *Emerald Isle*, adding how sorry he was that he hadn't had the chance to 'catch up' with the family, but that he'd see them all in a couple of days time and they could all have a 'rare old chin-wag' then. The receiver was returned to its perch triumphantly and Jacob flung himself back onto Alison's sofa satisfied with his days work so far.

12:45PM.

*

The moment his eyes opened they scanned the room for the clock. It read 13:05PM. No dreams had punctuated the twenty-or-so minutes that Jacob had lain unconscious half slumped on Alison's sofa. It was still raining outside. He stood up a little shakily, straightened his, or rather Alison's, dressing gown and checked his scarecrow appearance in the large mirror above the mantelpiece.

'What the fuck are we going to do for the rest of the day then handsome?' Making his way through to the kitchen, Jacob clicked on the overworked kettle for

132

what seemed like the hundredth time that day, but quickly flicked it off again. 'I am so sick of fucking coffee! There must be something else I can do to pass the time?' Jacob looked frantically around the flat in search of entertainment. A few dog-eared paperbacks festered on Alison's bookshelf, which on closer inspection looked like they'd been read a thousand times or more by some greasy tramp. Jacob decided against perusal. 'Not my type anyway…bit girly.' he reasoned as his hand recoiled in disgust. The newspapers in the magazine rack by the fireplace had been dead for weeks and the only other thing in there was a year old Argos catalogue. Defeated, Jacob collapsed back into the armchair and fingered the remote control. 'Fucking hypno-box, mindless shite, brainwashing torture…' He muttered, but switched the television on anyway.

There was a specially cut daytime rerun of a popular evening show on. Some half-witted TV personality, or *celebrity*, to give them their contemporary classification, was busy gushing about how taking part in this banal excuse for a game-show had changed her life. She was babbling on about the friends she had made, the discipline she had learned, the humility… 'For fuck sake, you haven't found a cure for fucking cancer love, you've just danced around a bit in front of a million morons with your tits hanging out! Take a fucking pill!' Jacob pictured himself as Elvis, pointing the remote gun-like at the TV image of the obsequious *celeb*', taking aim… 'Right between the fucking eyes…' Finger on the red button…'Thank you very much…' He pulled the trigger, '…Goodnight!' And she blinked out of existence.

Settling back into the suffocation of boredom, Jacob lit another cigarette - it was his last one. Soon he would have to put on some clothes and force his arse out into the miserable cold and damp. The rain was still teaming down drumming on the apartment windows. Jacob tried hard but could not remember the last time he had seen a clear blue sky. Glasgow, and indeed the rest of Scotland seemed to be eternally enclosed in a grey blanket. Offering up a short prayer for sunshine, Jacob then cursed the institution of bank holiday Monday.

13:13PM

*

Bored…

Reminiscing over the previous evenings' sexual exploits as he pulled on his t-shirt and fastened his trousers, Jacob was jolted back into the present by screaming coming from the back garden and raced through to investigate. From the kitchen window he could see two hoodies + dog, busy terrorising a cat they had trapped up on the bin-shed roof. Torn by the compulsion to interject and save the poor creature and his pressing need to urinate, Jacob judged the latter to be of far greater importance, and resigned to relieve himself and then, once in a fitter state to do so, head for the back garden to rescue the cat.

He arrived on the scene just in time to see one of the neds score a direct hit with a half-brick. The dog, some sort of bull terrier by the look of it, was small and quick, jumping to catch the poor feline in its' powerful jaws as it fell. A terrible fusion of angry growling, pained screeching and ugly laughter erupted as the powerfully muscled dog tore the poor cat to pieces and the two young men looked on.

'Hoi, ya sick wee bastards! What the fuck do you think you're playing at?' Jacob ranted as he strode towards the carnage. The two youths looked up cruel smiles slashed across their faces. The taller of the two fixed Jacob with an unrepentant stare.

'What the fuck are you wanting ya fuckin' auld prick? Ye want us tae set the fuckin' dug oan you anaw?' Jacob halted in his tracks and regarded the blood stained dog which had also now turned its' attention to him. Suddenly feeling very exposed, he thought about running. They did have a vicious looking beast with them and there were two of them, even if they did only have a combined height of around ten feet. The odds seemed stacked against him.

'But the cat must be dead by now anyway.' Thought Jacob and turned back toward the house. He has almost reached the entrance when one of the hoodies shouted after him.

'Aye ye know whit's good fur ye ya shitein' prick!' It was at that moment that Jacob lost control and turned to frantically search the ground for ammunition. Several large, painted beach pebbles decorated one of Alison's neighbours' garden planters; Jacob grabbed one of the larger ones, took aim and threw it as hard as he could. The dog gave a sharp yelp as the small bolder thudded into the top of its' back left leg. It immediately turned-tail and scampered off down the back lane.

'Watch ma fucking dug ya arse-hole... al rip you ya bam!' One of the neds screamed at him, but Jacob was unrepentant and had already grabbed up another stone and was aiming it directly at one of the boys' heads. It narrowly missed his target, landing him a glancing blow to the right shoulder. Fortified by the young mans' agonised screams, Jacob quickly grabbed up another stone. The two boys, realizing they were completely outgunned, jumped the back fence and sprinted after the dog. Jacob gave chase to the end of the garden and stepped over into the lane. The boys were quite a way off and moving rapidly, but Jacob knew that he

136

could make the shot. Pulling his arm back for one last great effort before letting the stone fly with all the power he could generate. As Jacob watched the projectile arch gracefully through the air and down the alleyway towards its ever retreating target he remembered, with an air of irony, how as a boy he had honed his aim by throwing stones at the cows and horses inhabiting in the green fields near his family home. There was a dull thumping sound as the stone struck the taller of the two boys between his shoulder-blades. He shrieked like a wounded animal and fell to the ground face first, the other boy stopping momentarily to look round at his prostrate friend then back down the lane. Jacob pretended to pull back his arm as if readying to throw another stone and the boy took off sideways into one of the other gardens and out of range. As the other flattened ned dragged himself up onto his knees and began to crawl over towards the side of the lane, Jacob couldn't help feeling a bit disappointed and thought of strolling down to finish him off with a good kicking. However, as he was trying to make up his mind, the other ned jumped out from his hiding place and dragged his friend to safety. Jacob could no longer hold back his satisfaction and let free a loud explosion of laughter into the alleyway.

'That'll teach you, ya wee bastards!' A few moments passed before he remembered what this was all about... the poor cat.

Back at the scene of the crime, there wasn't much left of the sorry creature; a bloodied mess of fur, entrails and crushed-broken bones, the mangled tail protruding upwards at an unnatural angle. Gingerly he took hold of it between the thumb and forefinger of his right hand, lifting the grisly remains into a dustbin. He took one last look at the carcass before dropping the lid, the echo of a tortured scream remained forever locked on its' broken face.

*

Safely back in Alison's flat, Jacob sat on the sofa shaking, half in exhilaration, half in terror, wrestling with his conscience. '

'What if they went to the police? What if they told their bigger, uglier brothers? What if they ran to their parents? 'No chance Jake, think about it... if they did that then they would have to explain the whole thing. There's no way that those two neds would admit to something like that and expect to get any sympathy, is there?. '* His brow creased temporarily. 'Suppose not.'

Jacob smiled remembering the feelings of complete satisfaction as all three stones connected with their intended targets.

'I feel a bit sorry for the dog though. At the end of the cliché it was only following orders.' He remarked to the wall, recalling the startled look in the dog's eyes when the stone had cracked into its' leg. *'It's crazy the blind panic that animals fly into when they're scared...'* mused Jacob *'...like a kind of paranoia. They'll bite, scratch, kick and generally do harm to anything or anyone near them.'* He recognised the reaction caused by pressing this metaphorical panic button only too well, although he was not entirely clear on how the mechanism behind it worked.

Fingering the empty cigarette packet Jacob sighed. There was no booze in the flat, he and Alison having finished the last of the wine the previous evening. The only thing he could find that was vaguely alcoholic was a bottle of Advocaat hidden in the far recesses of one of the kitchen cupboards, but god only knew how long that had been in there! 'Tastes like monkey spunk anyway.' He stood up and looked out of the large bay window at the already fading afternoon. Going to the shops was not an option for Jacob right now as he considered that the neds he stomped could still be hanging around, and may even have pulled a team together by now and be on the prowl. SO he though it better to lie low for a while, maybe even grow a beard and develop a limp.

A light-bulb flickered into life above Jacob's head causing him to leap up and make a dash for the hallway. In the his inside pocket was his wallet; inside his wallet was another little pocket; in this pocket was...

'A double fucking dipped fucking strawberry!' A not insignificant amount of Lysergic acid diethylamide.   14:57PM

Sitting by the empty window, his steely blue eyes with pinpricks of black at the centre, barely visible, fixed straight ahead. But like the painted eyes of a doll they see nothing of the obvious world. Not the raindrops that patter against the glass nor his breath that steams it cloudy. His is a hidden secret world where he is both supreme ruler and prisoner.

ACID RAIN

It had been just over fifteen minutes since Jacob swallowed the drug, and the atmosphere was beginning to alter. He was now finding the wallpaper extremely interesting. It could have been seconds, minutes or even hours later that Jacob noticed his hands - the hair on their backs dancing like tiny worms, to an inner, unheard rhythm. A beam of light sheared through a gap in the curtained window and onto Jacob's chest. It burned and tingled and his breath quickened as the sensation spread out through the rest of his body. Jacob began to dissolve and merge with all he touched, becoming one with everything, metamorphosis into Christ, Satan, his father, Alison... He was lifted into the air on a radiant cloud, then further up to the stars, his soul exploding in a brilliantly colourful orgasm of cosmic proportions!

The moon had risen.

Jacob drifted feather-light back down to earth, the lumpy sofa feeling like a million down-filled silk cushions under the weight of his body. He was at peace with the universe and felt... hungry.

The ten feet or so to the kitchen seemed to take an eternity to walk, the carpet underfoot swirling all the while like some vast tempestuous ocean. Jacob stared down into the abyss and lost himself for a while. He tried hard to focus on his feet which appeared to be a mile or more beneath his head, eyes peering out from every darkened corner of the flat, shadow people moving stealthily just out of direct vision. Geometric shapes sprung from the walls and flitted through the air as Jacob snapped on the kitchen light. He allowed these dancing shapes to entertain him for a short time before remembering his mission.

In the kitchen the cupboard was populated by a variety of tinned foods, but fearing a disaster of nuclear proportions, Jacob decided against preparing anything that would require the use of tin-openers or electricity. He closed the cupboard door to disappointed metallic shouts, opting instead for an altogether safer sandwich. The bread appeared to be viable, still soft and no visible signs of mould. A cluster of air-bubbles on one slice of bread reminded Jacob of his brother.

From inside Alison's cold and desolate fridge, Jacob rescued a slightly shrivelled tomato and the remnants of a block of cheese. An open packet of wafer thin smoked ham waved temptingly at him, but on closer inspection Jacob noted that it was covered in a pulsating green-black mould and decided not to disturb it. Jacob opened the cutlery drawer with the intention of retrieving a knife with which to cut his food into sandwich sized slices; but images of gushing arteries and severed fingers flooded his minds-eye and the drawer was immediately slammed shut. Using instead his hands to rip the tomato in two, seed-filled juice spurted from the uneven split spilling onto hands and dripped on the counter and floor. The remnant mush was squashed on top of one of the slices of bread and spread unsuccessfully by Jacob using his right index finger. Next the block of cheese was lifted to his mouth and two large lumps bitten off and spat out on top of the improvised sandwich; the whole car crash finally being concealed under another piece of bread. When at last Jacob lifted the horrible, moist concoction carefully off the surface and brought it upwards in the direction of his open, waiting mouth, a large proportion of the sandwich attempted to escape by throwing itself down onto his shirt. He observed in wonder the reddish-yellow blobs slip and crawl down the material munching away on his sandwich at the same time. The food felt cool and good in his mouth as Jacob chewed, and when he swallowed it rippled and fizzed in the descent to the pit of his belly.

'If a crappy, horrible sandwich tastes and feels this good, what the fucking hell is sex going to be like!' He pondered as his body attempted to digest.

Jacob thought of Alison, wondered where she might be, when she would be home, if he should ring her? And as he did so was engulfed by an unexpectedly and incredible feeling of unease. What if he couldn't hold it together when she got back? Maybe Alison didn't approve? She might be disgusted by him? Would she leave him? He had to get his head straight, there was no way he could talk to Alison in this condition. He had to get out before she called the flat, or worse, actually arrived back home!

*

Gliding darkly along the orange-grey pavements of the Glasgow night, the streetlamps buzzed a concerto in the smirr and Jacob could feel their electricity channelling through his body. He continued walking chanting a half breath mantra,

'I can feel it, I can feel it, I can feel it, breathe, deeply in, slowly out, deeply in, slowly out...' All around him was stained wet sepia and brown save for the blue-black-grey of the unrelenting sky. The rain, although not heavy, followed Jacob loyally in an incessant dense mist. '...breathe...' Disembodied voices visited his ears from time to time, drifting in and out before his brain had time to decode what they were saying. An echoed footstep stopped Jacob dead in his tracks. He looked around, but there was no-one, only trees, hedges, cars, lamp-posts, shadows... 'Yes the shadow people are always with me... I can feel it, I can feel it...'

Jacob turned a corner - made another; there were bright lights in the street ahead., he tried to focus. The first signs of any other humanity on the outside world was a twenty-four hour petrol station. The sight of it filled Jacob's mind with the comforting thoughts of cigarette smoke and chocolate. A voice whispered '*camera ...film*' in his ear. 'Yes film for the camera... excellent! Thanks for reminding me.' He remarked loudly to no-one, then pondered whether the words had actually been spoken at all.

144

Jacob stood with his shadows for a while summoning up the courage to walk amongst and interact with other human beings, talking himself out of it on more than one occasion. However, the magnet of consumer goods was too powerful. He steeled himself for his quest, focused on his goal, 'You can do it, you can do it...'

'Breathe – remember to breathe.' The shadow people encouraged Jacob and he threw his body forward and strode into the light.

*

The piercing neon bright inside the garage shop burned Jacob's eyes and he staggered back from the doorway to let his vision adjust. The automatic glass doors unable to decide whether to open or close resigned to do both. Gradually, a sharp white interior blurred into focus and Jacob stepped forward, immediately zoning in on the counter to his immediate right, behind which stood a long haired teenage male. He couldn't be sure, but it looked as though the long-hair was smiling at him.

'Can I help you?' This was it, first contact.

'Breathe, breathe...' Jacob took three side-steps towards the counter.

'Eh... hmm... camera? Film?' A faint ripple of puzzlement swept over the young assistant's eyes, but his brows quickly rose to a crest as he regained his composure. Through his innocent corporate smile the assistant spoke in strained teenage tones, pointing as he did so over and beyond Jacob's right shoulder.

'Just over there … on the shelf behind the crisps.' Jacob tired to smile, but succeeded only in convincing the left half of his mouth to contract into a brief upward twitch. Venturing where directed, he picked up two thirty-five millimetre thirty-six exposure films, returning them quickly to the counter and grabbing a Mars Bar, a Topic and a Twix en-route.

'Is that everything?' Asked the assistant. Jacob deemed this line of questioning a bit too interrogatory. Considering the assistant might be growing suspicious, Jacob thought about running.

'Come on now Jake, play it cool Jake… play it cool…'

'No… eh… that wont be all, actually…eh, I will also need twenty Marlborough and a box of matches please.'

'That's my boy Jake! You really showed him, didn't you!' As the assistant rung up the till, Jacob fumbled in his wallet and took out what he hoped was a twenty pound note

'Okay…twelve pounds sixty-eight please.' The total seemed a bit too much, but Jacob quickly handed over the money anyway, desperate to escape back into the safety of the obscure night.

'And that's seven pounds twelve pence.' Said the assistant as he counted out the money onto Jacob's upturned palm. He stared at the pile of money in his hand, trying to work out if it was right or not, but found it hard to recognise and differentiate between the various coins and notes.

'Is everything okay?' Enquired the shop assistant with fake sincerity. Jacob grunted and nodded affirmation then stuffed the money hurriedly into his jacket pocket and hurried towards the door. He had almost made the exit when the assistants shout stopped him dead in his tracks.

'Excuse me mate!' What had he done? Put something in his pocket and forgotten to pay for it? Jacob tried desperately to replay the last few minutes of his life, but his brain had failed to press the record button.

'What the fuck am I going to do? How can I defend myself in this state? What if they call the police? I won't survive a jail cell in this condition!' He prepared to make a bolt for it.

'Steady Jake... just relax now...breathe... breathe...' The assistant's voice broke in again, closer this time.

'Wait there...' Jacob looked up to see the assistant's face reflected in the glass of the door, he was right behind him, there would be no escape tonight.

'You forgot your shopping mate.' The reflected assistant was holding out a white carrier bag. Jacob half turned and grudgingly accepted the goods from the smiling teenager, again twitching the corner of his mouth in appreciation before exiting the premises at high speed!

Hitting the forecourt running, Jacob made for the dark side of the pavement. There, concealed in a cloak of night once again he began to relax. Rustling around in the carrier bag until he found the cigarettes and box of matches, Jacob quickly ripped away the cellophane and let it fall free in the wind. Completing the ritual by pulling out the small piece of silver paper to expose twenty filter tips, Jacob then liberated one of the cigarettes and lit it up using three matches. He watched their flame rapidly flicker and die in the cutting breeze. The smoke felt warm and good, comforting Jacob as he stood in the shadows. He smoked a little too quickly, watching the assortment of human traffic come and go from the petrol station. A silver coloured VW Beetle, one of the old models, rolled noisily up to sit parallel with the doors. A young looking man, early twenties maybe, it was hard to tell at this distance and in this light, bounced out of the driver-side door and entered the station shop. There was a woman waiting in the front passenger seat, her profile seemed familiar.

Jacob finished the cigarette and threw it to the ground, watching it skitter across the pavement driven by the wind, orange sparks trailing behind it. A brief fantasy barged its way into Jacob's mind in which a trail of petrol was set alight causing a river of fire to race towards the station consuming everything in its path before climaxing in an apocalyptic explosion lighting up the Glasgow skyline like a million suns and wiping out all life within a ten mile radius. He quickly scurried after the escaping fag end and stamped out its' murderous light. Looking back over towards the silver Beetle, a little closer now, the female passenger came into focus. Jacob felt his heart leap and was instantaneously filled with a irresistible radiance - it was Alison.

'I don't know if you should go over there Jake, not in this state' But Jacob really wanted more than anything else in the world at that moment to be with her. *'But would you be able to keep it together Jake?'* Anticipatory vibrations filled his body, he struggled to contain them.

'But I love her... I need to be with her...Fuck it!' Jacob had made up his mind, he was going over. Half way through his first step forward from his seclusion he froze. The young VW driver had re-emerged from the station shop carrying an identical carrier-bag to the one Jacob was holding. In his excitement at seeing Alison he had completely forgotten about her young companion. *'Who the hell are you boy, and what the fuck are you doing with my woman?'* Jacob tried to convince his legs to carry on forward, but they refused and he remained frozen in the shadows, watching as the young man got back into the car, handed the bag to Alison and kissed her tenderly on the cheek. *'Calm down now son... breathe Jake... fucking breathe...'* Betrayed, confused, angry, drained, unable to move, Jacob looked on helplessly as Alison and her mystery man drove off into the night laughing.

Stepping back into the shadows, heart pounding, head throbbing Jacob grabbed his aching stomach, doubled over and vomited the steaming contents of his stomach onto the pavement. 'How could she... why?' He implored the night, wiping the dripping spew from his mouth on a coat sleeve. Unfolding himself upright he took a deep breath, his despair turning swiftly to anger. 'Fucking bitch! Who the fuck was he? Little runt! Half her age... stupid cow! I'll fucking sort them both out... I'll fucking...' A quavering voice spoke from behind.

'You alright mister?' Startled, Jacob spun round and in the same motion punched the old face of a concerned man who immediately collapsed with a sickening crunch. Breathing heavily, Jacob stared down at the crumpled pensioner bleeding on the ground in front of him.

'Oh fuck, I've killed him! What the fuck am I going to...?' A pained groan interrupted his panic. The old man twitched.

'It's okay Jake, the silly old cunt is still alive. Now get yourself the fuck out of here pronto!' And with that Jacob turned tail and ran as fast as he could.

*

He ran all the way home, heart booming in his ears, feeling as though it could burst its way through his chest at any moment.

'Maybe it was nothing? It wasn't as if it was a full on French kiss, just a peck on the cheek really. But why didn't she tell me where she was going? Why did she lie to me?' Jacob could barely climb the two flights of stairs to his front door. Once inside, out of breath, exhausted he stripped naked and slumped in the bath twisting on the shower as he descended. His skin felt oily and unclean and blood

stained his hands, but Jacob was unable to discern whether it was the old man's or his own which was seeping from a small but deep gash on his right index knuckle. Jacob trembled as he cold water fell, knees pulled up to his chest, rocking rhythmically back and forth. 'The water will wash away all the dirt and the filth...'

*

The mirror reflected a stranger's face. 'Who are you? Who am I?' All around rolled lush-green country, capped with blue sky. The colours seemed ultra intense, hyper-real. 'Where am I? What is this place?' A beautiful woman walked darkly along in front of him, completely naked. Jacob reached out and took her gently by the wrist pulling her toward him. 'I'm so sorry to bother you, but I feel a little lost. Could you tell me where this is?' The woman smiled knowingly at Jacob and stroked his cheek, but said nothing. The silence caused him to grow anxious. 'Do you know me? Who am I? Why am I here?' But still the woman remained silent and placed her index finger on Jacob's lips to quiet him, her intense eyes penetrating his. As the woman brought her face close to his, Jacob felt her hot quick breath on his open mouth - he could smell her dusky perfume, their lips almost touching.

A sharp rapping at the front door dragged Jacob brutally from dreaming. He was still sat in the bath, the shower water ran ice-cold, but felt somehow cleansing and pure. The front door was rattled again three times - he knew it was Alison and considered ignoring her for the briefest of moments before leaping up out of the freezing water, throwing on his robe and sprinting down the hall.

By the time Jacob had unlocked and opened the door, she had already begun walking back down the stairs, although hadn't gotten very far. She turned her head and smiled.

'I didn't think you were in... I was just away to go back home...' As Alison re-ascended the stairs towards him, Jacob recognised the plastic bag she was carrying. It was the one from the petrol station, the one that *he* had emerged with in his grubby, little mitt. '...I know I should have called first, but I... I just wanted to get here as quickly as I could...' She was right in front of him now. Jacob had still not said a word. 'What happened to you last night Jacob? When I got back you were gone. I tried ringing, but there was no answer. I left a really stupid message on your voice-mail, talk about hysterical mad-woman! I was really worried Jacob, I thought that something might have happened to you ... I've missed you so much Jacob.' Alison reached up and brushed his cheek with her left hand as she let her lips tenderly caress his.

'Yes I bet she has Jake! The lying, cheating, deceitful little whore!'

'Yeah, sorry, I just had to get back and sort things out... you know, the funeral and all that kinda stuff. After a while it all got a bit much, needed some time to think, you know? So I switched off all the phones; I'm sorry that you were worried, I just didn't think... should've left you a note or something, I guess?'

152

'Oh, don't be so daft, I completely understand. I didn't get back till late, and I was completely knackered anyway; wouldn't have been much good for anything, if you know what I mean!'

'She's all but bloody well admitted it! The two-timing cow!'

'Listen Alison, don't worry about it… oh, and apologies for taking so long to answer the door, I was in the shower…' Jacob gestured drawing Alison's attention to his wet hair. '…and what the hell are we doing discussing our private lives on the doorstep? Come on in for god sake!' Jacob continued, waving Alison past with a sweep of his free hand. She walked forward pausing briefly to kiss him once again on the cheek as she passed. Jacob felt blood flush his face hot. Pulse quickening and fists clenched he threw shut the door behind them. *'Betrayer!* So what's in the bag then?' Jacob enquired following Alison into the kitchen. She pulled a bottle of white wine from the plastic bag and held it up by the side of her face.

'I thought that we deserved a little treat; some lunch, some wine and an afternoon of general relaxation… you haven't made other plans have you?'

'He bought that wine for her last night, didn't he? The little bitch is rubbing your nose in it… No, nothing planned. I haven't got much food in though. Do you fancy ordering a pizza?' Alison was busy rummaging in the drawer searching for a corkscrew.

'Oh yes, that sounds perfect… one of those spicy chicken pizzas if you can.' Jacob forced a smile.

'Okay, I'll just go and phone the takeaway then.' Alison was still rummaging around in the cutlery drawer.

'I can't find the bloody corkscrew.' Jacob about-turned, opened another drawer and fished around for a moment before pulling out an ancient, rather dangerous looking wooden handled corkscrew.

'Here try this.' He said sliding it along the work surface. Alison lifted up the corkscrew and stared at it.

'Where the hell did you find this thing? Looks like something from the dark ages!'

'It was my father's actually.'

'Oh shit… I am so sorry Jacob… I didn't mean anything by it.'

'Don't worry about it babe. Can you manage with that old thing? It is a bit tricky to handle.' Alison turned the corkscrew over in her hand; the initials 'A.A.D.' were burned into the handle. She frowned and turned it towards Jacob.

'Your dad's initials?'

'Yeah, 'Adam Alexander Douglas' Ade to his friends, of whom there were very few.' Alison frowned almost imperceptibly then attempted to pierce the cork, but succeeded only in ricocheting off the neck and almost skewering her hand.

'Here let me do it; such a dangerous bloody thing.' Said Jacob, grabbing the bottle and corkscrew from her. 'Exactly like my father used to be.' He continued, stabbing the point into the cork and grinding it down noisily and hard. 'Should have got rid of it years ago, but sentimental value and all that.' The cork pulled out with a thunk, some wine escaping like a vapour trail in its wake. 'Just got to have the knack I suppose.' He placed the bottle down on the side and laid the corkscrew next to it. 'I'll call for that pizza now, yeah? Could you pour us out a couple of glasses babe?' Alison seemed a little distracted.

'What? Oh yes no problem, just ask them to hurry it up I'm starving!' Jacob could hear her softly singing in the kitchen as he ordered the food. It was an old song, familiar, but he couldn't quite place it.

'Acting as if nothing's happened...like everything is hunky-fucking-dory! Pizza will be about forty minutes...lunchtime...you know...they're really busy.' He shouted through to Alison as the telephone was hung up. Jacob had resolved to use this intermission to confront Alison about her infidelity. He braced himself and begun the slow march through to the kitchen. 'Alison, there's something I need to talk to you about, can you come into the...' Jacob's voice dried up and trailed off as he turned the corner to see Alison standing there wearing a black satin corset, suspenders, fish-net stockings and stilettos. She was holding a large glass of wine in either hand.

'You fancy joining me in the bedroom for a wee drink big boy?' Jacob's cock told him that the confrontation could wait.

*

Their post-coital cigarette was interrupted by a loud bang on the front door.
'That'll be the pizza.' Said Jacob lazily and made to get out of bed, but before he could rise, Alison had placed a hand on his chest to prevent him doing so.
'No babe, you lie there and relax, I'll get it, I need to pee anyway.' She stubbed the dying cigarette out in the ashtray then lowered herself down onto the bedroom floor. Jacob examined every detail with increasing intensity as Alison hobbled across the room. He studied every naked inch, every blemish and line - the small pinkish scar towards the mid-line of her shoulders, the clover shaped birth mark just above her left buttock. Even with the handicap of her cut and bandaged leg, Alison still somehow managed to hold herself proudly, to smoulder, to exude sheer femininity and sensuality. She dreamily lifted Jacob's shirt from the chair and wafted it round her shoulders, paused, looked up with heavy lidded eyes. 'You don't mind, do you?'
'Absolutely not lover,' replied Jacob, the words dripping unconsciously from his lips. It was the shirt he had bought to wear at his father's funeral. Jacob was entranced watching Alison adjust herself in the mirror. He thought to himself how that shirt would never again look the same. It would always remind him of her, of

this moment, of how good she looked wrapped up in it. This memory could never be tainted, it had to be preserved. As he grabbed up his cigarettes from the nightstand and quickly lit one up, Jacob vowed never to wear the shirt again. The door was wrapped once again, this time harder, more urgent.

'I'll be right there!' Shouted Alison as she finished fixing her hair in the hall mirror.

'Would you like me to get it babe, give you time to put your face on?' Commented Jacob sarcastically from the bedroom. Alison shot him a mock offended look as she unlocked and answered the door. The delivery man looked a bit surprised to see her standing in front of him semi-naked.

'Eh…six-fifty please missus.' He stammered sliding the pizza box out of the heatproof bag and offering it over.

'Oh shit…eh sorry…' exclaimed Alison '…kinda forgot I needed money. Could you just hold on for two seconds? I'll be right back.' She continued accepting the pizza box and half closing the door. Alison padded hurriedly back along the hallway to the bedroom and entered to a blinding flash of light! Jacob had found the film he bought last night and loaded his camera. 'Bloody hell a flasher!' Shouted Alison.

'Yeah baby! Work that booty! Come on now, don't be shy, show me your best moves, give me that pure animal sex appeal.' Shouted Jacob, imitating a fashion photographer…very badly. He reeled off shot after shot, Alison striking sexy poses like a real pro. 'You seem a bit too good at this Alison. Now either you're a natural, or, I'm guessing, this isn't your first time.'

'Money?' Asked Alison, breaking her routine.

'Not until the shots are published darling.'

'No, for the pizza you silly man.' Jacob thought about being offended for a second, but pointed to a crumpled heap of clothes in the corner by the window.

'There should be some in my wallet there…in my trouser pocket.' He lifted his cigarette from the ashtray and took a drag as he photographed Alison rescuing his wallet from amongst the wreckage of their cast off clothing. Jacob continued to take photographs as she limped back off down the hallway, zooming in on her and the delivery driver's hands as she gave him the money.

Within the space of five minutes an entire thirty-six exposure film had been finished off. Jacob photographed Alison disappearing into the kitchen then photographed the empty space she had left behind. A strange melancholia hollowed a void in the pit of his stomach. Dropping the camera on the bed, he leaned back against the headboard, lifted his glass from the night-stand and attempted to fill the emptiness with look-warm white wine.

A short time later Alison reappeared from the kitchen brandishing a kitchen roll and the pizza sliced into neat triangles and displayed over a large wooden chopping board.

'Put it down here.' Said Jacob, picking up the camera and smoothing out an area of quilt in the middle of the bed. He attempted to take a picture of Alison placing the food down, but the camera flashed red, beeped and began to purr and whirr.

'Run out of film?' Quizzed Alison sitting down next to Jacob.

'Yeah, not quite dragged myself into the digital age yet.'

'Stick with what you know eh?' The camera creaked to a halt and Jacob flicked open the back and shook the film out.

'Got another film in here though.' Continued Jacob, leaning down to lift a carrier bag from underneath the bed. He noticed Alison's eyebrows rise slightly as she recognised the logo on the bag from the garage.

'Where did you buy the film?' Asked Alison. Jacob stared intently into her eyes but pretended not to hear as he tore open the box and loaded the film.

'Can't keep eye contact... looks like a guilty conscience to me Jake. Sorry? What did you say?'

'The film? Where did you get it? That bag - if you bought it at that garage it must have cost you a fortune.' The camera door clicked shut and Jacob looked up. Alison's gaze had not moved. She half smiled.

'There we go. Ready to shoot.' Alison tried again.

'So where did you get it then? The film I mean?' Jacob again chose not to answer and instead picked the bag up by its' bottom and emptied out two remaining chocolate bars over towards Alison.

'And there's dessert!' He hesitated, trying to read Alison's mood. 'Some twenty-four-hour petrol station, the one on Woodlands Road I think. Do you know it?' It was a hollow question, rhetorical, but she still replied all the same.

'Yes, I think I know it. Just along from that all night café.' There was not even the merest hint of deceit in her voice.

'She thinks she knows it? Bared face lies!'

Jacob aimed the camera at Alison's face, zoomed in on her eyes and shot.

*

They ate largely in silence, Jacob draining the last of the wine directly from the bottle after Alison had politely declined a second glass. He was aching to ask about her liaison of the previous evening, but this was not the right time.

When the couple had finished eating, Jacob cleared away the leftovers to make space in preparation for another bout of passion; but Alison had already stood up and was sorting out her clothes.

'So what do you fancy doing for the rest of the day?' She asked reaching round and fastening her bra. Jacob felt cheated, it was quite obvious what he had in mind for the remainder of the afternoon, and probably much of the evening, but that option had been snatched from the table.

'We could go for a walk?' He offered, unimaginatively. Alison pulled back the corner of a curtain and peered out of the bedroom window.

'But it's still pissing down with rain!'

'I don't mind the rain actually… it washes away all the dirt and the filth.'

'And you can splash in the puddles as well!' Added Alison glibly.

'Splash in puddles? What the fuck? Does she think you're, a fucking child? 'Yes, absolutely, that sounds like tremendous fun!' Jacob lied, painfully dragging his sorry carcass out of bed for a second time that day. Alison was putting the finishing touches to dressing, fastening the buckles on her brown leather shoes, while Jacob was still hopping around the bedroom trying to pull on his socks. He tugged on his battered jeans then searched for a shirt amongst the debris strewn across the bedroom floor. Already Alison was busy fixing her hair and makeup in the hall mirror when Jacob shouted through to her.

'We could go for ice-cream? I know this wonderful little Italian place along Great Western Road.'

'Sounds perfect, babe, ice-cream on a cold miserable day!'

'They also do the best hot chocolate, so thick you could stand a spoon up in it.'

'Now you're talking my language Mr Douglas! You got any cash? I forgot to lift my purse on the way out earlier, in too much of a rush to get over here.' Jacob felt his cock stiffen slightly at the thought of Alison hurrying over to his place with sex on her mind.

'Check in my wallet wherever you left it... I think there should be enough for a couple of drinks. We can stop at a hole-in-the-wall on the way if we need to though.'

'Your wallet's right here on the hall table, babe, I'll just have a nosey.'

Jacob finished getting dressed then examined his camera. Nine exposures used, that left about twenty-seven, plenty for that afternoon. Sensing a presence, he looked up to see Alison standing in the doorway. She was holding his wallet loosely, almost unconsciously in her left hand, whilst something in her right hand held her gaze transfixed.

'You okay Alison?' She said nothing. Jacob gave her a moment then tried again. 'Is there something wrong?' His second enquiry seemed to pop her bubble of solitary concentration.

'What? Eh... no... nothing.' She seemed startled, as if Jacob had broken in on her silent prayer.

'Is everything okay babe?' Alison raised her gaze and looked straight at Jacob.

'Who's this?' She enquired holding out a black and white photograph towards him. What the hell had she found out? Was it one of the others? Jacob was frightened for a moment, adrenalin pumping. Muscles tensed, he took a step towards her and the photograph came into focus. Jacob breathed a huge sigh of relief and began to smile involuntarily - it was the photograph he had found in his father's wallet. 'So who are they then?' Alison insisted. Relaxed now, Jacob answered.

'Oh that's just... well actually, to be perfectly honest I've got no idea who the young woman is, but the fine looking gentleman on the left is my late father. I expect the woman was one of his many floozies. Dad had, according to my mother, rather a *roving eye* in his younger and more foolish days.' What Jacob really wanted to say was that it was probably one of the many poor bastards that his father, the adulterous old letch that he was, fucked then discarded like yesterday's newspapers when she no longer interested him, but his mother had always taught him not to speak ill of the dead. Alison was still staring at him. 'So did you find any money in there as well?'

'What?'

'Money... in my wallet? For the drinks... remember?'

'Yeah... there's about twenty quid. And the change from the pizza is on the dressing table there behind you.' Jacob turned round to grab the small pile of coins and stuffed them into his trouser pocket.

'You ready to make a move then babe?' Alison seemed distant, as if off in a dream somewhere.

'Eh? Yes, of course, let's get the hell out of here.' She slid the photograph carefully back into Jacob's wallet and threw it over to him, but he fumbled the catch, the wallet bouncing off the bedpost and onto the floor in front of him.

163

'Thanks, I think?' He muttered sarcastically, but Alison seemed oblivious having already turned her back and begun to walk away. Jacob quickly tied up his shoes and stuffed the wallet into his jeans pocket, the noise of the front door being unlocked and creaking open hurrying him to his feet.

'Hold on a minute babe... don't leave me behind!' But Alison had already descended the top three stairs. 'What's the rush babe?' Shouted Jacob, stumbling out the door, grabbing his coat and umbrella on the way. By the time he locked the door and made it to the top of the stairs, Alison was out of sight, the sound of her receding footsteps echoing up the close. Jacob broke into a sprint trying to catch her up, losing grip of his umbrella as he accelerated. It clattered down the stairs in front almost tripping him up. Jacob regained his umbrella and his composure and picked up the pace. 'Where's the bloody fire Alison?' No response, only the noise of her footsteps getting further away.

He caught her up half-way along the street by the traffic lights. The phone box which had once stood on the corner had now been completely removed, some scatterings of shattered glass, the only evidence of the previous day's drama. A stiff breeze had flown in to join the rain and Jacob struggled to unleash his large golfing umbrella. 'What's the matter Alison? Why the rush?' Alison stopped by the kerb and pressed the crossing button. She turned her face towards Jacob's and looked deep into his eyes. It made him feel weak, uneasy. 'What? What is it? Have I done something wrong? Have I offended you in some way? What?'

Alison opened her mouth to speak, but no words came. The crossing screamed at them to comply, and she turned quickly away heading for the other side of the road. Jacob remained frozen, staring at the falling rain where Alison had stood only moments before. *'Come on now, act like a man, let the stupid cow go. Don't let her fuck with your head. Just turn your back on her and walk away. It's as simple as that.* Alison you're scaring me here. Will you please just tell me what the hell is wrong?' Jacob shouted as he ran across the road behind her. Alison reached the opposite pavement just ahead of him and made for the shelter of a doorway. Jacob hesitated, looked for some recognition, a hint of invitation. Her eyes were soft, her lips almost smiling. He walked the nine steps over and joined her. Alison flashed a gaze at him then turned her attention to the wet pavement.

'Alison, darling, why the hell are you being like this? Is there someone else?'

'There's no-one else Jacob, only you... there's only ever been you. And you've done nothing wrong.' She placed the side of her head on Jacob's chest and wrapped her arms around his waist. His stomach was burning; he had seen her with his own eyes, kissing another man and was bursting to tell her so, to shout it in her face.

'Why can't you just be fucking honest with me? I love you... I forgive you!'

Jacob put his hand under her chin and lifted her face up to his.

'Whatever it is we can fix it. Okay?' Alison attempted to smile.

'I guess I'm just a little bit tired. The medication I suppose. Do you mind if I skip the hot chocolate today? Think I just need to go home and get some rest.'

'Sure…absolutely no problem babe. We could snuggle up on the couch, watch an old movie…'

'No Jacob, I think I need some time on my own, to relax properly… to sleep. You don't mind do you?' The words were like a knife in Jacob's heart. He felt his knees start to buckle and a heavy darkness descend upon him.

'The bitch! She's going to see him isn't she? Conning, deceitful lying cunt!' 'Of course babe, I understand… and I don't mind at all. You take as long as you need to get yourself sorted out, I'll be waiting for you. Come on, I'll walk you home.' Replied Jacob putting an arm around Alison's shoulder. She pulled away leaving him feeling crushed and rejected.

'No it's okay Jacob, you don't have to do that. If it's all the same to you I think I'd like to walk on my own, clear my head, you know?' Jacob's fist tightened around the grip of his umbrella; he felt the scab on his knuckle stretch and tear.

'Just try and hold it together, relax… breathe… slowly in; slowly out… Well at least take this to keep you dry.' He spat through gritted teeth offering Alison the umbrella. She took it reluctantly.

'Thanks. I'll give you a call tomorrow.'

'Be sure and do that, just to let me know that you're okay if nothing else.' Alison fired Jacob an incomplete glance then kissed him fleetingly on the right cheek.

166

His eyes covered every millimetre of her face, every feature, every line and blemish. He could not be sure whether it was rain water or teardrops that stained her face as she turned and limped away.

Jacob watched Alison grow smaller then vanish round a corner. He wanted so much to run after her, to tell her that he knew everything and that it didn't matter; he forgave her, they could get through this, it would make them stronger... he loved her. But instead Jacob checked his watch - three-fifty-seven - and walked a short distance to the off-licence with the intent of purchasing enough whisky to kill a baby elephant.

*

Jacob pulled up in the car park behind the bank and thought more than twice before turning the engine off. It was Thursday afternoon 3pm, he knew she'd have to be at work. Her afternoon break was three-thirty, so she should be able to see him, even if it was for just ten minutes. Jacob stopped the car, started it again, let it run for a few seconds, thought of reverse gear and screeching out of here. He turned the engine off.
'You owe me at least ten minutes Alison.'

*

There was a queue of three waiting for a free window. The Customer Services desk was unmanned. Jacob took his place at the back of the impatient line. There was only one window open, the bank clerk busy going through a young

167

woman's personal account attempting to track down a mystery charge that had caused her account to plunge five pounds into the red. Jacob thought about leaving and coming back later, but he knew that if he went now he would never return. He wanted… needed to see her. A tallish blond-bobbed woman who looked to be in her late thirties maybe even early forties (it was difficult to be precise given the depth of her make-up) in blue uniform and red-neckerchief, emerged from a door at the far side of the service windows. She glided towards the Customer Service desk, situated on a raised wooden island behind and left of where Jacob stood. Jacob ducked under the roped off queuing snake and headed towards her. The woman sensed Jacob's movements and prepared the way with a corporate smile.

'How can I help you today sir?' Not an unpleasant voice, but one tempered with a cold professionalism.

'I hope so. I need to speak to someone, an employee. She works here, her name is Alison…Alison Clark. Do you know if she's around?' The woman's shoulders relaxed almost imperceptibly. Her features softening.

'Are you Jacob?'

'Yes! Alison told you about me?'

'Well, not exactly. She did say that you might be in looking for her, that she had missed you or something like that? That she didn't have the chance to explain something to you? Does that make any sense?'

168

'Is she here? Can I see her?'

'No Alison's on annual leave right now. But she did say you might be in while she was away. She left a letter for you, said it would explain things. I'll go and fetch it from through the back.'

Jacob's heart sunk as the woman descended from her perch and exited through the same door from whence she had came. There welled up a strange cocktail of emotions; he was saddened and frustrated that Alison was not here, but also filled with anticipation, excitement, trepidation that he was about to get an explanation of her sudden and absolute disappearance.

The woman reappeared after only a short time clutching a small white envelope. Jacob felt strangely disappointed by the size of the letter, as if a larger envelope would have conveyed a deeper sentiment.

'Here you go Jacob.' Said the woman offering him the letter. 'I'm sure this will explain everything.'

'So when will Alison be back at work then?' The woman looked at Jacob with a rather puzzled expression.

'I suppose it'll be in the letter, but Alison wont be coming back to work, well at least not here. She's transferred to a branch up north, Aberdeen somewhere I think? Or is it Inverness? Anyway, I'm sure it'll all be explained in there.' She gestured to the envelope now resting unconsciously in Jacob's hand. He felt numb.

'Yes, I suppose it will be.' His voice replied from somewhere far below him. '

Thanks…thanks a lot.' His voice continued with all the emotion of an

automaton. Jacob's right hand stuffed the letter into his coat pocket and his

legs carried him towards the door.

'No problem Jacob. Take care now!'

THE LETTER

Dear Jacob

This is the hardest letter I've ever had to write. I can only begin to imagine what you must be thinking and feeling. I am really sorry for the way I just vanished out of your life. The last thing I ever wanted to do was hurt you, but if you are feeling half as bad as I'm feeling now then I've failed miserably. Maybe sometime in the future I'll actually be able to sit down with you and talk about this whole mess, try and explain everything to you. But for now you're going to have to trust me when I say that it's better you don't know right now. Believe me, it'll be better in the long run. And believe me when I tell you that I had to leave not because I don't love you but because I do, I really, really do.

Forever yours

Alison

Dreaming was now a strange and unnerving experience. They still presented vivid, wild and fantastical landscapes, but when he begun to awaken it was into a pitch-dark room where dawn would never break.

THE PASSENGER

Jacob found himself sitting in the passenger seat of the old family car, a silver Volvo 265 estate. Looking to his right he became aware that it was his father who was driving, customary non-tipped cigarette hanging from the corner of his mouth. 'Where the hell are we going dad?' Mr Douglas Senior sucked long and hard on his cigarette then exhaled a steady stream of smoke. Still saying nothing, dead dad scrutinised the glowing orange tip then took one more quick drag and flicked the inch long butt out of the drivers-side window. Finally he acknowledged his son's question.

'Don't you recognise this road then J.J.? We've been up this way many times before.' Jacob wound down the passenger side window and looked out. There was no road beneath them, only a vast expanse of unmoving dark water.

'Are we going fishing dad?'

'No, we're not going fishing this time son, just out for a drive.' Dead dad took out and lit another cigarette, offering the open packet up to Jacob.

'Fancy a smoke J.J.?' Jacob waved the packet away.

'No thanks... not for me dad... too strong.' His father flicked the box lid closed with his thumb and slid it back into the breast pocket of his short-sleeved white cotton shirt.

'Yes, very wise, these things will kill you right enough son. I can safely say that without any fear of contradiction.' Jacob looked over the vast forbidding waters. It seemed to stretch on forever.

'So what's this all about then dad?' Dead dad cleared his throat, spitting the resulting phlegm out towards the water. He took another drag on his cigarette.

'I told you to watch yourself with that woman son, didn't I? I've told you about a thousand times boy, they're all the bloody same! You can't trust any of them.'

'But Alison is different dad, I'm sure of it. I just know she is. I really love this woman dad, and even with everything that's happened I know that she loves me.' Jacob watched his father's brows cut a deep furrow and braced himself against the storm that was gathering within those eyes.

'Yes I'll bet she bloody loves you alright... because you're such a fucking soft touch! She clicks her fingers and you jump up and go running like a wee fucking dog!'

'No dad... it's not like... it's not like that at all... Alison is...' Jacob's father cut him off angrily.

'Don't you sit there and tell me what it's bloody like! I am still your father young man! I'll tell you exactly what it's fucking like! You're an absolute bloody fool boy! She's ripping the fucking pish out of you! It will end up like the last time, you mark my words Jacob, and only this time you might not be as bloody lucky! Idiot, bloody idiot! Nearly fucking killed your-self! Do you have any idea what

174

that whole episode did to your poor old mother? Well do you boy?'

'I am so sorry dad... so, so sorry.' Jacob began to cry.

'Come on now son, pull yourself together... for heaven's sake, be a man. Be honest with yourself for once in your life. You know as well as I do that it could never work, that one's a tease son. Just use her then dump the cow, she'll only mess you around otherwise. Listen to your old man J.J. you know I'm speaking the truth.' Dead dad slowed the ancient Volvo to a creaking halt. 'Right son, we're here.' Jacob turned to face his father.

'What? Where are we exactly?' He turned his attention to the surrounding emptiness.

'This is your stop son.'

'My stop? Are you not coming too?' Jacob's father looked him in the eyes deep and long and smiled a father's smile. He gave Jacob a manly pat on the back as he spoke.

'Sorry son, but you're on your own from here.' Then leaned across and opened the passenger side door for him. Jacob exited the car without question.

'I love you dad' His father said nothing as the door slammed shut, and instantly Jacob was alone in inestimable darkness. The far off echo of his father's voice penetrated the black infinity.

'Remember what I said son... be a man!'

Jacob stared down to the dark undulating waters far beneath, and he was falling, falling, falling! His body broke the surface with the faintness of a butterfly's wing-beat, and submerged deep into the ethereal depths. Jacob glided in ghostlike silence under the midnight waves. In the black nothing a pinprick of white grew ever larger, hurtling towards him on a collision course. A face.... frightening velocity... accelerating still... impact imminent! He screamed a last desperate warning.

'Alison!'

*

The clock screamed 8:05AM.

Jacob thought about the dream as it quickly dissolved into the stale morning; about the relationship his father had alluded to, a relationship that had nearly cost him so dearly. As he sifted through memories of a relationship he had so carefully packed and hidden away, Jacob wondered how it was that he had managed to spend almost two years of his life with a woman that he really didn't like? A woman, who had bled him dry, drove him deep into a dark hole, devastated his self-confidence, and kept his heart imprisoned by making him feel sorry for her? He might have been able to understand it if she had been attractive or sexy or even, at a stretch, if she had been a good cook or kept a tidy house! But *the bitch* had been none of these things.

'Ugly, overweight, selfish, blinkered, two faced, liar, untidy, vindictive, immature, parasitic, venomous, bitter… I mean… what the fuck J.J?'

He had never loved her; could not even stand to be in the same room with her most of the time! Then it struck him, they had hooked up when he was at a low ebb and extremely vulnerable. Jacob's mother had died only days before *she* descended upon him during a party. He had been completely fucked out of his head on god-knows-what cocktail of drugs and booze when *she* latched on and dug in her fangs. By the time Jacob had straightened up he was a thirty years old and she had moved in with her manky old cat who made his flat stink of its piss! 'What in gods name was I thinking?'

Jacob rolled out of bed and staggered towards the hall, still drunk from last night's bingeing. There was not a hope in hell that he would be able to drive to the ferry port this morning. Grabbing the receiver at the third attempt, Jacob struggled to telephone his brother, asking him if they could meet at the pub in Central Station in an hour, giving the excuse that his car was dead. His fingers automatically dialled Alison's home then mobile numbers… again. Same result… no answer, no reply. With the exception of three or so hours of sleep, or, to be more accurate, unconsciousness, Jacob had been calling her continually since around eight-thirty the previous evening. Sporadic and rambling messages had been dictated to Alison's various answering services since that last time they had been together in the street. Jacob had tried hard to give her the space she said she

177

needed, but last night, with the trip to Ireland imminent, the truth had hit him hard and he had really needed to see her; but Alison had vanished beneath his radar. 'Why won't you talk to me Alison?' Jacob returned the handset to its cradle a little too vigorously and stared at it accusingly.

He thought about a shower and maybe some breakfast, but resigned himself to yet another cigarette and a generous measure of the hair of the dog that had bitten him so hard the night before. Throwing the sitting-room curtain aside, the light stabbed at his eyes causing a fleeting moment of bright yellow blindness and a hasty retreat into the relative shadows. His vision slowly adjusted to cold sharp daylight and Jacob turned to survey the miscellany of his life, searching hopelessly for a sign. The mantle-clock informed that it was now nearing half-past-eight. 'Better get the proverbial fucking roller-skates on boy!' Jacob shouted at no-one before draining his whisky and staggering off to the bedroom to pack.

*

The taxi driver *peeped* his arrival just after nine a.m. Jacob threw back the dregs of his second morning whisky then grabbed his bag and headed for the door. It struck him as he was about to take hold of the handle to twist.

'Oh for fuck sake!' He cursed and doubled back to the sitting room to locate his forgotten wallet. He found it lounging on the side table by the phone. 'One last time… before we go?' Said Jacob, his hand hovering over the receiver. The taxi driver's impatient horn repeated from the street outside. 'Oh fuck it!' Spat Jacob grabbing up his wallet.

*

Some fifteen minutes later Jacob was climbing the steps rather unsteadily to the railway station bar. Shadows crowded the corners inside, occasionally spilling out into the yellow-lit bar area at the front and centre of the pub to have their glasses refilled, before quickly shuffling back to seclusion. Jacob found the dimness soothing, his eyes still stinging and watering in reaction to the daylight. A quick scan round on his way to the bar informed him that his brother had not yet arrived. The only figures Jacob could make out seemed to be railway workers and post-men.

'What can I get you pal?' The barman seemed unusually energetic and friendly, it made Jacob feel uncomfortable.

'Eh... a pint of heavy please.' Replied Jacob, not really knowing where this order had come from as he was really after more whisky... cold and raw. But there was plenty of time to remedy the situation. 'Oh... and could I get a whisky with that as well please?' The barman looked up from the pint he was pouring without moving his head and acknowledged Jacob's request with the faintest raise of his eyebrows. When he had finished pouring Jacob's pint the barman sat it on top of the bar towel in front of him.

'Do you want to order any breakfast?' It was not the response that Jacob was expecting, he just wanted to be left alone with his drink. The situation made him feel under pressure, anxious.

'No... eh... no thank you... no breakfast for me this morning...I'm just waiting for my brother. We're on our way to our father's funeral...he's being buried in Ireland... he was born there. We're taking him back to the old country...' Jacob was no longer in control of his mouth; he was aware of speaking, but had absolutely no idea what was being said. He felt dislocated, as though he were floating somewhere behind watching all this going on, the words were coming out of his mouth, but they seemed to come from somewhere else... from someone else.

'Any preference?' The barman broke in.

'Eh?' Jacob was suddenly pulled back into his body in a state of utter confusion.

'What kind of whisky would you like?'

'And breathe...'

'Oh right, I see. Anything at all mate... Grouse?'

'The Famous Grouse it is then.' The barman pirouetted rather athletically for such a rotund man, and drained an optic into a small shot glass. The barman retraced his pirouette through ninety degrees and placed the whisky beside Jacob's pint. 'Have the dram is on me... for your dad an' that.' Jacob could feel that old lump rising in his throat. He swallowed hard.

'Thank you; thank you very much, that's… very kind of you.' He lifted the whisky in salute. 'Here's to you dad, you cantankerous old swine. God bless you.' And with that Jacob drained his glass in one gulp, the whisky burning lava-like all the way down, bringing warmth to the emptiness within him.

'That'll be two-fifty-five please pal.' Confusion engulfed Jacob once again.

'Eh?'

'For the pint of heavy; two-pounds and fifty-five pence please sir.' Jacob pulled out his wallet and rescued a solitary tattered fiver.

'Better nip out and hit the cash-point after this.' He thought out loud handing the money over. The barman took the five and rung it up.

'Aye, we've all got tae go sometime I suppose. It's a hard, hard road right enough…' Jacob was staring at the head of his pint and thinking of her.

'You're better off without her J.J., be a man.' His heart beat into overdrive and he looked up to see the round red face of the barman smiling apologetically.

'What did you say?'

'Two-forty-five... your change.' Jacob apprehensively held out an upturned palm and accepted the cash.

'You alright mate?' The barman enquired. Jacob's vision was blurring, sweat dripped cold down his spine.

'Yes…I'm…I'm fine. Just been a bit of a shitty week, you know, father dying, funeral arrangements all that shite.' The barman pursed his thin purple lips and shot Jacob one of those knowing looks that all good barmen have.

'Yep, been there myself not that long ago. My old mum, god rest her. Ninety-seven years old she was at the end, but it was still a bit of a shock, I don't mind telling you. I'll away and leave you in peace, gie's a shout if you need anything.' Jacob took two huge gulps of his pint, his cheeks bulging like Sachmo hitting a high 'c' with each one, as he watched the barman waddle off to the other end of the bar and bury his face in a newspaper.

*

Half way down his pint Jacob decided it was time to order more whisky and held up his empty glass to catch the barman's attention

'I'll get that...' Shouted Simon approaching from the doorway, '...and a pint of lager as well please.' Simon turned his attention from the barman to his brother. 'Looks like you've been here all night bro.' Jacob again resisted the urge to punch his brother square in the kisser.

'Good to see you too Si! But listen, we'll need to neck these drinks kinda sharpish - the train'll be leaving in about fifteen minutes.' The corpulent barman wobbled back with their drinks and positioned them carefully on the gold coloured draining board in front of them.

'Is this your brother?' He enquired addressing Jacob, who greedily took up his whisky and despatched it with a swift flick if the wrist.

182

'Correct! This is orphan number two.'

'Hi there...' Said Simon fumbling in his jacket in an attempt to locate his wallet. '...How much do I owe you for the drinks mate?' The barman put up both his hands as if readying him-self to face a penalty kick.

'No, no, son. You put away your money, we all have to pay respect to your dear departed father... it's a hard, hard road.' Simon stared at the barman puzzled and ever so slightly bemused.

'Eh? I mean, thanks very much mate.' The barman gave what appeared to be a small bow then returned to his roost at the end of the bar. Simon turned to his brother. 'What the fuck was all that about?'

'Oh, I went and told him about the funeral and that. Fat cunt made me pay for my pint though, why the fuck did you get the special treatment? Probably fucking fancies ye the dirty auld bastard!' Simon was busy demolishing his lager with huge, hungry gulps.

'Just my natural charm and charisma I suppose bro.' He belched, lager dripping from his chin. Jacob stared accusingly at the barman who in reply smiled at the brothers over the top of his newspaper. Jacob ruminated, philosophised and calculated; he had only had to pay for one drink out of the three - that was two drinks for free. His brother had only gotten one out of the deal, but he hadn't had to pay at all.

'Fat auld cunt.' He muttered under his breath.

'I've got some goodies for the journey Jake,' Simon breathed loudly from the corner of his mouth patting the left breast pocket of his faded denim jacket. Jacob tried hard not to appear too excited.

'You got some hash?' He whispered back, shiftily eyeing either side of the bar through his bloodshot slits. Simon gave a sly grin.

'Well, yes…amongst other things!'

'Not acid I hope? I'm not going near that stuff again. I don't think my nut could take it!' Jacob unconsciously rubbed the scab on his right hand as he spoke.

'Better than that bro, Coke! Pharmaceutical grade, the good stuff man! Got a contact at the Western Infirmary. Oh, I nearly forgot… here, something to liven up the ferry crossing.' Simon pushed a small, rectangular object into Jacob's hand below bar level.

'So what's this then Si? Fart sweeties?' Said Jacob opening his hand to inspect the contents, causing Simon to spit the mouthful of beer he had just sucked up back into his glass, the head frothing up creamily and almost spilling over.

'For fuck sake! Are you trying to get us arrested? Quick man, put it away!' Urged Simon surveying the bar for undercover operatives. Jacob frowned at his brother and slipped the package into the breast pocket of his coat.

'Okay little brother keep your fucking knickers on. So what is it then, heroin or something?'

'No it's just speed, but remember I've got about five grams of coke in my bag, if I get caught with that I'm, no hold on, scratch that, *we* are going down for a good few years.' Jacob scowled at his brother,

'What do you mean *we,* they're your drugs.'

'What the fuck Jake? So you're happy to swallow, smoke or snort anything I throw at you, but if it came to the crunch you'd let me take the rap on my own? Well thank you very fucking much dear brother of mine.' Jacob put his arm round Simon's shoulder.

'Come on Si, I'm only pulling your plonker. Of course I wouldn't let you take the rapp, excuse the pun, and just stand back and look. We're brothers, you know, *room on my horse for two* and all that shite?' Simon's face softened into a smile.

'Trust you to quote Rolf fucking Harris in a situation like this.' Jacob let go of his brother's shoulder and lifted the remnants of his lager.

'Now come on, drink up, we've got a train to catch and some evidence to swallow.' Jacob threw back his drink in one and watched as Simon gulped down the last of his pint before lifting up his bag. 'You not going to drink that?' Said Jacob pointing at Simon's untouched whisky.

'Nope, can't stand the fucking stuff. You can have it if you like.' Jacob raised his eyebrows, shook his head.

'I don't understand the younger generation with your designer beers and your alco-pops.' He lifted the glass from the bar and drained the whisky, inhaling sharply through gritted teeth as the golden liquid bit his throat. 'Absolutely no fucking respect for tradition.' Simon had already started down the steps towards the station. Jacob thumbed the wrap of amphetamine in his pocket and pictured the five small bags of coke nestling at the bottom of his brother's bag. He envisaged police dogs sniffing it out, handcuffs, anal examinations, cold grey prison, sharing a cell with an eighteen-stone gorilla who called him honey-bunch and thought quietly to himself, *'Fuck Rolf Harris!'*

*

They stopped three times on the way to the train; once at the cash-point to top up their wallets, once at the ticket office, despite the protestations from Simon who claimed that the inspectors hardly ever checked anyone for tickets these days, and once at a fancy station shop to buy too many cans of overpriced foreign beer, the name of which neither man could pronounce with any confidence.

Jacob and Simon, or 'Pierre and Jean' as they were referring to each other, boarded the train a little after ten-fifteen. It was not yet too busy and they had no problem finding a pair of seats with a table. Both sat down by the window facing each other, placing the beer filled carrier bag on the table in front and between them. Jacob took out two cans and slid one over the formica top to Simon.

'Cheers bro.' Said Simon immediately snapping the can open and taking a swig.

'You fancy a wee smoke to pass the time?' Jacob snapped back the ring-pull on his own can sending a small geyser of beer fizzing up and over.

'Oh ya cunt!' He spat clamping his lips over the can to stem the flow.

'Ya daft big shite!' Laughed Simon as his brother gagged down the bubbling liquid, grimacing with the bitter-sweet taste.

'Yeuch! Man… that is rank! Anyway, I don't think you're allowed to smoke on the train these days.' Simon gave a small false laugh.

'Chill out old man, keep your tartan slippers on! We can have a smoke in the toilet once the train gets going, even the clippies do it. I'll head off first, get a number together, have a wee blast and then I'll come back and give you the goods. It'll be cool, no worries at all big bro.' *Big bro* gave a capitulatory grunt, braced himself and took another swig of his beer.

As the train pulled away Simon stood up, winked at his brother and skipped off in what he hoped was the direction of the toilet. Once Simon was out of sight, Jacob pulled the mobile phone from his jacket pocket. No messages… no missed calls. Almost unconsciously his fingers began typing a text message to Alison;

'Of 2 Irlnd 2 bry Dd-rlly ms u :(

Bck Sun-c u whn gt hme?

Lve u – J.J.xx'

The *send* button depressed and Jacob watched a tiny animated envelope fly off into infinity. He was still staring at the blank screen as Simon returned.

'Who you calling bro?' Jacob looked up lazily.

'Oh no one, just checking my messages, you know?' But Simon had already lost interest; he placed his tobacco tin on the table.

'Here you go Jake. Word of warning though, that in there...' he said gesturing towards the tin, '...is an almost ninety-nine per-cent grass joint. There's just a smidgeon of tobacco rolled in to help keep it alight. So if you're not very, *very* careful it will blow your bloody socks clean off!' In reality, Jacob did not really need or want any more depressants, but the way Simon spoke made it sound like a challenge.

'Yeah, okay little brother, but I have done this before you know. In fact I was smoking joints while you were still playing with your fucking dolls!' Simon threw up his hands in mock defence.

'Alright, cool your jets big man! All I'm saying is go easy, it's extremely potent weed. Oh and they weren't dolls, they were action men actually.' Jacob puffed out his chest and grabbed the tin.

'Whatever you say...Barbie!' He spat like a petulant teenager, but was feeling more like a doddering old fogey.

*

Once inside, Jacob pushed the large black button to lock the toilet door, and a red 'ENGAGED' sign lit up on the wall. He checked his mobile phone again; still no contact. Thoughts of Alison lying unconscious in a hospital bed, the result of some terrible accident flowed through Jacob's head. He considered his reflection in the scuffed mirror - tired, growing older by the second.

'But surely someone would have called me? She must have told at least one of her friends about us by now?'

He unclipped the lid of Simon's tobacco tin, the pungent smell of marijuana slapping him in the face. Jacob lifted out the half joint apprehensively and lit it up. The smoke felt really smooth and cooling as he sucked it into his lungs, not like the harsh stinging sensation from the usual shit resin. A faded reflection stared back at Jacob puffing away greedily, reminiscent of an old paddle steamer chugging down the summer-time Clyde. 'What the fuck did Si mean *be careful*? Silly cunt! I could smoke this stuff all day…piece of pish!'

*

A loud banging off in the distance somewhere grew louder and louder, until…it was right above his head. An angry voice was shouting,

'C'mon tae fuck mate! I'm bursting for a pish!' Jacob was slumped in the corner of the toilet, his face resting against the small metal sink. He had no idea how long he had been there, but his watch read five past eleven.

189

'Holy shit!' He exclaimed, rubbing his head and standing up rather shakily. Jacob attempted to wash his face in the sink, but no water came from the tap, so he straightening up his appearance as best he could and made to leave. He pressed the release button and waited as the door slid slowly and creakily back. Something glinted at the corner and caught his eye - it was Simon's tobacco tin. Jacob snatched and stuffed it in his trouser pocket in one smooth movement just as the door juddered all the way open to reveal a short, stocky and extremely irate looking man. Jacob wondered if his face was so red from being overweight or as a result of having to hold in his pee for so long. It seemed to be growing ever redder by the second as if being fanned from some invisible heat source. Jacob thought it better to keep it simple. 'Sorry mate, fell asleep.' He offered timidly and shuffled quickly to the side. The fat, red man said nothing, but the dagger-look he shot pushing past into the empty toilet spoke volumes.

Half way along the carriage Jacob spotted Simon standing up and pulling on his jacket. The train juddered violently causing Jacob to stagger and fall backwards across the laps of an elderly couple. He looked up into their surprised and disgusted faces. 'A thousand apologies people... just woke up... still a bit wobbly.' Simon's voice broke in above him.

'Come on Jake leave this nice young couple alone, they don't want to play with you...' He offered Jacob an outstretched hand and pulled him back up onto his feet. 'I'm so sorry if my brother bothered you...' Simon continued, '... he's just trying to be friendly, doesn't get out much you see. Come on you, ya cheeky young scamp!' Simon put his arm round Jacob's shoulder and marched him off towards their seat. 'So, back in the land of the living at last bro? I was just on my way to look for you; we'll be arriving at the station in about five minutes.'

His arse safely relocated on the seat across from Simon, Jacob considered reproaching his brother for failing to come to find him sooner. But remembering his blatant disregard for the warning dished out before heading for the toilet and cannabis oblivion, Jacob decided against a reprimand, and instead picked up and guzzled down his warm beer.

'How long was I in there?'

'About twenty minutes I guess... Might even have been a bit longer, that dope has kinda messed with the space time continuum, know what I mean? I did tell you to be careful though.' Jacob wanted to disagree with Simon, to tell him that it wasn't the drugs that it was because he hadn't been sleeping. His woman had vanished from the face of the earth, probably run off with a man half her age, leaving him broken and hollow, but how would Simon be able to understand? He had never been in love. In fact Jacob could not remember ever seeing his brother with a woman.

'Yes okay... you were right Si, I won't be making that mistake again.'

'Here, take this.' Said Simon gesturing to his hand with a nod of the head. He dropped a screwed up piece of paper into his brother's outspread palm. Jacob raised an eyebrow.

'What is it?'

'Put a bit of speed in a fag paper for you. I had a dab while you were, how should I say…indisposed? Swallow it down then man, it'll perk you right up.' Jacob had deep reservations about putting any more drugs into his already over-loaded system. But he felt totally exhausted; he needed something, and he needed it quick, so without any more wasted thought he quickly tossed the tiny parcel into his mouth and worked it down with a gulp of his brother's beer.

*

Jumping into a taxi at the rank outside the station, they were at the ferry port within five minutes. The amphetamine Jacob had ingested on the train was beginning to kick in and, to his utter amazement he was actually feeling a lot better.

'How you doing Jake?' Enquired Simon as they made their way to the booking office.

'Remarkably well as a matter of fact… apart from a bit of a headache I feel, well… surprisingly good.'

'Good drugs mate, no shite mixed in with it. It's all the crap that the scum-bag dealers cut their powders with that fucks everyone up.' Simon answered with a smile. Again Jacob really wanted to disagree with his brother, and in particular with his pro-drug point of view, but at that particular moment in time thought it would be more than a little hypocritical to argue and so instead gave a nod of the head and said nothing.

*

The brothers Douglas located the booking office and collected their boarding passes in record time. There was just over twenty minutes until the boat sailed, but it was unanimously decided to get on board and find the bar. To their horror, a metal shutter was pulled down over the bar. Jacob attempted to pull it up by the handle, but it didn't budge.

'Sorry boys, the bar doesn't open until we set sail.' A serious looking young man in uniform informed them, positioning himself between the brothers and the bar as he did so. Jacob was wondering if they had time to make it to the nearest pub and back before the gang-plank was raised as Simon clicked his fingers and lifted the bag of beer, or what was left of it, and had a look inside.

'Two cans left Jake... keep us going till this thing opens, eh?' He said nodding towards the bar.

They climbed the narrow stairwell to the upper deck where they were greeted by a bitter, biting wind blowing straight in off the Atlantic and whipping up the Firth. It was just starting to rain.

'Nice day for it.' Commented Jacob ironically, accepting a can from Simon and cracking it open. He shuddered as the liquid fizzed down his throat and into his empty stomach. Jacob had given up on the concept of breakfast recently, but was surprised not to be feeling hungry.

'Wait till the boat pulls out then we'll neck some more of that speed, what do you think?' Remarked Simon between gulps from his can. Jacob absorbed the words, but remained silent, lost somewhere on the red horizon. 'You still seeing that woman Jake?' Continued Simon. Jacob felt a burning rage boil below the void of his stomach. He did not take his eyes from the horizon as he spoke.

'The truth is Simon, I don't really know. I haven't seen or heard from her for a couple of days, I've left messages, been round her house... It's like she's just... disappeared.' Simon looked genuinely concerned.

'Did you have a fight or something bro?'

'No, that's the weird thing about it, we were getting on really well. I mean really, really well. I thought that she might even be *the one* you know?' Simon visibly stiffened.

'Come on Jake, I mean, you've only been seeing her for what... a couple of weeks at the most? You hardly fucking know the woman!' The words seemed to snap

Jacob from his trance. He turned quickly on his brother.

'What the fuck would you know Simon? You never even met her did you! I know her all right, better than anyone, better than she knows herself! It doesn't matter how long you've known someone, we had, I mean, we *have* a connection, we were meant to be together. That's what makes this thing so fucking confusing. And I know she feels the same as me. I just don't understand what the fuck has happened! The whole business just makes no any fucking sense what so ever.' Jacob's eyes were pleading. Simon placed a hand on his brother's shoulder.

'Maybe... well maybe it just isn't the right time or something? Or maybe she isn't *the one* for you?' He felt cheated; Jacob expected empathy, genuine concern, not some patronising clichés. The boat juddered into life beneath their feet. 'That's us away Jake... come on, let's go get a drink.' Continued Simon. Jacob finished the dregs of his can and tossed it into the sea. He had one last look at the quayside, vainly hoping, praying, but there was still nothing but empty space where she should have been.

*

The ferry crossing was all a bit of a blur for the brother's Douglas; the boys spending most of their time staggering between the bar, where they swallowed far too much alcohol, and the toilets, absorbing a number of banned substances utilising a variety of methods. When the captain announced over the loudspeaker that the boat would soon be arriving at Belfast quay, the brother's, rather shortsightedly perhaps, decided that they had better pull themselves together and ordered two double espressos in place of the usual whisky. At this point Jacob was seeing three blurred images of everything and closed one eye to get a better aim at the coffee cup. It didn't help.

'Fuck it!' He stammered, somewhat to the surprise of Simon who was concentrating hard on not falling off his chair, and went for the cup in the middle.

 The boat lurched to the right knocking Simon to the floor. Jacob went with the sway, his hand brushing the side of the hot cup. 'Aha! Ya fucking beauty! Izza one on the right Si!' He shouted triumphantly and delicately lifted the cup between right thumb and forefinger, pinkie cocked. A whisky reflex tipped the tiny cup's entire scalding contents into Jacob's open smiling mouth, frazzling the fuck out of his tongue. Simon looked up towards Jacob from his new horizontal cruciform position on the floor, just in time to see the lava-hot coffee eject from his mouth at light speed into the air. He could not discern exactly what language his brother was speaking, or rather shouting, as he spat out the steaming coffee, but could tell that it was not an expression of pleasure at the excellent quality of the beans, the full bodied, deep, pungent flavour with excellent acidity and a hint of smokiness.

*

As the ship juddered, screeched and banged its' way into port, Jacob and Simon finished off what remained of their coffees and looked at each other for inspiration. The other passengers were already busily shuffling past them on their way to the exits. Simon raised himself up on one elbow and ventured reticently,

'Well bro, you ready to go meet rest of the clan?'

'Suppose we'll have to… got no fucking choice now, have we?' Jacob slurred in reply and clambered unsteadily to his feet. He offered a helping hand to his brother who still lay on the floor; Simon took it and Jacob staggered backward pulling him to his feet, Simon immediately having to reciprocate to stop Jacob catapulting backwards into the quickly emptying bar room. They shakily made their way towards and down the gangway, glad of the jostling crowd who were helping them to remain upright and moving in the right direction.

Uncle Andrew and younger cousin Peter stood waving and smiling solemnly by the dockside. Peter was a lot bigger and taller than Jacob remembered, but some quick mental arithmetic brought the realisation that the last time he had seen Peter was seven years ago at their grandmother's funeral. Much vigorous handshaking ensued, punctuated by conciliatory phrases such as,

'…I wish we were meeting again under happier circumstances…'

And,

'…He was a fine man…'

Or,

'…It must have been such a shock…'

Also,

'…It is a very sad occasion.'

*

The journey to the family home normally took just under an hour, but about thirty minutes in Jacob's bladder felt like it was about to explode.

'Is there any chance of pulling in Uncle Andrew? Need to drain the python… know what I mean?' Uncle Andrew gave no indication of slowing down.

'Can you not hold it for a bit longer Jacob? It's not too far to go now, and the family's expecting us.' Jacob winced, his face contorting into an ugly grimace.

'I really don't think that I can Uncle Andrew.' He looked to his younger brother for support, moral and physical. Simon seemed slow to get the message, but eventually caught on.

'Yeah, I need to go too Uncle Andrew, the toilets on the ferry were really manky.' Uncle Andrew harrumphed and pulled the car to a halt at the side of the road.

'Right then boys, if you've got to go I suppose you've got to go. But don't be too long now, okay. Squeeze it out as quickly as you can, your Aunty Esther will have a fit if I'm late back.' Jacob had barely undone his flies when the floodgates opened.

'Ah sweet release!' He shouted at some passing sheep. Somewhere amongst the undergrowth he heard his brother laugh. The pee just kept on coming, Jacob had

198

no idea that his bladder was capable of holding so much! The image of Uncle Andrew sitting at the wheel of his car growing increasingly impatient kept popping into Jacob's head; he knew exactly what his Uncle was worried about - Aunty Esther was a stern woman, obsessively punctual and precise. His father had told him of a time when he and Andrew had been out at the St Patrick's Day races at Down Royal, a trip they had both planned and saved for throughout the year. Much of *the black stuff* had been imbibed that day and they had missed the train back home and had to catch a bus. This had the unfortunate result of making Andrew over two hours late and Aunty Esther had not been best pleased, to say the least. Poor Uncle Andrew found out just how angry he had made his wife when he woke up in hospital two days later with a fractured scull, the result of a heavy blow from Aunty Esther's cast iron skillet. For the sake of Uncle Andrew's noggin, Jacob tried to push a little harder.

As he struggled and strained, hidden amongst a sparse scattering of trees, Jacob looked out over the rolling Irish countryside. The green-brown scrubland meandered down to where it was intersected by the irregular, wandering line of a river, dividing it from a fall of grey scree that climbed up to the mountains on the other side. Jacob noticed someone down by the river standing by the water's edge, a man.

'What's that silly bugger up to?' He thought feeling inside his pocket with his free hand for his glasses. Opening out the legs using his mouth, Jacob then

pushed the glasses on. The lenses were scratched and cloudy from never being put to bed in a proper case, always stuffed in a pocket or left on the nearest available surface. Jacob squinted through the fog of inebriation and ruined glass to see the man, dressed in a brown three piece suit, white shirt black tie; he was just standing there in the middle of this sodden wilderness, staring down intently into the feral waters of the river. *'A suit? A shirt and tie? What the fuck is the old boy playing at? The man's a fucking idiot! Dressed like that down there... he'll get fucking maukit!'* Jacob pushed harder still attempting to squeeze out the remainder of his piss. 'Come on, come on... onward and outward!' He urged his bladder, picturing it as the inflatable girlfriend he used to date at Art School: slowly rolling her up after a brief explosion of teenage lust, expelling every last drop of air before slipping her inside the discreet nylon carry-bag and hiding her at the back of the wardrobe under his collection of Commando magazines. *'Ah, Li-Lola...'*

Jacob's attention was again captured by the river man. There was something familiar about him. 'Who the fuck are you queer fellow?' The last few dribbles were leaking from Jacob's wizened cock. He looked down to make sure he wasn't dribbling on his shoes, the end of his mammoth pissing session now in sight. Relaxed and very relieved he again focused on the river man, who had now moved a bit closer and was walking towards him. Jacob concentrated through his battered spectacles on the strangers face, and gradually it sharpened into focus.

'No… it's impossible…it can't be him?' But there was no mistake, Jacob was looking into the eyes of his dead father.

'Simon! Simon! Come over here, quick!' He shouted over his shoulder.

'Okay Jacob, don't panic, I'll be right there, don't move!' The sound of his brother's racing feet grew louder as he approached. Jacob looked again towards the river man; he was waving at him now, smiling. He could swear it was him, definitely his father. 'But how?' A warmth spread over Jacob's thigh as urine soaked through the leg of his trousers 'Oh for fuck sake!' He snapped, jumping back in a vain attempt to get away from his own penis. Shaking off the last dregs of piss, Jacob flopped his dick back into its lair and zipped it secure. Simon arrived on the scene out of breath, and panting like an asthmatic rapist.

'What's up bro? I thought the fucking yokels had got you, or you'd stood in a bear trap or something!'

'Over there!' Urged Jacob, gesturing towards the river. His brother immediately whipping round to take a look.

'Yes, very scenic, now what the fuck are you so wound up about?' Jacob frowned in incredulity.

'The man, over there by the river! Can't you see him?' Simon raised an eyebrow and had another look.

'What the hell are you on about Jake? There's fuck all down there but muck and sheep!' Jacob scanned the unforgiving panorama. There was nothing for miles but harsh, open country, no place to hide.

'But he was right there…I saw him? Unless he went into the river? We have to go and help him Simon!' Simon caught his brother by the shoulders to stop him from running. 'Just whoa there now big man! Let's just take a minute to think about this. Now listen, I was looking down towards that exact same spot just before my pissing was so rudely interrupted by my insane older brother who I thought was being fucking attacked by the way he was yelling. There was no-one there, trust me.' Jacob was still staring towards the river, looking for signs of life. Simon took him by the shoulders and pulled him round. 'Jacob, look at me; we have been, if fact scratch that, we *are* under a lot of stress at the moment. Come on Jake try and focus! Think about it…we've drunk more booze than George Best on a bender and taken enough drugs to kill a rhino. In short, we are both extremely fucked and liable to see and do strange and stupid things. Now take a look bro…' Simon turned his brother back towards the river, '…there's nobody down there, no-one has fallen in the fucking river and there is not a hope in hell that I am letting you go anywhere other than Uncle Andrew's house in this state.' Jacob broke his gaze and stared hard into his brother's eyes. He knew that what Simon was saying made absolute sense, but was also absolutely convinced that there had been a man down by the river; and that man had been his father. The image of him smiling and waving replayed with crystal clarity in Jacob's mind. Uncle Andrew's car horn car cut in through the trees.

'Come on Jake, we better hoof it, Andy-boy will be shitting his pants that auld Esther's waiting for him with the frying pan!' The boys turned and begun to make tracks. When he was sure that Simon had focused his full attention on the trail, Jacob twisted back and searched the empty landscape one last time before following his brother to the impatient car.

*

Waiting by the door as the car pulled into the driveway was Peter's older brother Mark, but there was no sign of Aunty Esther. Jacob saw Uncle Andrew's shoulders tighten and his small, dark eyes grow wide, darting around looking for danger signs. Mark approached the car and pulled open the rear-left door.

'Well hello there Scottish cousins! How about the both of you then?' He took Jacob by the hand as he clambered out, and shook it a little too vigorously, his firm grip knocking free the scab from Jacob's knuckle, yet again. Mark noticed the crimson smudge over the horse-shoe of his hand between thumb and forefinger. 'I didn't think I gripped you that hard Jake... you okay?' Jacob placed his thumb over the trickle of blood and pressed down hard.

'Yeah, sure Mark, it's nothing, just a scratch really. Must have caught it on the edge of a table in the studio or something... can't really remember how I did it to be honest.' Mark looked again at the red and swollen flesh around Jacob's wound.

'That looks to me as though it might be infected. Maybe should have a doctor take look at it?'

'No, really Mark, it's not that bad, it looks worse than it is.'

'Well at least let me clean it out and dress it properly for you' Mark was really beginning to annoy him now and Jacob decided to change the subject.

'So you're looking well; how's the family?' Mark looked back at him a little bemused.

'You haven't heard then?' Of course Jacob had *heard*, but this was a diversionary tactic. He acted dumb.

'I'm sorry Mark, heard what exactly?' During the course of their interaction Simon had hauled himself up and out at the other side of the car. He threw Mark a wave and his cousin reciprocated before turning his attention quickly back to Jacob.

'I honestly thought you would have heard by now Jacob, but Gayle and me split up, what... must be over six months ago now. She took the baby and the house... oh, and my car and I got to keep the mortgage.' Jacob pretended to be shocked.

'My god Mark, I had no idea. I'm really sorry to hear that mate, especially the bit about the mortgage!'

'Yeah, you and me both! I've been living back here ever since. Ach, I can't really complain, it's not that bad. Bit of a trek into the city for work and stuff, but apart from that it suits me fine. Gayle's even letting me see wee Siona at the weekend now.' Jacob continued with the pretence of ignorance.

'So tell me, what happened with you two then?' Mark hesitated to answer. 'You're right, it's none of my business, forget I said anything.' Mark shook his head.

'No, no, it's fine sure... really. It'd be better coming from me than from anyone else I suppose. Well you know how Gayle can be a little, how shall I put it...irrational? You must remember that much about her Jake, don't you?' Jacob nodded, although the description he would have used was *crazy psycho bitch*. Mark continued. 'The slightest little thing set her off, you know? So, we hadn't been getting on for a wee while, just arguing and stuff, and she takes to going out to the bingo of a Friday evening, leaving me at home with the baby. I mean, the wee one is great and everything, but I'm a grown man. Once she had gone down, normally around seven-thirty, I was left on my own with nothing to do. So I took up a hobby to entertain myself. Everything was going along smoothly for a while. In fact we were even beginning to treat each other like human beings again. Then one night Carol arrives back from the bingo two hours early, one of her friends had been ill or something, haven't been able to get the details from her as yet, and she walks in on me *entertaining myself* and goes right off on one. I thought she was going to have a bloody stroke or something...oh fuck, sorry Jake, I didn't mean to...'Jacob tried to suppress a smile.

'Please Mark… don't worry about it, no offence taken and all that shite. But tell me cousin, how exactly were you *entertaining yourself?*' Mark smiled ironically, rubbed the back of his neck.

'I suppose you could call it the ultimate home shopping experience. I was indulging in the many delights offered by a checkout girl from Tesco by the name of Claire! A delightful little creature, hair as dark as night and tits like ripe peaches. So that, as they say, was that.' He concluded with a wave of the hand. 'Come on now the both of you, will you not come away into the house, you look like you could use a drink. The old folks are dying to see you. Holy shit! I've done it again, many apologies once more for my unfortunate choice of phrase.'

And that was typical Mark - womaniser, unconscious comedian, always the life and soul of the party, the total opposite to his brother Peter, the quiet one. The quiet one who, at the age of seven, was caught tying kittens to his mother's washing line and shooting them with an air rifle. Who by the ripe old age of ten had managed to get himself thrown into a children's home for stabbing his best friend in the eye with a pencil; and who, by sixteen had graduated to the heady heights of a young offender's institution, charged this time with kidnap and torture.

Peter had broken into a farmhouse about two miles down the road with the intention of robbing its occupant, one Sandy Cole, an old farmer in his seventies, and a good friend of Peter's own father. Thinking he would be in bed, Peter had entered the house simply by breaking the glass in the kitchen door and undoing the latch.   Once inside he knew exactly where to go, he'd been in that house a thousand times before. He made straight for the living room where the old man kept a biscuit tin full of money hidden in a cupboard next to the fireplace. However, what Peter didn't know was that Mr Cole had gotten into the habit of downing a quarter-bottle of Whyte & MacKay in front of the evening television and crashing out on his sofa.   The old boy was shocked awake by Peter rummaging through the cupboard searching for the biscuit tin and jumped up in a vain attempt to defend his home and himself. But old Sandy was still half-drunk and Peter reacted cold and fast, catching the poor bugger with an upper cut square on the chin.   As his victim lay on the floor in an unconscious crumpled, bleeding heap, Peter improvised his plan, running out the back door and cutting down the washing line with a steak knife from the kitchen which he then used to tie helpless old Sandy to a chair.   The house was then well and truly ransacked, Peter seizing anything he thought was remotely of value.

He thought that he had hit the jackpot when he found two bank-cards and a credit card in a bedside cabinet.   For the next two and a half hours Peter employed various modes of torture - slashing with razor-blades, needles under finger-nails, burning with a cigarette, electric shocks to the genitals – to name but a few - in an attempt to get old Sandy to divulge the pin numbers.   Finally, just wanting the whole ordeal to be over, the old man cracked.   But Peter had only just started;

untying his victim and pulling him to his feet, *the quiet one* then proceeded to batter seven shades of shit out of the old man, just for the hell of it! When he got bored of that game, Peter lifted the keys to the elderly farmer's Landrover and made for the ferry in Belfast, stopping on the way to withdraw as much money as he could from the two bank accounts. He did not, however, get very much further.

Ironically, one of the Landrover's taillights was broken, and when the police tried to pull him over Peter, thinking that somehow the old farmer had managed to raise the alarm, tried to make a run for it. The police easily ran him off the road on the outskirts of the city, and he was apprehended and taken into custody. But it was not until the next day, when the police attempted to contact the owner of the stolen vehicle that the true horror of Peter's crime was fully discovered. He was subsequently tried and sentenced to just two years and six months in a young offender's institution for the perpetration of these horrific acts. The old farmer never recovered from the ordeal; he died in hospital six weeks later completely broken by the experience.

The Douglas brothers entered the house and were immediately greeted by the diminutive but substantial figure of Aunty Esther.

'Hello there boys, and aren't you two looking so handsome and distinguished these days. Come on now and give your old Aunty a hug.' They dared each other to go first; Jacob quickly capitulating, feeling it his duty as the senior representative, he leaned forward and embraced his Aunt.

'It's good to see you again Aunt Esther.' Said Jacob stepping back and nudging his reluctant brother forward as he did so.

'Yes, really good to see you too Aunt Esther.' Added Simon, embracing his Aunt with all the tenderness of a hedgehog.

'Peter, take the boys' bags up to their room please, there's a good boy.' Aunt Esther shouted over to their psychotic cousin, before turning her attention quickly back to the brothers. 'Now I'll bet you two young fellows could do with a drink.' Both of the *young fellows* shrugged, smiled then nodded their heads in freaky unison. 'Well will you come away through to the kitchen then, there are a few people here already.'

The Douglas brothers trailed their Aunt through the narrow dark hallway and on into the kitchen. There were already around five or six other mourners in there, amongst them the familiar faces of Uncle Matthew's widow Auntie Anne and her children, cousins Thomas, Philip and Jessie - together with their respective spouses -Rachel, Isobel and Kevin. Uncle Matthew had been killed in a motor cycle accident aged only forty-seven, and it had then been a mad dash among his progeny to pop out a male child upon who would be conferred the filial crown of Matthew. Thomas and Rachel were first to bloom, but an abject lack of male genitalia resulted in the rather unfortunate Matilda. Next up to the plate were Philip and Isobel; but they could only manage an Emma. It was left to little Jessie - an impish, porcelain blonde-thing of barely sixteen years. Unmarried and suspended from school for non-attendance, she consummated her three week relationship with spotty Kevin - unemployed, but with a keen interest in automobiles and herbal medicines. Nine months on Matthew (junior) arrived on the scene, a boy at last for *proud* grandmother Annie.

As the Douglas boys nodded their hellos, a member of the clergy sprung forward and, with a practiced, silent and concerned purse of the lips and nod of the head handed them each a can of Guinness and a couple of whiskeys. He reminded Jacob of the barman from the train station. Aunt Esther standing between the brothers took them by the elbows to focus their attention on her,
'I'm sure you two boys want to be left to pay your respects, so I'll just away now and check the oven, don't want to burn the sausage rolls now do I!' And off she waddled, disappearing through a doorway at the other side of the room. The boys looked at each other a bit puzzled, but resolved to neck their whiskeys and crack open the cans of Guinness. Jacob took a big gulp; it was bitter and room

temperature, but it went down well.

'What do you think she meant by paying our respects Si? Do you reckon that we have to tip the priest or something?' Simon was looking the other way; he said nothing. Jacob tried again. 'Simon…did you hear me?'

'Holy shit Jacob, take a look at this!' Urged Simon, taking hold of his brother's shoulder and spinning him round. There laid out on the kitchen table in his best suit, grinning like only he knew the punch-line to the joke, was their dead father. Jacob's jaw bounced off the linoleum.

'Fuck me! I'd forgotten they still did all this kind of jiggery-pokery over here!'

'Did they not have Granny Sarah laid out for her funeral?' Simon asked, looking a tad perplexed.

'Oh no, of course… don't you remember how the old bird went in the end?' Simon frowned, slightly confused.

'It was a heart attack wasn't it?'

'Well, yes… that's what they reckon killed her in the first place, but when she keeled over out of her armchair, she fell face-first onto her old two bar electric fire. There wasn't really a lot left of the upper part of her body by the time she was found. Aunty Esther knew right away it was her though, she recognised the slippers she'd bought her for Christmas.'

The brothers Douglas approached the corpse of their deceased father nervously.

'He's a bit waxy looking isn't he? Wonder what he feels like?' Whispered Simon, a strange hybrid of apprehension and revulsion tinting his voice.

'Touch him and find out.' Dared Jacob. Simon appeared uneasy about the idea.

'Eh…don't know if I can bro… this is all a bit weird.' Jacob egged his brother on, 'Go on Si… he won't bite you.' Simon extended his hand towards dead dad, but it froze in mid-air.

'I can't do it Jacob. I'm totally shiteing myself.'

'Okay Si, we'll do it together.' Jacob extended his left hand bringing it up parallel to his brother's. 'Okay, now you take the right cheek and I'll take the left. Ready?' Jacob said looking intently at Simon. Simon signalled his readiness by a raising of his eyebrows and a tightening of his lips. Their hands hovered over dead dad's face waiting for the signal. Jacob nodded his head. 'Go!' Mr Douglas senior felt unusually cold to the touch, like a side of chilled beef. Simon immediately withdrew his hand as if in receipt of and electric shock.

'Jeez! That's the freakiest thing. He doesn't feel… real Jake.' Jacob's hand had remained on his father's left cheek for a moment longer, before slowly retreating.

'No Simon, he doesn't seem real at all does he? But I suppose this is as real as it gets Si.' Jacob's gaze was transfixed. 'Is it really dad though? It's just…well he's so cold.' Simon looked hard at the corpse.

'I suppose? Check out that smile; the old boy looks like he's about to get up at any moment and start laughing at us all for being so bloody stupid!'

'Yeah Si, this could all just be one enormous hoax. Maybe you should bend down and check that he's not breathing!' Jacob knew that his brother would go with the joke. As Simon leant his ear down towards dead-dad's breathless mouth, Jacob surreptitiously slid his hand under Mr Douglas Senior's dead hand and lifted it onto the back of his younger brother's head, moaning, 'Aaaaaaaaaaaaaaaaahhhhhhhhhh!'

'Holy fuck!' Shouted Simon, jumping back almost pulling dead-dad from the kitchen table. You absolute wanker Jake!' But big brother paid no attention, and was laughing so hysterically he was almost unable to breathe.

When Jacob had at last managed to regain control, sniffed up the snot and wiped the tears from his eyes, a room filled with rather concerned looking faces washed into focus. All eyes were fixed staring over at him and his father's dangling, dead arm. Jacob composed himself as best he could.

'Well I'm sure that *he* would have appreciated the joke.' No-one said a word. Sensing that all was not well, Jacob stepped forward and returned his father's arm to its' former position, then turned to face Simon who was still looking extremely pissed off. 'I think I'll go upstairs to have a bit of a lie down...suddenly feeling very tired. See you later Si.'

Jacob made his way unsteadily to a door which lead to the stairs. He paused as he took hold of the handle and looked over his left shoulder at Simon, mouthing the word 'sorry'.   Simon frowned, shook his head and mouthed the word

'CUNT!'

Dear Alison,

It seems like forever since I last saw you, where did you go? Did you run off on holiday and forget to tell me? Have you fallen on your head and forgotten who I am? I've racked my brain for an explanation of your vanishing, but so far I have come up with exactly... nothing! Did I do something wrong? What did I do? Please tell me and I'll fix it if I can. Please, please contact me, whatever it is I know we can work it out. I'm in Ireland right now for my dad's funeral and I am absolutely dreading it. I wish you were here to hold me up, I really need you, please come back to me. There is no need to worry about anything, whatever is done is done as far as I am concerned. I can forgive you anything, never even speak of it again, just come back?

I love you

Jacob

Jacob found himself at the bottom of a dark oak staircase. He began to climb. The stairs seemed to get longer and steeper the more he ascended. Exhausted and frustrated, he was about to give up when the top came into view - a landing dim and long. Doors lined the walls evaporating into points of equal darkness on either side. Jacob sat down on the uppermost stair unsure which way to go or what door to try. A heavy oak panelled door third on the right, began to slowly creak open, leaking dim yellow light into the hallway. He hesitated for a moment, uncertain and afraid; but, little by little, begun to creep warily forward on hands and knees towards the light. Inside, the room looked familiar - a log fire was crackling and dancing on an old brick hearth, two male figures silhouetted in its warm glow. One of the men leant by an elbow on the mantelpiece, the other sat hunched upon a battered armchair. From behind the door to the right, Jacob's father poked his head round.

'Hello there J.J. my boy, come away in and warm your-self by the fire. Uncle Mattie has got it blazing away fine there.' Encouraged, but still reticent, Jacob crawled further into the room. On closer inspection he recognised the other two men as his Grandfather Joseph and his Uncle Matthew. In the company of ancestors Jacob felt small, almost childlike.

'I've really missed you dad... Simon has too.' He said, climbing to his feet. His father lit a cigarette using a taper from the fire, and inhaled deeply.

'Well as you can plainly see, I'm doing just fine here son. We all are.' He replied, gesturing to the other two men with a sweep of his hand and billowing smoke from his lungs into the room as he did so. 'You've just missed your ma and grandma son, they're off out gallivanting, probably at that bloody bingo again! But are you not going to say hello to your granda and uncle J.J.?' He continued. Jacob shrugged apologetically and moved towards the fireside.

'Hello Gramps, hello Uncle Mattie, how you both doing?' Both men smiled warmly and answered in a single voice,

'I'm fine Jacob my lad, and how are you?' Jacob took a step closer, feeling the warmth of the fire on his face and hands.

'Can't complain, you know. I really miss you all though.'

'We miss you too, but we will always be here if you need us Jacob, just look in the shadows and dark places.' Jacob turned his attentions to his father again.

'It's been really hard without you dad.' His father took a drag of his cigarette and stared far into the fire beyond the ballet of flames, but said nothing. Jacob spoke again. 'Why did you have to leave me dad?' Mr Douglas Senior flicked the dying butt of his cigarette into the grate, a look of resignation washing over his face.

'It was just my time to go son, simple as that, nothing personal.'

The light in the room started to dim, slowly at first like a cloud passing in front of the sun.

'What's happening dad? Hadn't you better put a light on or something?' But then, as quick as a blink, the remaining light was sucked out of the room, his father's face fading into the gloom until all Jacob could see was the fire reflected in his eyes. He spoke to Jacob one last time.

'Whatever happens Jacob just remember that I always wanted the best for you…I love you son…' And with that last remark echoing in the infinite dark, Jacob felt himself dragged away into an ink-black void of nothingness and again he was falling…

*

Eyes opened to stare at the cracks on the swirling Artexed ceiling, spreading out in yellowing tributaries. A painful emptiness filled in the hollow gouged in Jacob's love and his head ached to the rhythm of a thousand stabbing knives. The curtains were already open and the tired sun was trying hard to push through a grey-white blanket of cloud. Somewhere in the murk birds cleared their throats. In the burgeoning chorus Jacob could distinguish the flute-like toot punctuated by an almost referee-like whistle at the end, of an early blackbird, and the unmistakable twiddle-oo, twiddle-eedee of a Robin. During long boyhood summers spent holidaying in Ireland, his father had taught him the calls of all the native birds.

Fragments of the dream flashed back in Jacob's head; he closed his eyes tight and tried hard to fall back to it, but his head became fuzzed with images of Alison.

Purring like a contented kitten not four feet to his left, was Simon. Afraid to be alone at such a raw time of day, Jacob thought of waking his brother; but the peacefull look on his face, serene almost, caused a reconsideration. He had always slept like that, childlike, still, happy. Jacob had always bore an absurd resentment towards his broher because of this, which was making it all the more difficult to resist the urge to shake Simon violently awake! Instead Jacob turned his back on temptation, closed his eyes tight and tried to imagine what his life would be like if *she* had never left him. *'If she called right now and wanted me to come home, I would just drop everything and go.'* Jacob thought about the soft touch of Alison's hands on his body, his caresseing her, a touch only they knew. He felt himself grow hard.

'You awake bro?' Simon broke in, quickly dragging Jacob back to cold reality. He hesitated trying hard to find her again, but she was gone.

'Nearly…you okay?' Jacob's eyes were open, but he still had his back to Simon who he could hear rumaging around on the floor. The unmistakable jingle of spare change in a pocket and the dull thump of a belt buckle falling on the carpeted bedroom floor confirmed to Jacob that Simon had found his jeans. More muffled fumbling ensewed, Jacob still resisting the urge to look round. The jeans carumped to the floor one last time and Jacob concluded that Simon must have found what he was looking for.

He could not remember hearing his brother light the joint up, perhaps he had dozed off fleetingly? But as the sweet aroma met Jacob's nostrils he whipped round to face Simon, eyes as wide as they were ever likley to get.

'Thought that might get your attention!' Said Simon, leaning back against the headboard, joint held carefully above an empty Guinness can. He took a deep, long drag before holding the joint and Guinness-can-ashtray out towards Jacob. 'Here you go Jake, get that into you. It'll put hair on you teeth.' The warm smoke caused Jacob's lungs to go into fibrillation and he began to cough uncontrolably. 'Fuck sake Bro, you want me to call an ambulance?' Jacob attempted to answer, but could not force out any words. Still barking like an asthmatic bulldog, he passed the joint back to Simon. 'Here bro, take a drink, clear your tubes out.' Said Simon, handing hisbrother a blue china cup. Jacob assumed that it was filled with water and took a huge, quenching gulp. The liquid blazed down his already scorched throat and chest like burning gasoline. 'Careful bro, that's raw alcohol!' But the advice was delivered, rather conveniently, thought Jacob, just a second too late. He felt the blood rush likeraw gurgling lava through his body, attempting to exit via his face.

Jacob was about to jump from his bed and beat Simon around the neck and head with the empty tea cup when intoxication intervened, descending upon him in a calming golden glow. His coughing fit subsided and the pounding headache disolved.

'Wonderful…I feel absolutely fucking wonderful Si! What the hell is that stuff? He equired, gesturing lazily towards the blue cup, which only moments ago had been a potential murder weapon.

'Pochine, straight from psycho Peter's still…moonshine, firewater, *the rare old mountain dew*! Come on now Jake, we had better start getting ourselves ready. You know what this lot are like, they've probably been up since the bloody crack of dawn!' Jacob rocked up into a sitting position, his head seeming to take a couple of seconds longer catching up with the rest of his body. Simon handed the last of the joint to Jacob, who eyed it with disgust, but accepted the offer anyway.

'This is all I'm bloody well needing Si!'

'Suck it up J.J., something tells me we'll need all the help we can get. I've got a feeling that today isn't going to be easy.' A shiver ran down Jacob's spine hearing the name *J.J.,* the name his father used to call him by. He was lost for a moment, but found himself again painfully, the joint burning his lips as he attempted to take a drag.

'Oh ya fucker!' Spat Jacob, and posted the butt into the empty Guinness can.

'Thanks for that, ya prick.' Simon turned round laughing.

'Don't mention it bro, it was starting to get a bit hot on my fingers too. Is this what you're wearing today then?' He was fingering the lapel of Jacob's black suit and tie suspended by a coat-hanger hooked over the wardrobe door.

'Yep; I was thinking of wearing the gold lamae, but decided against it at the last minute.'

'Aye, very funny Jake… and where's your shirt?' Continued Simon, lifting open the jacket. As Jacob looked up at his empty suit, he remembered the white shirt bought specially for today and smelling Alison on it. He had been unable to bring himself to pack it. But it now dawned that he had also neglected to pack a replacement.

'Oh for fuck sake! The bloody thing must still be lying on my bed back in Glasgow!' He lied.

'Don't stress bro, I'll nip downstairs and see if you can borrow one of cousin Mark's, you're both roughly the same size.' Said Simon, scrutinizing his brother's physique before exiting the bedroom at high speed. Jacob's attention fixed on the empty suit and on the absence of his shirt. He thought of it lying on his bed back in Glasgow, vacant and alone.

*

Jacob stayed in the bathroom as long as he could, listening to the muffled voices of his relatives through the floor and walls as they readied themselves for the long day ahead.

'Jacob, it's time to go son.' Uncle Andrew shouted up the stairs to him.

'Okay, be there in a minute.' Jacob shouted in reply through the closed bathroom door then rose to confirm his reflection in the mirror one last time. *'Well here we go then J.J.'*

Downstairs people were saying their final goodbyes to Mr Douglas senior before the coffin lid would be screwed down by the undertakers the last time. The scene Jacob drifted down into seemed unreal, almost like he was watching it all on a giant cinema screen. Simon moved in from rear-left and caught his brother by the elbow.

'Come on Jacob, we had better go and say goodbye.' He whispered and led Jacob reluctantly towards the coffin. 'And no more of your stupid jokes Jake, not today.' Added Simon firmly as they approached the edge of the table.

Looking down intently at the corpse formerly known as *dad* for the second time in as many days, Jacob felt his heart quicken. Somehow his father looked *different* from the previous night; a more relaxed and less mischievous expression. Simon was busy whispering something in his ear, but Jacob felt at such a distance during that particular moment that he was unable to make it out. In an effort to focus on his brother's words, Jacob turned his head to face him; but Simon's eyes were fixed on the departed. Jacob witnessed the birth of a single tear and traced its brief descent from his brother's eye, down onto their father's dead face. Simon covered his eyes with a hand, clearly very upset, then hurried away towards the back door.

Suddenly all the eyes of the room were again concentrated on Jacob. Unable to think of anything fitting and poignant to say or do, Jacob panicked and gave in too instinct. Moving reflexively he bent down and kissed his father's cold forehead.

The grey imprint of Jacob's kiss remained just above dead-dad's left eyebrow, some of the embalmers' heavy make-up having come away with Jacob's lips. He ran his tongue quickly around the outside of his mouth trying frantically to lick the makeup off before any of the mourners noticed. It tasted oily and bitter and he started to gag, bile rising through his stomach and saliva beginning to gather and pool in his mouth. Jacob was going to be sick.

'Oh no...not on dad's corpse!' Thought Jacob, ramming a hand against his quivering mouth and racing off in the direction of the back garden. Outside was busy with smoking mourners, Jacob's eyes were watering, his sight blurring; an eruption was most definitely imminent. Spotting a small garden shed through his tears, Jacob made a desperate break for it. The puke had already invaded his mouth and was beginning to seep through the gaps between his fingers. At the back side of the shed Jacob vomited the meagre contents of his guts into a vacant terracotta flower pot.

'The funeral procession is about to depart from the front of the house, can family members make their way to the cars please!' Announced one of the funeral directors from the kitchen door. Jacob sniffed and wiped his mouth on the sleeve of his jacket. He noticed that it left a strange flesh coloured stain which puzzled him for a moment before he recognised it as the make-up he had only minutes before kissed from his father's lifeless grey head. Jacob felt his stomach begin to somersault all over again.

*

The sky was low and gun-metal-grey over the ragged, broken landscape. Jacob watched the tidy curtains of the village houses wink as the funeral cortege passed by. A group of three old men waiting at a bus stop removed their caps, looks of genuine sympathy and understanding invading their eyes.

'These are the people who know death better than most.' Mothers hurried little feet in through the primary school gates towards the north end of the village, shielding inquisitive, innocent eyes with their bodies and glancing apprehensively, warily, over their shoulders to make sure that dark shadows were not following them.

Heading out of the village, the procession road started to climb the hill towards the church. The sky bruised purple-black over the ruined monastery as they trundled wearily past; it appeared much smaller than Jacob remembered. From this vantage point he could see the snaking outline of the river, entwining the hill's foot, where dad had taken *his boys* fishing during many childhood summers. It was a small, fast river, brown with peat. Simon had once claimed to have seen a salmon leaping upstream, but Jacob had never been so lucky.

Finally, the road levelled off as they approached the church. A raw cutting headwind had picked up and the rain was getting heavier. Already some black figures had gathered by the main entrance, huddled together, sheltering under the sombre grey stone arch of the doorway. The procession crunched ever slowing along the gravel drive, entering a pocket of liquid silence as the engines were turned off. For the briefest moment Jacob felt outside of time, calm; there was no howling wind, no droning motors, no tap-tapping of rain, no sniffing relatives; only the steady rhythmic whisper of his own breathing. *'Slowly in... slowly out... '*

But this serenity was quickly and brutally fractured as the door swung open and a man in black ushered him out into cold reality. Jacob felt paralysed.

'You coming then Jake?' asked Simon from somewhere far off on the right hand side. Jacob concentrated, trying desperately to make his body respond, but no sound came from his lips and he remained motionless. All around mourners poured blackly onto the sober gravel, shuffling hunched against the weather towards the church. As Jacob watched the undertakers open the back of the hearse, bow to the coffin and slide it out, the controlled stern voice of Auntie Esther close beside took him by surprise.

'Come away Jacob, it's time to do your duty now.' His automatic pilot kicked in responding to the cue and he stepped from the car. Simon had already walked round to meet him.

'How you doing bro?' Jacob responded with an iron smile.

'Oh, tickety-fucking-boo Si!' Simon curled a reassuring arm round his brother's shoulder and they turned to watch as their father was carried shoulder high into the church. The boys hesitated, looked intensely into solemn reflected eyes, breathed deeply. Earnest faces rose into acquiescence and the brothers Douglas followed on. No words were spoken.

Yet another undertaker led Jacob and Simon to the front-left of the church, 'Could the elder brother be seated towards the aisle please?' Jacob shot him a questioning look as he took his seat and the man in black crooked his long frame down and spoke softy. 'It makes it easier to get to the lectern for the eulogy sir.' Sharp electric panic detonated in Jacob's brain, the inner shock and turmoil manifesting in totally unconscious outward expression. Noticing Jacob's increasingly worried look, the undertaker leaned in again, 'Don't worry sir, the minister will introduce you.' Jacob looked to his brother for support, for an answer, for...something! But Simon just showed him two empty palms and shrugged. *'What the fuck am I going to say?'* Thought Jacob, frantically racking the far corners of his brain, desperately trying to dust off some old memories of his *dear departed* father. Sweat begun to bead on is forehead, his stomach cramped and he thought he might be sick again. The perspiration nipped at Jacob's eyes causing him to blink uncontrollably. He wiped his face with a jacket sleeve and swallowed dry and hard.

Far off behind, the church door banged shut. The echoes still reverberated in the damp and musty air as the minister, hunched and grey, entered through a door to the front-right of the church and, seemingly unaware of the congregation, limped slowly up the three steps into his pulpit. Without looking up he raised both arms into the air, one hand open with fingers spread, the other clutching firmly an austerely black, leather-bound bible, its' gold edged pages flashing as he spoke.

'Brothers and sisters, please join with me in offering up a prayer for our dearly departed brother.' Jacob's head bowed automatically, but his eyes remained open, staring down past the flaking oak pews to his shoes. His feet felt damp inside - he had never gotten round to buying a new pair. They reminded him of meeting Alison in the café, a day that now seemed so long ago. 'Dear Lord, our heavenly father. We humbly commend our brother to your eternal care, and ask that you help us find the fortitude to see us through this sorrowful day. Amen'

The minister surveyed the congregation with a practised, mournful expression. 'And Jesus spoke unto the people of Bethany, 'Lazarus is dead.' There had been no happier home anywhere else in this small village. The family loved each other and they had a love for Jesus. There was no where on earth where Jesus felt more at home than when he was with Lazarus, Mary and Martha...' The coffin constructed of polished walnut, its brass handles gleaming, appeared somehow more sharply focused, solid and real than everything else in Jacob's line of vision.

'What would you have said dad... I just don't have the words.'

'...They had all a family could possibly need; a comfortable home, ample amounts of food and many, many good and kind friends. But now Lazarus, the head of their household, the family's' protector and provider could no longer share their laughter and their tears. The once happy home, a home that had always been a place where people would go to sing and dance was now filled with darkness and despair...'

'Come on now, enough! Just try to relax... breath, slowly in; slowly out. Slowly in; slowly out...'

'...From the very first day of his illness, Lazarus's two sisters had nursed him with tender care. Many times these sisters had anxiously confided to one another, 'If only Jesus would come.' The Holy Bible tells us that Jesus loved Lazarus and his two sisters, but when he heard that Lazarus was sick, he remained where he was two more days. In the meantime Lazarus grew ever sicker, and eventually, he died. Why we ask ourselves was Lazarus allowed to suffer so? Why did Jesus allow his friend Lazarus to die?

'Sometimes we need a little help, its okay, that's not a weakness. Just let go and the words will come.'

'...Love does not always do what we expect. Jesus stayed away until Lazarus had been prepared for burial and put it into his tomb before he gathered with his disciples in an upper room in Jerusalem where they witnessed the resurrection of Lazarus. Jesus had stayed away for so long *because* he loved Lazarus and his sisters so much. This may seem extremely odd to us, perhaps even the opposite of what we would expect. But God, in all his infinite wisdom sometimes delays or refuses to act as we would like him to. For God, death is not the end, it is simply a transition. There is a power greater than death, and that power is in Jesus Christ. More precious than preserving life, are events which bring others to believe in Jesus Christ. Christ loves us and he comes to us through tragedy and grief. To believe in Jesus Christ is to triumph over death. Let us pray...'

'Alison, I need you, please come back to me!'

'...Jesus is the resurrection and the life. He calls us to die with him, that we might live and inherit the treasures of heaven. Trust ye in Jesus for he comes to be with us in our pain, he weeps with us and gives himself for us to the glory of the Father, the Son, and the Holy Ghost. Amen.' Jacob's eyes broke from the sadness of his shoes. He tried hard not to look at the coffin, but its' stark magnetism proved too great. The minister quenched his rasping throat with a sip of water before continuing.

'Brothers and sisters, our faithful and beloved friend Adam Alexander Douglas has entered into the eternal rest and salvation that awaits all of Gods' children. We have lost a dear, dear friend and an honoured brother, and I am sure you would not be satisfied, any more than myself, if I did not attempt to give some expression to our grief for the loss we have sustained...'

'Come on now, enough of this nonsense; this is neither the time nor the place. Just get her right out of your head boy, try to focus… you need to focus.'

'…We bless God almighty for the mercy shown in delivering His servant out of the miseries of this sinful world; taking our brother Adam in the fullness of his age, so gently unto Himself to the haven where he would be. I could say much more than I propose to do about our friend, but I am restrained, not only by my own feelings, and the sense of what is fitting, but also by the knowledge of how distasteful anything that seemed to savour of parade or praise, or glorification from this place would have been to Adam. But there was just one prominent trait in his character that I must for a few moments refer to; his unselfish heart. Rich and poor alike knew that they could always depend upon Adam, that they were always sure of his understanding and of his willingness to help if he could. Brothers and sisters, we have lost a dear and respected friend. His big heart has ceased to beat, his voice has been hushed by the solemn stillness of death, but his legacy and his memory remains and will endure. He leaves behind two devoted sons, Jacob and Simon. Jacob would like to say a few words in tribute to his father.'

'This is it then… no turning back now. Time to be a man J.J.!' Jacob looked up to see the minister, arms outstretched, beckoning him forward. He had to concentrate hard to convince his legs to carry him shakily up to the pulpit. A

231

deathly hush fell over the congregation as all eyes fixed on Jacob. He held onto the lectern, steadied himself.

'What the fuck am I supposed to do now?' He thought, eyes darting round nervously scanning the assembled serious faces. *'Just relax J.J. Let go and the words will come.* Jacob closed his eyes took a deep breath then began.

'Well, eh… I'd just like to kick off by saying thank you to everyone for coming out today in such miserable weather. Eh… *Breathe, J.J., breathe…'* He cleared his throat and continued. 'The man who has had the most influence on my life and the most influence on the man that I have become, passed away on September the fifteenth. Adam Alexander Dougas was only sixty-three years old They say that the loss of a parent is one of the most devastating events in your life. As many of you will know my mother passed away just over a year and a half ago. It was a very traumatic time for us all. I don't think dad ever got over it. And now he's gone, well…I guess that me and my brother Simon are orphans! People keep telling me that, in time, the pain will fade. Well all Ican say is, I hope they're right. But I do get great comfort from the thought that mum and dad are together again and this time they can never be parted. Dad and me had a really simple, loving relationship. He was a good man, a loving father and a loyal husband. He worked hard all his life, built his company from nothing. The thing I remember most about my father is his hands; rough as grade ten sandpaper from all the hours he spent grafting in his factories.

Dad used to take my brother and me for long country walks on Sunday afternoons, up by Loch Lomond. We fished together out of his old rowing-boat on the loch. I think that we tried just about everything, worms, maggots, fish eggs, lures, flies…even tried bread and bacon one time! We never seemed to catch anything, but it didn't matter. He took us up to Maryhill to watch Partick Thistle every second Saturday of the season without fail. I could never work out if that was a treat or a punishment though! We used to spend the summer holidays touring the north of Scotland or the wild Irish countryside in the battered old family caravan.

I remember these things as if we had done them all last week. His big hands, like sandpaper, outstretched leadng me everywhere, and because he did, we will always travel together. I love you dad and I miss you.' Jacob tried in vain to choke back the sudden and immense surge of grief, but it engulfed him.

As he staggered back to his seat through the tears he saw one solitary dark figure standing in front of the doors at the back of the church. 'Dad?' Croaked Jacob as Simon stood to embrace him.

'Yes I know Jake, it really brought it home to me too. That was…well, beautiful bro.' As the noise of the church organ echoed and filled the cold air, Jacob turned his head and looked toward the back of the church, but the figure was gone. The minister now back in position at the alter announced a hymn:

'Page one-hundred and seven, Abide With Me.' Whilst aware of everyone standing up around him, this time Jacob was unable to make his body obey. He tried to follow the hymn, but his tears fell onto the pages, blistering the fine paper and causing the words of the song to smudge and run. Head bowed low to avoid eye contact, Jacob noticed his shoes again. Simon looked down and placed a consoling hand on his brother's shoulders which had begun to shudder with uncontrollable emotion.

*

The remainder of the funeral appeared to Jacob as a series of broken events: the coffin being carried to the graveside; the weight of his father suspended from one of six cords as he was lowered into the ground; a prayer; dirt thrown on the coffin lid; another hymn… It all seemed disjointed and fragmented, the only constant being the inscesant driving rain.

*

Back outside the church, cars had gathered, black and shining, in readyness to ferry the assorted mourners back to the family home for a cold buffet lunch and *light refreshments*. Following on three steps behind his brother, automatic pilot fully engaged, trudged Jacob. They were heading towards the lead car, but something stopped brother Douglas senior a few feet short.

'Simon, I think I'm going to walk back to the house, clear my head a bit.' Simon straightened up and re-exited the car door which has just been opened for him; his brows furrowed.

'But it's pissing down Jake, you'll get soaked!' Jacob turned his face upward and regarded the angry heavens.

'Ach away and stop fussing like an old woman. I'll be fine... the rain's easing off a bit now anyway.' He lied; Simon looked exasperated.

'I'll come along with you then.' He said, taking a step towards his brother, but Jacob came forward to meet him half way. He took hold of Simon's shoulders and looked him in straight in the eyes.

'Listen to me Simon, I'm fine... really. I just need some time on my own, some quiet time to try and get my head straight before I face the rest of the tribe. I'll see you back at the house.' Simon took Jacob's hand from his right shoulder in both of his and kissed it.

'Okay bro, have it you're way. But understand that I'm not happy. I don't think you should be on your own, not today, but I suppose I can't stop you, can I?' He looked at his watch. 'I'll give you an hour, if you're not back at the house by then I'll be coming to look for you...and the first place I'll be looking is the pub Jake!' And with that, the brothers Douglas shared a hug, mirrored a cheerless smile and went their separate ways. A few steps along the road the soft whirring of an electric window behind Jacob preceded Simon's urgent voice beside him.

'Seriously though Jake, keep your mobile swiched on, and call if you need me, none of this texting shite, okay?' Jacob turned fully around to acknowledge his brother's proclaimation.

'Right you are Si. Save me an eggy sandwich! I'll see you soon, okay.' That now all too familiar lump blocked Jacob's throat again in response to his brother's expression of genuine concern. He gave Simon a wave and turned his face quickly downward to avoid eye contact, hoping that the drizzle had disguised his tears.

Walking downhill away from the church, the road snaked round in a bend at the bottom and over a small, ancient stone bridge. Jacob remembered his father talking about this bridge, how a local farmer had lost control of his trailer after taking the corner too tightly and knocked half the left-hand side wall into the river. One of the builders employed to repair the damage had found an earthernware jar concealed amongst the mortar and stones during the bridge's construction. It contained a yellowed piece of paper upon which was written the names of the two men who had originally built the bridge and the date it was completed. The names of the bridge builders had long since faded from Jacob's memory, but the date, 1557, had somehow stuck. He recalled how surprised he had been hearing that a couple of Irish labourers had actually been able to read and write in 1557. His father had laughed at this assertion. 'Perhaps it was just another one your yarns dad?' As he crossed the bridge, Jacob paused at the centre and tried hard to remember the builders names, hoping the very fabric of their labours would provide him with inspiration. But nothing came. Looking over the low wall, he was captivated by the raw energy of the river, its eddys and whirlpools gushing and swooshing below before racing off up towards the moors and dark blue hills. He watched the brown water rush angrily past under his feet, off into the coutryside, the river a violent hurry of power and motion. The sheer intensty made Jacob feel dizzy and he had to kneel down on one knee to steady himself. Enraged grey and black clouds kissed the hill-tops, threatening to descend so low that Jacob would have to find his way home from amongst them. He glanced up the hill towards the church and considered heading back there to try and beg a lift from one of the stragglers; but something on the periphery of vision caught his attention. About a quarter mile downriver stood a man dressed in a brown suit.

Using a hand to shield his eyes from the rain, Jacob tried hard to distinguish through the mist the solitary, mysterious figure. A dark sillouette perched precariously on top of a wet-black rock overhanging the vicious flood. Jacob had already begun to walk forward to the edge of the bridge, straining to focus on the shadow man's face. 'No?' Jacob shook his head. 'It can't be... it's not possible!' He wiped the rain from his eyes and stared back hard again. His dead father smiled and waved casually back at him. Racing round the side of the bridge, Jacob then stumbled painfully down the embankment direction riverside, determined not to let his father get away this time. Speed escalating the further he descended; momentum carrying him forward at increasing pace; the fierce waters rushing towards him; Jacob was unable now to resist the magnetic embrace of gravity.

The river was almost upon him, a despairing hand shot out involuntarily managing to grasp the inquiring arm of a passing hawthorn tree. Jacob screamed, primal, reflexive, as it's thorns penetrated the soft flesh of his palm. But hung on through the pain ever tighter fearing the alternative and came to a skidding halt in the mud banking, a single foot slipping over the edge to dangle for a moment in space before being pulled quickly back to onto terra-firma. Leaning his full weight back against the mud and the moss, breathing heavily, heart pounding, head pulsating; Jacob dug in one heel after another and begun to push himself slowly up the banking. The steep angle gradually levelled off onto a tiny footpath, but it was just enough to enable him to regain his balance and stand upright. Jacob hadn't noticed the hawthorn branch still tightly gripped in his right hand. He winced as the slender bough was set free, whipping away and tearing back its bloodied thorns. The path was about ten feet up from the river; Jacob traced the deep parallel troughs left by his retreating shoes to a point approximately three quarters of the way down. He had only scrambled up around seven feet or so but it felt as though he had just scaled Everest. Further inspection revealed that there was nothing between the spot where Jacob had come so violently to rest and the cruel unforgiving waters but approximately five feet of Irish air.

'Another narrow escape Mr Douglas…' He stopped his mind imagining what nearly was and re-focused on what had brought him here in the first place. A thick overhang of trees obscured the view down the river, so Jacob climbed up the banking a little and stretched and strained his neck to get a better look. He jumped up on one leg and caught a fleeting glimpse of the spot, but his father was long gone. 'Where did you go?'

'You all right son?' Enquired a familiar voice from somewhere above and behind. 'What the fuck?' Startled, Jacob spun round too quickly, losing his footing and stumbling, slipping backward.

'Jacob!' Echoed above him as he fell. A dark figure on the banking reaching out a despairing hand, receding, as the overpowering icy-brown rush and thunder of the river took him under.

*

Shadow people moved around Jacob's frozen form.

'It is time…it is time…is he? Yes…it is time. Cover his body with the funeral shroud. Entomb him within this sacred stone.' Jacob tried desperately to move, but could not even twitch a finger. In his mind he was screaming, but his mouth made no sound. Darkness fell upon him like a crushing rock. His chest laboured to rise and allow him to breathe.

'Is this death? Am I dying?' The noise of Jacob's voice resonated inside his head like a million cathedral bells. *'Is this the end?'*

And with that thought, Jacob relaxed. The pressure on his chest lightened, his breathing eased and deepened, until he was no longer aware of the process. Rising up, his body dissolving into silver vapour, merging with the atmosphere leaving only tranquil consciousness. He no longer felt afraid. *'Peace at last...peace...'*

*

Light stabbed like a shard of white-hot glass through Jacob's eyes into his brain. 'You awake Jake?' He attempted to blink away the pain as the outline of his brother slowly materialised through the sunlight. Pushing down on his elbows, Jacob made to sit up, but collapsed back onto the bed, his muscles failing him. 'Whoa right there cowboy!' Urged Simon jumping forward, pushing the air between them with both hands. 'You've been out of it for nearly three days bro. Give yourself time to come round properly.' Jacob's brow creased in consternation.

'Three days? He croaked - his throat fiery and dry.

'Yeah man, you were sort of waking up now and again, babbling nonsense and stuff. Your eyes were open, but they were completely dead. You were completely away with the fairies man! We were just happy to get some water into you while we could.

'Water?' Realisation unfurled Jacob's brow. 'Oh yes... I remember now...' He shot Simon a quizzical glance. '...I remember seeing someone just before I hit the water. He shouted out my name.'

'Yeah, that would have been Uncle Andy. He was driving past when he saw you disappear down the banking. He thought that you might be in trouble and pulled over to take a look. Lucky he did, eh bro?' Jacob felt strangely disappointed.

'Uncle Andy? Yeah... I suppose I was a lucky man right enough.'

'No suppose about it Jake, the current dragged you right under and carried you way down river. If Uncle Andy hadn't been there, well... he saved your life bro!' Looking out through the cosy window, Jacob observed that it was still raining.

'So what about the ferry tickets?' He said at last, trying hard to suppress the memory of Alison's face.

'No problem, I phoned up and explained the situation. They were brilliant about the whole thing, agreed to keep the tickets open for another week. We just have to give them at least twenty-four hours notice to be added to the passenger list.' Alison's smile was proving irrepressible.

'Good. You'd better get onto them right away then.' Simon's face went from smile to scowl in a microsecond.

'Are you fucking crazy man?' He pleaded hopelessly. 'You've just been delirious for the guts of seventy-two hours, prior to which you nearly fucking drowned, and you think that you're fit enough to travel all that distance?' Jacob looked at his brother and yawned.

'Correct. Look at it this way Simon, I've been well taken care of here, had a good long rest. I really appreciate Auntie Esther and Uncle Andrew putting themselves out like this, but I don't want to outstay my welcome, be a burden on them. I just want to go home where I can recuperate in familiar surroundings.'

'But the doc said that you should stay in bed for at least a week to ten days.' Cramping electric pain shot from Jacob's toes straight through to the crown of his head as he dragged his carcass up into a sitting position.

'I feel absolutely fine, honestly; and I promise as soon as we hit Glasgow I'll go straight to bed.' Simon looked unconvinced, concerned. It was time for Jacob to play his joker. 'I won't be able to relax here Simon. In fact, it would probably take me even longer to get back on my feet. All I need is to go home and get into my own bed.' A faint ringing in Jacob's ears was growing louder and his vision was beginning to blur. He quickly fixed Simon with his *older brother* look, the same look he had used so many times down the years to emphasise his rank I the pecking order or to get what he wanted. The ringing was now accompanied by a whooshing, wave-like sensation. Jacob struggled to keep himself upright, pouring a hand over the bedpost and holding on tight. *'Come on for fuck sake Si!'* Simon frowned, sighed, slapped his knees and jumped to his feet.

'Okay... okay Jake, you win.' He acquiesced, 'But I'm putting you to bed myself the minute we get back.' Jacob's shoulder relaxed.'

'Thanks Si, it's a deal.' As Simon strode towards the door, his older brother exhaled and the dark corners of the room came racing in to meet him.

'I'll away and phone the ferry company now then, see if we can get booked on for tomorrow morning.' Said Simon turning the groaning brass door handle. 'In the meantime try and get some sleep bro. Just bang on the ceiling if you need anything.' As the door slammed shut, Jacob let go of the bedpost and fell back into numb forgetfulness. The room racing off along a dark tunnel until it was no more than a pin-prick of light in the limitless velvet black.

He moved gingerly towards where the door last was; baby steps. He finds it easiest barefoot – more sensation – sensing the coldness of obstructions through his blackened toes.

Dear Alison,

I write these words as I cross the waves back into your arms and heart my love. I have just lain dead for three days, but am now resurrected, reborn. I know what happened and I forgive you. I feel that I've been given a second chance, and if someone as undeserving as me can get a second chance, then I think that it's only fair that I offer you, a beautiful, caring woman, someone who really does deserve it, the opportunity. I know about the other man, I saw you that night at the petrol station; I was there in the shadows, watching. Please don't think that I'm being judgmental, but he does seem a bit young for you. Not that you're too old, you look fantastic and you have an amazing body, and I miss it all. But what we had, what we can still have, is real. I love you with every inch of my being and I just know that you feel the same, so come back to me Alison I know we can work it out. I will never even mention that other man ever again. We can take up where we left off, pretend this mess never happened, treat it all like the bad dream that my life has become since you took your love away.

Please, please call me Alison.

All my love, Forever

Eternally yours

Jacob

Dear Alison,

You have abandoned and broken me, left me with photographs and cold memories. You spent more time looking at yourself than looking at me. Why did I not see it coming? The signs were right there in front of me from the start. I should have run over and spoke to you at the petrol garage that night, got it out in the open, dealt with it. But I was frozen by your betrayal. Standing there in the rain watching you with him, it felt as though you had stretched a silken scarf across my face, it was getting wetter and wetter, clinging to me, suffocating me. The cold September wind blew through my clothes as I watched you disappear with him into the orange gloom. Where did you go? I spend hours staring at your pictures, staring at myself, asking my reflection what I did wrong. I only see darkness and blue fire in my eyes. I used to be able to see you in my head all the time, but lately you have not appeared to me much, except in the thin way that dreams appear. Your face is

247

just an extra in a cast of thousands. Do you even remember our first kiss? We had only known each other for a short time before I encircled you and we silenced the world for the longest moment. Our lips met and parted without embarrassment and your seed was sown. It grows in my head like a cancer now, slowly spreading through my whole body. It makes my hands and feet burn and itch and cold-sweats my back. My stomach is cramped and sick. I fall to the floor and writhe in agony, imprisoned, as I am, within my own inconsequential universe, celebrating how beautiful the pain of love can be. You have left me trapped in this bad dream with your dark lies. I remember your love in scarlet and gold spinning out searching thoughts to every excess of my finite mind. Now I am the condemned man with no hope of reprieve. I stand by my window, dark and empty pleading with God to forgive me my love of falsehood. I was looking for love, for myself, in your eyes, only to suffer the indignity of rejection. I am alone and lost in a labyrinth of time where I can perceive change, but cannot feel it in my soul. I am too infantile and incomplete, my life is thin and unreal, it does not seem like mine anymore. No control, I am moved by others and doubt everyone. I wish that I were falling on my feet instead of just falling. I long to be the person I used to be, someone who accepted being who he is, not this creature I have become who constantly questions every thought and fear. I thought that everything you said to me was the truth, I trusted you. Did you ever tell me the truth? You have left me with nothing I am destroyed; and yet I long for you. I stayed up for three days painting a portrait of you from my photographs. The morning woke me from a memory replayed and I found myself covered in you. It was hours before every piece of you was washed away. I cried for hours afterwards because I had lost you again. In those photographs you looked like a stranger to me, I almost convinced myself that our past never existed. But I found a strand of your hair on the hall table underneath the mirror. I remembered your constant preening and gesturing, your superficiality your need for reaffirmation. If it was not anger that killed our love, could it have been vanity? If I close my eyes tight and shut out the world I can almost hear your voice. I still dream of you, wake up in the night

calling your name, the scent of your hair lingering for a moment

on my pillow before evaporating into the cold unforgiving black.

Love to me is like your voice hanging on the wind, I can almost

make it out, but it always fades into the distance before I can grasp

its meaning. When you first left I really wanted to hate you, so I

took all the bad things I've ever felt and put them into a bowl and

mixed and ground and pounded them to a pulp. I put the pulp into

a syringe with the intention of injecting myself with enough bad

feeling to make me hate you. But when I felt the cold sharp point

of the needle against my arm, I thought,

WHY?

I realised that it was not the bad things that would make me hate

you, but the fact that you had left and taken the good times with

you. You tore my soul from deep within me, left an empty void

where our love once lived. I sit here numb, unable to feel anything

at all. Like a vampire you have drained me, but still I cannot hate you. I am empty, emotionless.

Jacob

His fingers searched the wasteland of the kitchen table like drunken spiders. He knew they must be here somewhere. The pack revealed itself to his touch and flicked open invisible, a well rehearsed routine. An index finger slid out a single cigarette to grasping length and he retrieved the lighter that hung by a shoelace around his neck and quickly lit up. The now familiar smell of burning hair no longer alarmed him.

INSOMNIA

It had been over two days now since he had last slept or ate. A rumbling, vacant stomach voiced disquiet at having been neglected for so long. Jacob considered eating something, but instead lit up another cigarette and stared out of his bedroom window at the wet-grey Glasgow streets. Thoughts of getting dressed were quickly dismissed as pointless. He took another drag on his cigarette then walked over to the bed and perched on the edge. The sky was growing darker now although it had not really been light at any time during that day.

Jacob finished his cigarette and tried to find a space in the ashtray to stub out the end; his over-enthusiastic attempts unbalancing the whole side-table and sending the assorted objects on its' surface (ashtray, alarm-clock and table lamp) crashing to the floor. When the jagged grey-brown mess had settled, he stood up and stared vacantly at it, desperately trying to feel... something. But there was no anger, no sentimentality, no regret; Jacob was empty of expression. Everything was just stuff, and sooner or later it would all end up as rubbish. Stepping casually around the debris, he headed for the living room, pausing fleetingly by the phone, willing it to ring; but there was only... silence. Jacob lifted the receiver thinking that maybe the line had been cut; but a crisp dialling tone addressed his ear.

'Might be something wrong with her phone? Not paid the bill on time and they've limited her to incoming calls only? Maybe she's had another accident?' His fingers began to punch in her number, it was ringing. This whole charade had been played out before on numerous occasions and Jacob had never, as yet, succeeded in convincing himself or completing the call. It was still ringing, but he was already resigning himself to yet another failure.

'Hello?' It was her!

'Alison? It's me, Jacob, I'm so happ…!'

'I'm sorry I can't come to the phone right now, but if you leave a message after the tone I'll get back to you…Beeeeeeeep!' Jacob choked back the anger and frustration and cleared his throat.

'Alison, it's me, Jacob. I know that you're around because you've changed the message on your answering machine. Why won't you just talk to me, tell me what I've done wrong? I just know we could fix it, whatever it is, it doesn't matter babe. But if you don't tell me what the problem is how the hell am I supposed to know what it is I have to do? Oh for god sake Alison! I'm just spending all day thinking myself into corners, I'm so confused. I don't know who I am any more. I can't eat, I can't sleep; sometimes I even have to concentrate to breathe. I'm shaking and crying like a lost child, my home doesn't feel like home… What the fuck is happening to me Alison? What have you done to me? I remember laughing together with you, so full of hope for the future. With you I felt for the first time in my entire pathetic little life that I belonged. Now there is nothing left inside of me Alison. How the hell did all this happen so quickly?' He hesitated, anxiously, hopelessly, waiting for an answer. But the line had already gone dead. Defeated, he returned the receiver to its cradle.

Following the retreating twilight into the sitting room, Jacob was drawn towards the mirror above the fireplace. He looked the same as always, but everything around him was alien. 'This life is a prison... a comfortable prison.' Jacob walked over and stared out of the window. 'And you all spy on me incessantly.' He spat and shivered in the cold draft Jacob longed for the freedom of summertime, getting drunk in the afternoon sun, kicking a ball around barefoot on the grass, smoking joints in the open air, not caring when, how or even *if* he got home. 'Well I guess we have to grow up sometime J.J.'

Dusk had fallen quickly over Glasgow, a chilled web of shadows spinning tightly through Jacob's flat. He took a thick woollen throw from the back of the armchair and wrapped himself against the dark chill, still refusing to be hungry.

*

The clock on his mantle-piece screamed four forty-six AM silently at Jacob. 'This is torture, absolute fucking torture...why can't I sleep?' He pleaded to the grey darkness. 'Why did you leave me Alison? Why have you done this to me? I think so hard about you that my mind hurts. The page refuses to turn, there is no way to begin the next chapter, and the old times will not die. I live in vivid dreams where I am king and you are my queen. Sometimes it's hard to believe that you were actually once here, that I held you in these arms and looked into your sincere eyes. Distant echoes, distant echoes. Mountain tops I cannot reach, the rock crumbles away to so much dust in my hands. Down again I fall, lost and forgotten, like it didn't happen, like *we* did not exist.'

The emptiness answered with silence.

Feeling dirty, filthy and putrid, and consumed with the irresistible desire to purge himself, to cleanse his soul; Jacob sprang from the armchair, ran to the bathroom and snapped on both taps. He stared at the bath as it bubbled and filled, wondering if it was big enough for the job. If this problem did not require immediate attention Jacob considered that a short walk to the river or a rather longer drive to Loch Lomond may have served his purpose more adequately.

The water kissed the rim, running over onto the floor as Jacob lowered himself in. The warm embrace was consoling, comforting. He felt like an infant protected in his mother's womb and relaxed for the first time in longer than he cared to remember, Jacob closed his eyes and allowed the stillness to take him.

*

He saw her everywhere these days. Jacob threw back the last dregs of his whisky and made for the door. The wet Glasgow afternoon air stung him like frostbite and he recoiled into the shelter of the pub doorway to light a cigarette. Another Alison doppelganger crossed the street in front of him and entered a corner shop. This one even had her walk the slight limp. Jacob watched her through the shop window pick a carton of milk out of the tall fridge and take it to the counter. She was so much like Alison, the same way of moving her head to flick the hair to one side.

'Alison?'

 Jacob threw his cigarette onto the pavement and started in the direction of the corner shop. He reached the door just as she was coming out.

'Alison?'

She looked startled, almost apologetic.

'Jacob...I... How are you?' Jacob struggled for words, felt his chest tighten.

'I'm okay, I guess? Where've you been? I've been trying to call you.'

'Oh just been busy with family and work stuff and that. I was going to give you a call when everything was a bit less crazy.'

'I've really missed you Alison. Did I do something wrong?' Alison shifted uncomfortably like a child caught red-handed.

'No you didn't do anything wrong Jacob. It's just... well let's just say there's been a lot going on recently. Tell you the truth it's a bit of a mess for me right now.'

'Maybe I could help? I'm a good listener.'

'Not this time Jacob, I'll have to sort this out myself.'

'You fancy coming round to mine for a coffee?'

'I actually a bit tired right now and I really should get back and put this in the fridge.' Alison held up the milk. Jacob felt like someone had just punched him in the guts.

'Oh… okay. You left some things at mine, now that I know that you're still alive I'll drop them round. I'm just heading home now so I'll could put your stuff in the car and meet you there if you like?'

'I'll probably be out Jacob.'

'But your milk?'

'What?' Jacob pointed to the carton of milk Alison held.

'You said you have to get your milk home. By the time you walk back I could be there with your things.'

'I don't want to put you to any trouble.'

'It's no trouble at all Alison. I'm not doing anything.' Replied Jacob, trying not to sound too desperate. Alison looked far away for a moment. Jacob steeled himself for another blow.

'I suppose I have time for one coffee. I could put my milk in your fridge for a bit.' Jacob struggled to control the smile exploding upwards on his face.

'Cool. Let's go then.'

*

The tail of Jacob's grey trench coat flicked the pile of mail that had teetered and grew unopened on the hall table for over a week. It cascaded to the floor like outsized weather-burned tickertape, where it skidded and stuck to the damp outside that he and Alison had just trodden into the flat. Jacob kicked and scraped the scattered mail under the hall table.

'Just junk and bills mainly. Nothing to worry about.' He said, ushering Alison in and closing the door behind her. 'Go through.' Jacob continued, 'You know where everything is.' Alison made instinctively for the kitchen. Jacob followed, reminding himself that this was actually happening, Alison was actually here in his flat. ' You want a drink Alison... tea, coffee?'

'You have anything a bit stronger?'

'I think there might be some wine in the fridge, or there's whisky if you like?' There was always whisky these days.

'Yeah, whisky would be good... take the edge off.' Jacob wanted to ask what that last remark actually meant, but he didn't want to complicate things. She was here and Jacob wanted her to stay as long as possible. He wasn't about to chase her off with difficult questions.

Jacob took the bottle from the side and slid it over to Alison before hurriedly washing up two glasses.

'I would have settled for a mug.'

'Ach they're done now.' Jacob replied, bringing the still dripping glasses to rest beside the whisky. Alison had already begun to unscrew the top.

'Large one?' Jacob quickly dismissed any subliminal message in Alison's remark.

' I'm game if you are.' Alison smiled and filled both glasses halfway up. Jacob watched as she placed the cap back on the bottle and turned it only once.

'Bottoms up.' Said Alison raising her glass then taking a swig. Jacob focused on her mouth; amber pouring softly over faint rose, a single droplet escaping onto her bottom lip. She chased it back into her mouth with the index finger of her right hand, and punctuated her coy smile with an 'Oops!'

There was so much that Jacob wanted to know, but he would have to be patient. He didn't want to scare her off. Better to try and act as casual as possible he thought.

'Have you had lunch Alison?'

'Yeah, had a sandwich earlier.'

'Okay. I'll just go and get your bits and pieces together then.' Alison nodded and took another sip of her whisky. 'Right then...I won't be long. Help yourself to anything.' Continued Jacob before exiting the kitchen, grabbing a carrier bag from a drawer on the way.

There wasn't really that much left of Alison in his flat. Just a couple of random CDs, a magazine, some clothes he had washed and folded and left on top of his chest of drawers just in case, just in case...

Jacob carefully placed Alison's things in the carrier bag and scanned the room for any items he might have missed. On the bedside table opposite his own sat her hairbrush, abandoned and alone, in the same position in which she had left it on that last day. Jacob sat down on the bed and picked it up. Alison's hair was woven thick between the many teeth, her scent still clinging. Jacob closed his eyes and inhaled her deeply.

'I never meant to hurt you Jacob.' For a moment he thought it might be another dream, a ghost whispering in his ear as had been happening more and more recently. '...It's just, it's just life got in the way. I promise I'll explain everything one day. I just can't deal with it all right now, my head's all over the place.' He opened his eyes and turned his face towards her where she stood in the doorway.

'But why wouldn't you talk to me? I left messages, I texted you, I even wrote you a letter, but nothing. Why Alison?' Her silhouette moved out of the doorframe and towards the bed. Alison sat down next to Jacob and hugging his arm two-handedly to her cheek she spoke just above her breath.

'I really wish I could tell you Jacob, but it's just not the right time. I promise I will though. Soon.'

'I don't know if I could stand losing you again Alison.' She turned her face upward. He could feel her breath on his cheek, the warm intoxicating aroma of *uisge beatha* carried on her words.

'You'll never lose me Jacob. I'll always be with you. We are connected forever.' Jacob turned his face to hers. They both hesitated for a moment locked in a gaze, before a kiss overtook them and they fell back onto the bed tearing at each other's clothes like starving men at a banquet.

*

She arose and departed without words, leaving a wet imprint of her body on the white sand. Jacob watched her recede and then stared at the damp shadow as it slowly evaporated in the afternoon sun.

A loud bump from somewhere in the flat startled him from dreaming. He sat up and reached instinctively to the bedside table for his phone, upsetting a glass of water that splashed and smashed to the floor.

'Fuck!' Exclaimed Jacob in hushed tones to the dark room, any element of surprise dissolve into the night air with his frosted breath.

'Alison… did you hear something? Alison?' He felt for her in the bed next to him, but there was only cold empty space. It sunk in that the band that had awakened him was probably the door slamming shut behind her. Jacob listened for the sound of footsteps on the stairs, the loud *thunk* of the heavy close security door. But all he could hear was the sound of his own breathing and the distant throb of motorway traffic. Jacob flicked on the light and searched the bedroom and then the rest of the flat for a note of explanation, but the only sign that she had ever been there was her lip-stain on a drained whisky glass. He parked himself in his armchair in the front room and lit a cigarette.

'Maybe it was just a dream? If it was I wish I could sleep forever.'

Clothes had proven an unexpected problem. He didn't really care what he wore, he never really went out anymore, didn't move around much either, the view was the same from everywhere anyway. He just picked the most comfortable things and put them on. However, alarmed by some of the more bizarre colour combinations, his brother had gone out and bought him a complete wardrobe of black clothing.

PARTY FEARS

The shrill scream of the telephone dragged Jacob from a dark dreamless sleep.

'Alison?' The water all around was freezing cold now and had numbed his body. Trying to move felt like fighting through heavy, deep snow. The telephone continued to ring, increasing Jacob's anxiety and frustration. 'Come on you fuckers!' He urged his petrified limbs. Neurons rapidly fired nervous electrical wake up messages, and, little by little, as Jacobs frozen synapses began to thaw, the transmissions reached their destinations. Slowly, painfully Jacob pushed himself up and out of the icy water. In stages he creaked along the hallway to the living room and picked up the insistent telephone. 'Hello? Alison?' A male voice answered.

'Who...what the hell are you on about? Is that you Jacob? Have I got the right number? Am I talking to that bloody machine again?' It was Justin his agent - Jacob felt like getting back into the bathtub.

'Yes, it's me Justin; now what the fuck do you want?'

'Well that's a charming welcome darling. You sound awful dear boy, have you been on the sauce?'

'No, no...just caught me sleeping, that's all. I'm fine.'

'Sleeping? At this time of day, are you ill?'

'No Justin, I told you. I'm fine. I just stayed up a bit too late finishing off some work. What time is it anyway?'

'It's about six o'clock.'

'P.M.?'

'What? Of course P.M! Now listen to me Jacob. I'm at the Aragon Bar on Byers Road, having a bit of a session with Quentin Davis…you know, the art critic with the Daily Telegraph?' Jacob answered with a 'Hmmph?' Impervious, Justin continued. 'Anyway, he's also a bit of a collector and, as it turns out, a bit of a fan. He owns a couple of your earlier works and, get this Jacob, he's really interested in commissioning a bloody portrait! Can you believe that this is really happening? This could be bloody huge for your career!' Jacob tried hard to muster some enthusiasm.

'Yeah, sounds great Justin. Can you take care of the details? I'm still a bit fucked.' There was a sharp intake of breath from the other end of the line, then a pause like the anticipatory silence before a baby starts screaming.

'What the hell do you mean you're a bit fucked? This could be the big one matey! I've sweated blood over the years trying to get you a break like this. It's not a question of how *you* fucking feel! Now pull yourself together man! Get your bloody skates on and deliver your arse down here pronto! I've worked far too hard on this one to have you go and fuck it up! Don't let me down Jacob or you're finished…I mean it…one word in the right ear and…'

'The self-righteous fucking leech!'

'Okay, okay Justin, keep you fucking knickers on! You're such an old drama queen! Sorry Justin, been a bit stressed out lately. But don't worry, I'll get my shit organised and be there as soon as I can.'

'Better be quick Jacob, the way Mr Davis is throwing back the single malt I doubt if he'll be coherent for very much longer.'

'Right Justin, I'll be there in about an hour.'

'Better make that twenty minutes or we're fucked my boy!'

'Twenty minutes? No chance Justin, that's imposs... Justin?'

But Justin had already hung up.

Shaking off the final vestiges of frostbite, Jacob limped back to the bathroom and quickly showered off the stale bathwater. A change of clothes and a quarter bottle of the cheapest whisky later and he was out the door and on his way. A bit too drunk and bit too confused to consider walking the half mile or so to the pub, Jacob instead steadied himself with the help of a lamp-post and attempted to hail a taxi. Two black cabs drove past, lights on, no passenger in the back, completely ignoring a manically waving Jacob. A quick check of his watch revealed that he was going to be late.

'Twenty minutes my arse!' He envisaged a fizzing, pissed off Justin trying desperately to keep a steaming red faced Mr Quentin Davis esq. from buggering off in search of a kebab. Drastic measures would have to be employed. Noticing another black cab slip into stealth mode by the tube station, Jacob levered himself upright, held his breath, and left the relative sanctuary of the pavement, stepping into the pathway of the speeding cab, arms raised.   There was a terrible screeching noise as the taxi rapidly decelerated; Jacob witnessing the panic stricken sagging features of the taxi-driver in vivid detail, illuminated by the orange street-lights, mouthing the universal idiom 'FUCK!' as he slammed on the brakes and swerved slightly, narrowly missing the statuesque Jacob.

 Jacob exhaled relief and hurried to into the back of the cab, before the driver came out of shock.

'You tryin' tae get yersel killed mate?'   Spat the taxi-driver through a small sliding window, arms gesturing wildly, clearly irate.   Jacob fumbled for the seatbelt, avoiding eye-contact.

'Eh? Sorry driver; macular degeneration.' he replied pointing at his eyes. The taxi-driver frowned and puckered his thin lips.

'Macu-whit?'

'Macular degeneration; my eye-sight is nearly away. Having trouble seeing where I'm going.' The driver eased his bulk back slightly into the front of the cab, perhaps fearful of contamination.

'Well should you no' be wearing yer glessees then mate?' Jacob fixed him with a grin.

'No use driver... nothing the doctors can do. My eyesight is just going to gradually get worse and worse until...' Jacob clicked his fingers, '...lights out!'

The driver raised his eyebrows and blew through pursed lips as if attempting to whistle.

'Aye well... I'm sorry to hear that mate, sounds like a terrible thing.' He said turning and re-setting the meter. His narrow bloodshot eyes habitually scanned Jacob's reflection in the rear-view mirror. 'Blin or no, ye'll need tae be a wee bit mair careful though, no' ivry-buddy's as wary a driver as me ye know.' He commented with sincerity and restarted the engine. 'Now then... where to sir?'

Jacob relaxed back in is seat and smiled.

'The Aragon Bar please driver.'

*

Five minutes later he was standing on the Byers Road pavement directly outside the pub. The taxi-driver, hurrying round upon their arrival, opened Jacob's door and offered to see him inside. Jacob thanked him but said that he could manage from here on his own; then waited until the driver had walked half-way round the cab before making his way towards the barbers shop next door and attempting to rattle open its' locked doors. Looking over to investigate the noise, the taxi-driver quickly doubled back to guide the poor blind man into the proper entrance. Jacob thanked the wheezing driver once again, trying hard to disguise the laughter in his voice.

Inside the pub was as busy and noisy, as usual. Through the bobbing heads Jacob located Justin at the other side of the bar and waved over to catch his attention as he fought through the throng. Half turning his head, Justin spotted Jacob's his wildly gesticulating hand poking out above the undulating wave of schmoozing boozers, and unfurled a long arm to beckon him forward.

Justin was a tall man of six feet two or three, whose willowy physique gave the illusion of being even taller. He accessorised his trademark ex-public-schoolboy floppy blonde hair with a *fuck you* smile and a large gin and tonic, lime not lemon, and definitely *no* ice. However, as he approached, Jacob noted by the large unmoving pupils and his hundred-yard stare that Justin had been indulging in something other than *mothers' ruin* that evening.

'So nice of you to finally grace us with your presence Jacob; we had just about given up on you.' Justin extended a long hand towards Jacob who reciprocated the gesture, grasping the agent's bony mitt with such vigour as to invoke a small wince and rapid withdrawal.

'I had trouble getting a cab. You know how the traffic is in this bloody city Justin!' He parried, with a slight shrug of the shoulders - Justin's *fuck you* expression turning to one more akin to a rabbit caught in the headlights of an onrushing car. The agent took a sip of his drink and composed himself for a second before continuing with the social formalities.

'Now then Jacob, I'd like you to meet a very good friend of mine…' He turned to the short, dapper, forty-something standing to his left. 'Allow me to introduce Mr Quentin Davis.' He continued, gesturing like a magician who had just inexplicably materialised this small, shiny man from the ether.

'I'm so pleased to finally meet you at last Mr Douglas.' Gushed Quentin, leaning forward into Jacob's space so rapidly that his head took a second to catch up with the rest of his body.

'Please, call me Jake.'

'Marvellous, Jake it is then; and you must call me Quentin. Now then Jakey, Justin has been enthusing all night about the painting you're working on at the moment; he said you were so excited by this particular piece of work that you could hardly drag yourself away from it to come here tonight.' Continued Quentin, caressing Jacob's hand like a damp, lukewarm flannel. 'I really would love to come up to your studio and have myself a sneaky wee peek at it! Is there any chance of a private viewing before it goes on public display? Oh please say that there is Jakey, oh please do! I'm such a big fan of yours.' Jacob was completely caught off guard by the camp intensity of this onslaught. And what was more, he had not a clue as to what the fuck this Ronnie Corbett look-a-like was going on about; he hadn't done any serious work in weeks, not since… Jacob figured that Justin must have been feeding the little man a line of bullshit to keep him interested. Catching Justin's eye Jacob tried desperately to psychically

271

connect and convey the message –

'Help me out here you lanky fuck! I haven't got the foggiest idea what the hell this joker is on about!' But Jacob's psychic powers failed him at the vital moment.

Placing a hand on his upper arm, Justin eased the diminutive Mr Davis to one side and spoke furtively from the corner of his mouth.

'What's this then…' interjected Jacob, '…you two 'brothers' discussing the agenda for the next lodge meeting?'

'Jacob, dear boy…' began Justin conciliatorily. '…I'm just explaining to Mr Davis here about the creative process - you know, how you, like most great artists, are… a perfectionist. Not until you are no less than one hundred and fifty percent certain that a piece is complete, that there is no more to be done to that particular work of art, then no-one, I repeat, no-one, will be permitted to cast the merest gaze upon it.' Jacob felt his shoulders relax. Maybe there was something to this telepathy shite after all? Quentin adopted the look of an elderly woman who had just been given the news that her beloved pet pooch would have to be put to sleep. His tepid, moist paw brushed the back of Jacob's hand again in resignation.

'I do understand Jacob, really I do. But not even the tiniest glimpse?'

'Not even if you were the Queen herself!' replied Jacob with a dismissive sweep of his hand. As Mr Davis sunk deflated back into his protective bubble, ever the salesman, Justin, swooped to the rescue.

'Quentin, my dear man; you can rest assured that the very moment Jacob has applied the final brush-stroke to *The Rape of Summers End*, yours will be the next two eyes to fall upon that canvas.' This was all, of course, total and utter crap; but that was Justin's job, and you had to hand it to the old queen, he was damned good at it! After giving Quentin a reassuring hug, which Jacob considered to last slightly too long and was a tad too passionate for a Glasgow bar, Justin focused his attention back on Jacob.

'Now Jake, pay attention - the agenda for this evening is as follows: Quentin has graciously invited us round to his place for drinks, and then afterwards we shall be attending the exhibition opening of an exciting new sculptor; an extremely gifted individual who I intend to take under my wing, and whose name, for some inexplicable reason, completely eludes me for the moment...' Justin furrowed his brows and stared at the ceiling as though he had written the sculptor's name there earlier in case he forgot.

'Poor bugger...' thought Jacob, '...won't even know what's hit him.' Justin snapped out of his reverie.

'No, it's gone... but nevertheless, the boy is an exceptional young talent and I am sure that you will find his work as fabulous as I do.' Quentin smiled politely and excused himself then minced off to the toilet. Justin's practiced smile went south as soon as Mr Davis was out of sight and he turned on Jacob, grabbing his jacket by the left shoulder. 'What the fuck do you think you're playing at you ungrateful little bastard? Look at you! You're a fucking mess, and you reek of whisky.' Jacob looked first at Justin's closed fist holding a grip of his sleeve, then right into his eyes.

'I think you had better move that before it gets broken.' He said without breaking eye contact, '…and if you speak to me like that again you'll be cleaning your arse with a tooth-brush. Do I make myself clear?' Justin's grip fell limp in unison with his jaw, his hand dropping flaccidly to the side.

'I'm just trying to look out for you Jake. You can be your own worse enemy sometimes.' He stammered in response, fumbling nervously in his inside-left coat pocket for a second before discretely palming something into Jacob's right hand. 'Go and get some of that into your system, it might straighten you out a bit.' Jacob looked down at the small bag of white powder, smiled up at Justin and turned toilet-ward. 'And for god sake sort your fucking hair out. You look like a bloody scarecrow!' Jacob paused and thought about smacking Justin in the mouth, but instead decided it easier just to take his reprimand… and his cocaine.

Swinging the toilet door open Jacob was greeted by the sight of Mr Quentin Davis busily fannying around in front of a mirror with the little black-grey hair he had left.

'*Fucking twat!*' thought Jacob.

'Hello there Jakey my boy! Is everything all right? You look a bit rough.' Chirped Quentin enthusiastically at Jacob's passing reflection. Jacob turned his face to acknowledge the greeting, catching himself in the mirror as he did so.

'Holy shit! You're not kidding are you? I look like the fucking wolf-man!' He ran both taps into one of the toilet sinks and scrubbed his face vigorously before pushing the hair back over his head using his hands like a comb. Quentin was laughing,

'But truthfully Jake, are you okay?' Jacob pulled a few paper towels and dried his face.

'Oh I'm just tickety-fucking-boo Quents, or, at least, I will be very shortly.' He replied shaking the bag of cocaine in front of him. 'Now, if you'll excuse me, but must go and powder my nose.' Jacob continued walking towards one of the toilet cubicles. Trailing not far behind Quentin's voice appealed.

'Would it be possible to cadge a quick line from you dear boy?'

Several minutes later and much to the delight of Justin, Jacob and his new best friend Quentin emerged from the bogs, arm in arm, laughing their heads off at nothing in particular.

*

Many rapidly imbibed malt whiskies followed before a fast-black-cab conveyed the trio to a luxury apartment building overlooking the River Clyde. As the men approached the grand glass entrance illuminated and reflected in the wet night time pavement, Quentin Davis frowned disdainfully at Jacob's offer of *a nose of coke*. 'Not until we're inside Jake, there's a whopping great tabloid newspaper office not one-hundred meters that way.' He said pointing far to the left with his eyes. 'This whole place is putrid with low-life paparazzi. For all we know there could be a camera pointed at us right now!' Jacob contemplated Quentin's statement for a microsecond then shrugged and dipped his finger into the bag. Scooping up a small heap of cocaine onto the tip, he stuffed it into his left nostril with a grinding sniff. Jacob's two companions hurried on inside and into the waiting shine of the elevator. Justin holding the door, a look of obvious concern inhabiting his face. He whispered loudly, impatiently to Jacob who had not even made it all the way into the atrium. 'Hurry along now for heavens sake Jake, before someone sees us!' Seemingly unconcerned, Jacob casually tucked the bag of cocaine into the breast pocket of his jacket like a silk handkerchief, and sauntered nonchalantly towards his anxious companions. The nervous electricity in the elevator subsiding as its' golden mirrored doors slid closed.

'You are a very naughty boy Jakey.' scolded Quentin gently, 'There are more cameras in this place than there are in the bloody BBC! I fear that the residents committee would take a very dim view of me allowing a drug crazed maniac into the building.' Jacob smiled and pulled the coke from his pocket.

'Do accept my humble apologies Mr Davis…' he said, offering the bags' open mouth to Quentin.

'Not until we are safely inside dear boy. If you could just curb your enthusiasm for a moment longer, I would be more than happy to join in the fun.'

The elevator smoothed to a halt somewhere in the early teens and the doors swished open. In the quiet hallway Quentin searched his ring of keys.

'Ah, here it is.' He announced, holding up a small silver key reminiscent of the type used to open a gym locker. 'I am quite positive that you two gentlemen are going to appreciate this…' he continued, beckoning his companions to follow which Justin and Jacob did without question. Quentin led the party three doors down to the left to what appeared to be a cupboard. 'Now boys, pay close attention,' whispered Quentin unlocking a small metal compartment on the wall to the right of the door, revealing a numeric keypad. 'All very James Bond, don't you think?' He continued using his body to discretely shield the number he was punching in. The muffled clunk of a lock was followed by a faint electric whirring. 'And here we are gentlemen…' announced Quentin opening the door with a camp flourish, '…our own private elevator.'

It was a snug fit with the three men inside, but the trio were in for less than a minute, ascending only one floor. The elevator door opened onto the generous white marbled entrance hall of Quentin's vast open planned living space. This room alone was larger than Jacob's entire flat! A huge wall of glass framed the Glasgow night skyline, looking out over the river towards Govan and the Southside. The electro-magnetic pulse of city lights punching holes through the black, attracting Jacob across the polished floors towards it.

'How much fucking dosh does that fucking rag pay you Quents?' Quentin was already busy chopping up three stiff lines of coke on the vast smoked glass top of the coffee table using his platinum Amex card; he paused for a second and lifted his head.

'Not enough to keep me in the manner I've become accustomed to dear boy. I have a *lot* of fingers in a *lot* of pies. Various investments, stocks and shares, art - of course, property... In fact, I own a couple of flats in this very building. I make over two grand a month rent from that little scam alone!' Quentin removed a twenty pound note from his wallet and began rolling it up. 'It's that old cliché Jacob, *you've got to speculate to accumulate*. If you keep all your eggs in the one basket, well, you're bound to drop the basket once in a while aren't you? Writing my columns for the paper and the glossies helps to keep my profile in the public eye, gives people confidence in me, gets me invited to things... like the exhibition opening tonight. This young sculptor we're seeing later is the next big thing Jake, and tonight's a chance to get in on the ground floor so to speak - invest in a piece before the prices skyrocket.'

'Okay if you've got the spare dosh to *invest* as you put it.' Replied Jacob. 'But some of us lesser mortals have to waste our hard-earned on necessities like food and electricity! Quentin flicked him a lizard smile and continued rolling up the twenty-pound note. He paused and held it up as he spoke.

'Do you know that in America the prevalence of cocaine on paper currency is so great that the police can no longer use it as admissible evidence against drug dealers?' Jacob dragged himself away from the window and sank into one of three huge black leather sofas, directly across from Quentin.

'I've never been in America Quentin... But I've been in some states!' Quentin raised his face from the table, the twenty pound note still protruding from his left nostril.

'Eh?' he mumbled through cocaine fuzz. Jacob immediately threw his hands up and shrugged apologetically.

'Never mind, it wasn't that funny anyway. Are you going to give anyone else a go at that then?' He said pointing at the mound of white. 'Or were you planning to snort it all yourself?' He continued, reaching over and snatching the note from his companion's beak. Jacob leaned down to the table-top and sniffed deep and long through the note, vacuuming up an entire fat line in one go.

'Where on earth has that agent of yours got to Jake?' Quentin's voice seemed very far away. Jacob tried in vain to bring his watery form into focus as a cocaine spark shot up his spine and set his brain on fire.

'Something? Calling ahead… gallery?' All memory of events leading up to and surrounding that moment - why he was here in the first place, Justin's phone call, the exhibition - were temporarily lost. Jacob felt like a disembodied spirit suspended at the centre of a black leather universe. Electricity shot out in colourful waves from his core. Off into the infinite dark they flew until… he was empty, floating in golden silence. A distant, infinitesimal speck rapidly grew and zipped towards him at incredible speed. Paralysed, Jacob was unable to avoid a direct hit. A huge ball of blue-white light penetrated the centre of his chest, immersing him in wave after wave of ecstasy. Jacob thought that he must surely die of pure pleasure, and hoped he would.

'Aaaaaaaaaaaaaaaaaaaaaaaaaaaaaaaaaaaaaaaaaaaaaaaaaaaaaaaaaaaaaaaaaaaa!'

'Fuck sake!' shouted Justin rushing into the room barely managing to keep the tray of drinks he was carrying balanced. 'What the hell is going on? Are you two pumping each other in here or something?'

'I haven't laid a finger on him… or anything else for that matter.' Countered Quentin defensively. Jacob watched the room slowly…slowly, and then quickly, melt into present time. He found himself standing up staring at the ceiling, hands in the air, the last utterance of his euphoric scream dripping from his lips.

'Holy fuck!' began Jacob, 'I've just had a cosmic orgasm! That must've been how Mary felt when the big man fucked her!' His two companions gawped in slack-jawed befuddlement.

'Hmmm... okay... very interesting indeed Jacob... right then.' interjected Justin, cracking the awkward silence. 'Here we go.' He continued, placing the tray of drinks on the coffee table. 'I do hope you don't mind Quentin, but I cracked open this rather nice single-malt you had nestling in the drinks cupboard.' Raised eyebrows, pursed his lips and a nod of the head signalled Quentin's acceptance. 'Now then gentlemen...' Justin began again, distributing a whisky to each of his companions as he spoke, '...the gallery are expecting their guests of honour, and I am referring to us there by the way, in approximately thirty minutes time. So I suggest we have our drinks then hot-foot it right over there.' Justin raised his drink initiating the salute, and all three chinked glasses and swigged at their whisky. Looking down at the table he pointed a long finger and feigned surprise. 'Oh and you left a little line for me, how sweet!'

*

'What are you up to in there? Having a wank or something?' Jacob shuddered awake to the sound of Justin's voice, his face cold against the porcelain of the washbasin. He was still on his feet, but was bent over at the waist, his upper body supported on the opulent marble top of a serpentine chestnut-wood vanity unit. He had no recollection of entering the toilet or of producing the small pyramid of vomit in the rather expensive looking sink to his immediate left. Snapping on an antique brass tap, Jacob worked his finger around breaking the pile of sick into smaller, easily washed away particles. He regarded his reflection in the grand Italianate gilt mirror.

'Well at least you're passing out in a better class of toilet these days J.J!'

'The taxi is here… it's waiting on us, or should I say, YOU!' Broke in Justin from the other type of the toilet door.

'Yeah, okay Justin - keep your fucking knickers on! I'll be there in a second!' Remembering the sculpture exhibition, Jacob splashed cold water over his face, letting some slip into his mouth and swishing it around, catching the spare lumps of puke and spitting them out into the sink. He dried his face and hair on a fluffy white, lavender scented towel then had a rummage in the medicine cabinet for something to make him smell a bit more pleasant. In amongst the various prescription medications and several tubes of lubricant jelly, Jacob discovered an entire shelf of the finest aftershaves. He selected the bottle of Creed Green Irish Tweed Cologne and sprayed it on liberally before exiting the toilet. Directly outside, waiting like an anxious parent at the school gates, stood Justin.

'I thought you'd flushed yourself away! Hurry now; come along; chop-chop!'

*

The rain was falling hard outside as they entered the taxi. It had only been a short walk of three metres or so from the front door to the roadside, but already, all three men were dripping wet.

'Should have ordered a bloody gondola instead of a cab!' quipped Justin.

'At least you two are dressed for it.' Remarked Jacob in reference to the long raincoats adorning both his companions. He tried hard to shake as much moisture as he could out from his battered black suit jacket, but quickly gave up and sank back into his seat and into a dream.

He tried to freeze time in his head and rewind back to that last night with Alison. *'What did I do wrong? Why did you leave me?'* He could find no answers, no comfort. The circular thinking made him dizzy, and he had to come up for air. Emerging back into the present, Jacob found himself staring out of the cab window holding a lit cigarette. He stared at it for a moment trying to figure out from where and when it had appeared, but drew a blank. He took a drag and re-focused on the streets; there was something familiar about the landscape. Then it struck him, they were near Alison's place. *'This is fate...Why else would you be thinking of her right at this moment, right at this place?* Stop the taxi!' Shouted Jacob, Justin and Quentin rounding on him in cloned astonishment as the can screeched to a halt.

'What the fuck do you think you're playing at Jacob?' shot Justin, 'We're already ten minutes late!'

'I know, I know... and I'm really sorry guys, but this is really important... an emergency! Can't believe I forgot... completely slipped my mind! There's someone I really need to go and see. Someone... it's really, really important, matter of life and death you might say.' The others just stared at Jacob bewildered, as the cab sat thrumming at the roadside.

'You getting' oot or whit mate?' Enquired the driver from the front.

'Yeah mate, just be a second. Jacob turned back to his companions. 'Honestly boys...' he pleaded, '...if it could wait...I'll only be half an hour tops. Just give me one of the invitations and I'll get there as soon as I can, okay?' Quentin sat back and puffed on his cigarette, seemingly unperturbed, but Justin was clearly seething. He leaned in toward Jacob and addressed him in a very quiet and intense tone, maintaining frowned eye contact throughout the exchange,

'This is a very, very important night for me Jacob and I don't intend to let anything or anyone fuck it up. Understand?' He slid a hand into his inside coat pocket. 'Here...' he continued withdrawing his hand, '...take this invitation and do not, under any circumstances, be any later than thirty minutes.' Jacob took the invite from Justin, trying hard to look as apologetic as possible.

'Cheers Justin, I owe you big time.' In reply the agent simply glared hard in silence then turned theatrically away. 'See you in half-an-hour Quentin,' added Jacob stepping from the cab. Quentin popped a smiling face around Justin's brooding form,

'Okay Jakey, just don't keep us waiting too long now. Missing you already!' Jacob slammed the door and watched it grunt off as he waited to cross the street.

When the traffic had cleared he hit the street running, crossing the road in the direction of Alison's flat. The rain had eased off to monsoon conditions, water soaking through Jacob's coat in seconds and beginning to run down his back. He ducked under a bus shelter and attempted to make himself more presentable. It was only a couple of minutes walk from the bus stop to Alison's flat. Jacob strained to see his reflection in the scored and graffitied Perspex. It looked like he had just swum the Channel fully clothed. Searching his pockets for something to dry himself with, Jacob unearthed a scrunched up ball of damp paper hankie. Unfolding the tissue carefully like some ancient priceless parchment, he then attempted to dry his face with it. But the soft paper caught and snagged on his five day stubble leaving a trail of confetti across his chin, which Jacob then had to erase using the lining of his jacket - using the same method, to towel off his hair as best he could before setting off.

Jacob's eyes ascended the three red-dark stories to the light in Alison's sitting room window. *'Do you really want to do this?'* It was a short jump up to the elevated security entrance on the front of the tenement building. Jacob's finger hovered above the call button, remembering the numerous times over the past few weeks that Alison had refused to answer the door. *'No, this time you have to use your head... be patient.'* Jacob went through a pantomime of patting his jacket, pretending to look for a key. Shaking his head in fake disbelief, he descended the stoop and started to walk off up the street, but ducked into the shadows beside the building only a few feet from the entrance, and waited.

The rain subsided to a torrential drizzle. Jacob searched for a smoke to pass the time, but the contents of his cigarette packet had turned to brown mush. 'Fuck it!' He spat and threw the packet onto the pavement. It hit with a dull thwack, and was swept off on a rivulet of drain-water, cascading from a broken down-pipe, a single filter-tip trying in vain to escape as the pack disappeared into the gutter. The sound of male voices echoed down the stairwell and out onto the street. The voices grew louder as their owners neared the entrance to Alison's tenement and Jacob primed for action.

Sticking carefully to the shadows, he approached the side of the stoop and observed through the safety glass of the security door two pairs of booted feet descend the final few stairs and exit the building. Jacob's eyes darted agonisingly between the slowly closing door and the two men as they retreated off down the street chatting loudly about football. He had to be sure. The men turned the corner and Jacob belted out hauling his body up the steps, catching the heavy security door just before it clicked shut.

*

Jacob crept up the stairs afraid to breathe and cursing his heart for beating so loudly. Rounding the corner at the stair-head he paused, took a deep breath and steadied himself. He was now only a few feet from Alison's door, the sound of running water trickling through into the corridor. As he approached Alison's singing voice drifted somewhere inside, her gentle song causing Jacob's anger to deepen.

'What the fuck has she got to be so happy about?' Jacob drew back his fist to bang on the door. *'No J.J. she'll phone the bloody police, play it cool.'* Jacob regained control, giving the door three short raps and standing to the side out of the spy-hole's range. The soft thudding of bare feet padded up towards the inner doorway.

'Who is it?' asked Alison from inside. Jacob felt strangely surprised to hear her voice; he was afraid to answer. 'Hello? Is there someone there?' Alison continued. Jacob imagined her body pressed against the cold wood just centimetres from his own, but could not bring himself to speak. Moving his head nearer he could hear the sound of her breathing close behind the door, she must have had her eye to the spy-hole. Another softer thud from inside as Alison came down off her tip-toes, was followed by her receding voice as she begun to pad back down the hall. 'Bloody kids!'

'Alison wait... it's me... Jacob!' He said unconsciously. There was an audible silence. Thinking that maybe she was looking through her spy-hole again, Jacob stepped out and back to make himself more visible. There was a brief pause.

'Please go away Jacob...' called Alison, breaking the silence '...this isn't a good time. I really can't see you right now.'

'Just five minutes Alison, that's all I ask. Surely you owe me that much? What have I done to you that is so awful Alison? What did I do to deserve being treated like this? Like… like… like a piece of shite scraped off the bottom of your shoe?' Pleaded Jacob.

'Really Jacob, I can't explain right now. Please, just go away. I promise I'll call you and we'll talk.' Alison's breathing had quickened. Jacob turned round and leaned his back on the door.

'Call me when Alison? When there's a proddy pope in the Vatican? I've left you a hundred or more messages and you haven't returned one yet, so why should I trust you now?'

'That was different Jacob. I promise, I *will* call you this time. As soon as I've worked things through in my head I will definitely call you. You have a right to know the truth. I'll call you as soon as I…'

'Just tell me now for fuck sake!' broke in Jacob, beginning to lose control.

'No Jacob, I can't… not yet… it's too… too… Just go Jacob! I'm begging you!'

'Oh Alison, where did I go wrong? What did I do? Why am I not good enough for you?' Jacob was sobbing uncontrollably.

'It's nothing you've done Jacob… honestly. It's just, well, things got too…I mean, things *are* too complicated.' He felt his stomach somersault.

'Three's a crowd, eh?'

'What the hell are you talking about Jacob? Listen, I have to get ready now, people are expecting me. I'll call you when all this has calmed down a bit.'

Hot date is it Alison?' Sneered Jacob.

'No, of course not. I'm going now Jacob.' Alison's voice was firmer.

'No time for me now, eh? I remembered you said you loved me Alison. LIAR!'

'Please go away Jacob; I really don't want to see you right now.' Alison replied maintaining her restraint

'What have I done to deserve this? Why wont you tell me what I've done?' Jacob turned to face the door.

'Just go away Jacob!'

'Not until I get some answers. Please Alison, open the door!'

'There is no way in hell that I'm opening this door. Now listen to me Jacob, you're making me late, I'm trying to get ready for a party.'

'I suppose that you'll be going with *him* then?'

'Going with who? What the hell are you talking about?' Jacob's mouth was parched; he attempted to lubricate his dry and cracked lips, but the saliva on his tongue was like glue.

'Alison I'm begging you… please open the door! I just want to see your face one last time then I'll go, I promise.' There was a pause.

'No chance Jacob. Now I really, *really* would like you to leave.' Jacob sensed a weakness.

'I love you Alison…please, just let me see your sweet face one last time; it haunts me. One brief look at your beautiful face then I'll go, I promise you.

'What is it about the word no that you don't understand Jacob?' But he was unrepentant.

'Just one last look Alison? Just ten seconds out of your life, that's all I'm asking. It wasn't all bad, was it? We had some good times? Just let me see your face one last time and then…and then I'll never bother you again. I give you my word, I swear it… on my father's grave!' There was another contemplative pause. Jacob held his breath.

'No more phone calls?'

'None, I promise.'

'Or turning up at the bank?'

'You have my word Alison; I'll be out of your life for good.' Another slight pause was followed by the scraping of a door-chain being put on from inside, then the rasp and click of a key entering and turning in the lock.

A small crack in the doorway broadened steadily into a narrow rectangle of light, framing Alison, clad only in a large bath towel. As Jacob stared in brooding desperation, she began to speak.

'You don't have to be out of my life forever Jacob. Sometime in the future I'll be able to explain everything to you, I promise. But right now I need you to leave me alone. I need time to work this whole mess out, I just… well, I just don't think that there is any way that you *could* understand right now.' Jacob could shelter from his inner storm no longer.

'Oh I understand everything perfectly my dear. You got bored and traded me in for a younger model!'

'What? No Jacob... that's not it at all, I...I...'

'Fuck you bitch, I should have known right from the fucking start! You're all the same! Fucking whore!' Jacob's body quaked and erupted, the door hitting Alison square in the face as he kicked in the flimsy chain. She reeled backward hitting the wall heavily, a torrent of blood flooding from her mouth and nose. Jacob found her stunned expression comical, a strange caricature and began to laugh. Coming too, Alison pushed herself up into a standing position and wiped at her bloodied face with an edge of the bath towel exposing her inner thighs. Jacob began to approach.

'Stay away from me you fucking madman! Get out of my house before I call the police!' Jacob was laughing hysterically as he smacked Alison hard across the cheek with the back of his hand, sending her falling back into a sitting position on the hall floor.

'Don't you realise how ridiculous you look Alison? Trying to give out orders with your cunt hanging out!'

Using her feet and hands, she pushed herself along backward away from her attacker, then quickly jumped up and raced towards the bathroom. 'Get back here bitch, I'm not finished with you yet.' Jacob shouted as he shot forwards and made a lunge for her. But Alison was too quick and the bathroom door slammed shut in his face followed quickly by the frenzied click of the bolt.

'Leave me alone Jacob! Get the fuck out of my house and leave me alone you fucking maniac!' Screamed Alison from inside. Jacob raised his foot to kick the door in, but quickly placed it back on the floor. Walking calmly back down the hall, he closed and locked the front door of the flat, removing the key from the mortis lock and tucking it into his trouser pocket. 'I'm not falling for that old trick… I know you're still out there Jacob. Do you think I'm stupid?'

'Not at all my love…' replied Jacob under his breath before running full-pelt down the hallway and throwing himself at the bathroom door. The tiny bolt pinged off like a teenage bra-strap; the door flying open to reveal Alison cowering between the toilet and the still running bath. She did not scream. 'Better shut this off before it overflows.' Said Jacob in disconcerting parental tones as he turned off the taps. In a reflexive, animalistic effort of self-preservation, Alison sprung up as Jacob leant forward over the bath and landed a blow to the back of his head with the heavy ceramic mermaid she had been hiding behind her back. The mermaid broke with a heavy thump causing Jacob to stumble and collapse into the bath. He stuck out a hand and grabbed Alison's wrist on his way, the sound of her screams diluted by rushing water as his head submersed momentarily beneath the surface. Using Alison's arm as an anchor, Jacob pushed and hauled himself quickly out of the water. As he emerged Alison confronted him brandishing. 'A toilet brush? For Christ sake Alison! I mean the ornament was a good idea, but a fucking lavvy brush?' Jacob became aware of his uncontrollable laughter once again; he wondered if he had ever stopped. Alison swung the toilet brush, stinging Jacob just above the left temple. 'Fucking cow... I only wanted to talk to you!' He shouted, connecting with a left hook on the point of her chin. She crumpled to the floor like a pile of dirty washing, a deep scarlet-purple gash opening on centre left of her bottom lip.

Semi-conscious, eyes rolling, Alison was mumbling, trying to say something. Jacob bent down to try and hear.

'Please... alone... leave... no, no... police...'

'Police! I'll give you the fucking police all right! I'm in control here, you fucking cow, not the police! They can't help you now; two-timing whore!' Jacob picked Alison up of the floor and perched her on the edge of the bath. 'Look at me Alison, focus!' He slapped her hard on both cheeks. 'Wake up! I'm not leaving until you apologise for what you've put me through.' But Alison was showing no signs of regaining consciousness. Jacob thought for a moment, then let her slip back into the bathwater. She sparked to life with a deep and frightened gasp almost instantaneously, and Jacob was upon her. 'What's his name bitch? What's his fucking name?' He shouted, restraining Alison by placing his hands on her shoulders. Alison was frightened, pleading.

'I.... I can't tell you Jacob, please leave me alone. I promise you I won't tell the police.' Unconvinced, fury intensifying, Jacob continued his interrogation..

'I've told you before bitch, I'm in control here!' He took a breath and seemed to calm himself. There was no laughter now. 'Alison, my love, please, just tell me his name.'

'No... please... I can't...not right now... you have to trust me!' Jacob's brief calm exterior evaporated

'Tell me his fucking name! Tell me you fucking whore! Tell me, Tell me TELL ME!'

Jacob was not sure how long he had been holding her head under the water. Alison's eyes stared widely back at him; she had stopped struggling and no breath broke the surface. He released the pressure and she floated upward. 'Now, all you have to do is tell me his name and this will all be over.' But for Alison it was already over. Her face bobbed just under the surface, eyes gazing intently at nothing, towel hanging loosely in the water exposing her breasts and upper torso. Jacob noticed the small raised scar just below her left nipple. She had told him it was the result of letting a pet hamster venture a little too far up her sleeve; the rodent had liked its new home so much that when she tried to remove it the little bastard anchored its teeth into the nearest part of naked flesh.

Sitting on the edge of the bath unable to tear his eyes away from her, the full impact of what had just happened begun to descend upon Jacob. He held his breath and listened, waiting for a shout of alarm, the thunder of running footsteps, the banging of fists on the door, shouting, sirens... But there was only the sound of his pounding heart hammering inside his head. Slowly, carefully he exhaled.

'What the fuck am I going to do now?' He asked Alison. But Alison offered nothing.

'Come on son, pull yourself together.' A voice; was it in his head? It sounded as if it was in the room.

'Who's there? Where are you?' Jacob stood up, looked around... nothing. The voice came again; it was familiar.

'I'm right here J.J. I've always been here. Now settle down and let's get this thing sorted.' 'Dad?'

'No time now son, get this place fixed up, we'll sort her out later.' Jacob did not question further and began picking up the debris scattered around the bathroom and hallway. *'Don't suppose this bint has a screwdriver knocking about lying around this joint?'*

'I don't think so dad, but I could get a butter knife from the kitchen drawer if that would be any good?'

'It'll have to do son, off you go.' Jacob found a butter knife in the kitchen drawer and ran back to the bathroom. *'Now get that lock screwed back on, and when you're finished with that you can start on the security chain on the front door.'*

The clean up was completed after mopping the floor using towels from the airing cupboard.

'Mind and take care of those wet towels J.J.'

'Yes dad, I will. Jacob's eyes caught Alison's as he leaned in and pulled out the bath plug. When she had sunk to the floor of the bath, he leaned in and lifted her out, placing her carefully onto the floor beside the bath.

'Come away now son, don't stare, you'll just upset yourself.' Jacob turned his back and quickly walked from the bathroom click-clocking the light off as he went.

'You need to get yourself to the gallery pronto. Better walk there though, you can't be placed anywhere near here… can't trust any of those big-mouthed taxi-drivers.'

'Yes dad, I'll go the back way, no-one will see me. I'll be like… a shadow.' Replied Jacob, putting the dirty-wet towels into the washing-machine.

'Nice touch son, but remember to put them in the tumble-dryer when you come back.'

'Are you coming with me to the gallery then dad?' Enquired an anxious Jacob.

'No son, I had better stay here and keep an eye on things. Now off you go J.J. and don't forget the keys, she keeps them on the hall table.'

'I know where the keys are dad, I have been here before you know.'

'And quietly does it son. We don't want any of the neighbours involved now, do we?'

'No we certainly wouldn't dad, things are messy enough. I'll be back as soon as I can. Thanks dad, I don't know what I would have done without you.'

'It's not finished yet son, but we're over the first hurdle at least. Now you had better get off before people start to miss you. Jacob looked around for someone to smile at, but only there were only shadows.

*

The corridor outside seemed darker somehow, the only noise was the echo of Jacob's heavy breath. Gradually, as he made his descent, the sounds of Saturday night, music, laughter, shouting, arguing, loving, begun to leak out from the various apartments and filter up the stairwell, mixing in a dissonant, deafening symphony of existence. Jacob shielded his ears, but must have trapped some vibrating airwaves with his hands as he did so because the noise was locked in his head. Picking up the pace, almost falling down the last few stairs, he made the exit and the pitiless freedom of the cold Glasgow streets.

Turning up his collar against the bitter wind and rain Jacob made for Great Western Road. A flash of car headlights edging round the corner caused him to spin and walk in the opposite direction. He turned off down the side of the building. There were no streetlights in the alley and the uneven cobbles caused him to stumble every now and then, but here Jacob was invisible. At the corner of the building he doubled back towards the street using a service road running between tenement blocks. Pausing to look up as he passed underneath Alison's flat, Jacob's saw the dark silhouette of a man illuminated from behind, in the kitchen window.

'Dad?' But by the time he had wiped the rain from his eyes the kitchen window was dark and empty. Head down and alone, Jacob hugged the shadows along the garden walls and continued on his way.

Further alley-ways and service roads provided an escape route to Great Western Road where Jacob merged easily with the flotsam and jetsam of the Saturday night throng. Trancelike, he glided rapidly along and over the Kelvin Bridge. Right turn, cross the road, left turn, down through Woodlands, no signs of slowing down, ignoring the growing stitch in his right side. *'Just got to keep going...'* Several minutes later Jacob's autopilot was navigating Sauchiehall Street. The gallery in sight he moved down to second gear and noticed that for the first time in what seemed like weeks it had actually stopped raining.

Outside the gallery Jacob found and carefully unfolded his sodden invitation. He flashed it to the men in black and was ushered inside to the main gallery, where he took up position at the top of the stairs to get a better view. At the far corner by the gents, surrounded by guffawing sycophants, stood the tidy figure of Mr Davis. Jacob pushed his way through the crowd towards him, grabbing a glass of complimentary champagne from one of the circulating waiting staff on the way.

'Jacob old boy, you made it!' Gushed Quentin in exaggerated tones, brushing his fan-club aside.

'I wouldn't have missed it for the world Quents!' Replied Jacob with equal artifice, icing the bull-shit cake with a counterfeit smile. 'So where's Justin then?'

'Oh you just missed him; gone to the little boy's room.' Quentin tapped the side of his nose and gave a playful wink and adding a rhetorical 'If you know what I mean...' Jacob reciprocated with a knowing smile and a slight nod of the head. Before Quentin could begin to introduce his entourage who were hovering like silent grinning morons waiting for an invite to the party. Jacob deftly parried and countered.

'Sounds like a plan to me Quentin! I think I might have to go and join him! Don't go away.' As he turned to go Quentin brushed a small hand over Jacob's cheek.

'I'll be waiting right here for you dear boy. And I promise, I won't move a muscle.' Jacob felt violated; he wanted to take Quentin's effeminate porcelain hand and crush it then watch that sleazy, smug expression twist and contort as his tiny bones snapped.

'But if things start to go pear-shaped, Quentin could prove a useful ally.' Much as he hated to admit it, Jacob needed to keep Quentin sweet... for now. *'Breathe, slowly in, slowly out...'* Antipathy subsiding Jacob unclenched his fists and

walked calmly to the gents. *'Slowly in, slowly out...'*

Every cubicle in the toilet was engaged. Bending down Jacob spotted Justin's tattered brown suede Hush Puppies shuffling awkwardly under the last door but one and hammered on the door with the side of his fist. 'Open up Mr Leitch, this is the fashion police! You're under arrest for gross miss-matching of certain items of clothing, namely blue trousers, a lime green shirt, an orange tie and that ridiculous sports jacket.' The door swung open to reveal a smiling Justin, the tip of his long aquiline nose frosted in white powder.

'Get in here you fool!' He urged grabbing Jacob by the lapels.

'Well, if you insist.' Replied Jacob as the agent manhandled him into the cubicle.

Jacob was managing to maintain a cool facade, but an inner storm was raging. He was quick to accept the offer of a small silver spoon piled with coke, greedily vacuuming it up his left nostril, eager for the hit to numb his senses and maybe make him forget who he was for a second or two.

'And when did *one* finally arrive then Mr Douglas?' Enquired Justin lighting two cigarettes and handing one to Jacob.

'About fifteen-twenty minutes ago.' He lied. 'Can't stay long though; need to see a woman about a shag.'

'You filthy slag!' replied Justin; Jacob gave him his best fake-rascal smile.

'Well at least you showed your face, that's the main thing.' continued Justin. 'Just be sure to get yourself photographed a couple of times before you go, we could really use the publicity.' Jacob nodded slowly and took a drag of his cigarette, blowing the smoke back into Justin's face.

'Yeah, whatever you say *boss*. So is this it for you Justin, or have you something else planned for later?'

'Not really planned as such; Quentin has invited me back to his place for a few drinks… you are welcome to join us of course.'

'Don't you remember? I've got a date.'

'Oh that's right, silly me!' replied Justin, relief apparent in his voice, 'Never mind, maybe some other time then.' Justin dug his little spoon into the bag of powder and sniffed deep. Jacob watched impatiently as the agent's eyes and nose began to stream. 'Here…' said Justin, pinching his nose with one hand and handing the bag and spoon to Jacob with the other, '…fill your boots!' Jacob eagerly accepted and dug in. Coming back down off the ceiling he actually had begun to feel human again; but it didn't last.

'Not my scene anyway.' Said Jacob handing the drugs back to Justin, who fixed him with a puzzled look. What the fuck are you talking about? What's not your scene?' Jacob looked at him and smiled,

'Playing gooseberry to a couple of old homosexuals.' Justin's expression changed to one of good hearted submission,

'And I thought I was being so cagey! It's nothing serious you understand. And even you must admit he is pretty fucking gorgeous.'

'Justin, you dirty big poof! Can you give me a fag for later, mine got mushed up by the rain. And it's one of the tobacco kind I'm after before you go getting any ideas.' Justin found his packet and offered Jacob a cigarette. He took three. 'Now I better go and say goodbye to Quentin. Are you coming?'

'Hopefully later!' Replied Justin with a smile that made Jacob's stomach turn and consider violence.

'Breath J.J. breathe! Just got keep it together for a little longer. Be out of here soon and then you'll be able to go home and relax for a bit before…'

As the two men exited the toilet, Quentin was busy chatting to a photographer from his newspaper. Spotting a gilt edged promotional opportunity, Justin grabbed Jacob by the elbow and hurried him over.

'Ah, there you two are.' Began Quentin, arms thrown out. 'Please, come and let my friend Brian here take your picture. I can assure you that he is very, very good…not a bad photographer either!' Brian visibly squirmed at Quentin's leering, but managed an awkward smile as he replied.

'No problem Quentin.' Then fired off five or six rapid shots. 'Got a few crackers there gents, should look good in the colour supplements this Sunday.' Brian spoke as speedily as his camera work. 'Anyway, must crack on, lots of faces to get around. Time getting on and all that.' The photographer shook each mans hand as he made his exit. 'Nice to meet you guys, and see you on Monday Quentin?'

'I won't be in the office until mid-week at the earliest Brian, few things to tidy up elsewhere.'

'Right you are Quentin,' replied Brian indifferently. A lizard smile slashed across his hungry mouth as he melted into the swarm.

A quickening in the pit of Jacob's stomach, urged him get out fast; he caught his agent's eye.

'I'm going to shoot off now too Justin; got to take care of that *thing* we talked about earlier.' Justin looked vacant for a second before recognition crashed into his eyes prompting a knowing smile.

'Okay Jake, your secret's safe with me. Mustn't keep your *thing* waiting, might go off the boil eh!' Jacob resisted the temptation to head-butt his agent and turned to Quentin.

'It's been really good to finally meet you at last Quentin, and thanks again for a great evening, it was... unreal!' Quentin took both of Jacob's hands in his and looked up into his eyes,

'Now Jacob, dear boy, are you sure you won't come back to my place for a night-cap?'

'*If you try and kiss me I'll fucking nut ye ya poof!*' Jacob managed to force a syrupy smile. 'No thank-you Quentin, wouldn't want to cramp your style, if you know what I mean? Two's company and all that crap.' He continued squeezing Quentin's hands so tightly that he felt him physically wince and pull away, giving

Jacob a huge rush of satisfaction. 'You two kids have a good night, but remember to be careful now. And don't be staying up too late!' He conclude turning to walk away. *That's it, always leave them laughing. They don't suspect a thing.*

The cold outside slapped him hard in the face, stinging salt-water from his eyes; Jacob sniffed and wiped the tears away with a jacket sleeve.

'Need to focus, need to focus, need to focus, need to focus, need to focus, need to...' he repeated, entering the long-night.

*

The aroma of strong coffee gave his flat a strangely comforting feel.

'You've got to be straight to do this J.J. If you get pulled over for drunk driving you've had it.' In the bedroom he rooted frantically around in his still packed luggage.

'It's got to be here somewhere!' More frenetic searching. 'BINGO!' Jacob shouted excitedly, pulling out the remnants of the bag of amphetamine from his father's funeral. 'This should do the trick.' He said, sucking his right index finger and eating the drug like a sherbet-dab.

Five cups of tar-like Colombian later, the clock told him that it was 12:30 am. 'Shit, still too early.' He thought about lying down on top of the bed for a while. 'Nope, can't risk falling asleep.' The absurdity of this thought made him laugh out loud. 'Who the fuck am I kidding? With the amount of stimulants circulating

304

in my bloodstream I'll be lucky to get any sleep in the next fucking month!' Jacob lay back on the couch and closed his eyes; but all he could see was her lifeless eyes staring out just below the water's surface. He got up and switched on the television. A daytime talk show, the British version of an American show where all the cheap, white trash go on to beat each other up, was being repeated for insomniacs. He stared blankly at the screen, not really taking anything in. 'Maybe a shower would pass the time?'

Entering the bathroom, images of Alison flooded Jacob's consciousness. He stared frozen at the bath.

'Snap out of it J.J. you've still got work to do.' He filled the washbasin from the blue tap, and submerged his head, the cold feeling good against his burning skin. Under the water Jacob opened his eyes to be confronted by Alison's dead face. His scream bubbled the water, evaporating into hoarse breath as Jacob threw himself back against the bathroom wall. *'It was only a bad dream J.J. that's all it was, only a bad dream.'* 'But I'm not asleep?' He sat against the wall shaking, eyes tightly shut, fists held against them, afraid to breathe. Time became an irrelevance.

'Come on now J.J. we've got to go'. Jacob's legs had cramped and were stubborn to comply when he tried to stand up, resulting in a staggering escape into the hallway. *'This needs to be over with.'* However, deep down Jacob knew that it would never be over.

*

Outside the air was still, dead silent. The engine of Jacob's car broke the calm like a brick through plate glass. Pulling out from the kerb, he quickly scanned the surrounding windows - no nets twitched, no lights snapped on. The five minute drive to Alison's flat seemed to take an eternity, Jacob making three stops on the way to check that he wasn't being followed. He pulled the car into an alleyway two buildings up from Alison's and used the service road running along the back to approach in stealth mode - headlights turned off. Sitting silently in his dark car, engine off, Jacob looked for signs of surveillance. When he was absolutely sure that no unwanted eyes were watching, he eased the car door gingerly open by instalments.

The back gate was bolted from the inside. Jacob tried but could not reach over far enough to release the catch. Keeping tight to the shadows, he edged cautiously around the side of the building and stood at the corner, out of the orange glare of the streetlamps and searched for signs of life. The coast appeared to be clear and Jacob ran quickly on tip-toe along the pavement and up the steps to the entrance. The key fumbled into the lock, turned and he was inside, hurrying upstairs. *'Secure your escape route J.J.'* Jacob stopped and jogged back downstairs to the rear exit and unlocked the door. *'The back gate!'*

In the garden he pulled back the large bolt and the gate swung loose. A number of green wheelie-bins standing to attention along the partition wall offered Jacob a method of transport from the backdoor to his car. He pulled one out, recoiling at the loud hollow scrape emitted as the bin was wrestled from its' bed and dragged it over beside the steps. *'Good improvising J.J., pity there's no easy way of getting her down here in the first place though.'* Jacob loosened his shoulders and began the ascent.

The silence in the hallway seemed to amplify each movement he made. Taking the key from his pocket sounded like the crash of a thousand cymbals falling onto rocks. Inside Alison's flat the air was uneasily calm. 'Dad?' whispered Jacob into the stillness, but there was no answer. He looked in the kitchen, the bedroom, the living-room, but there was no sign of his father. 'Are you still in the bathroom dad?' The light caught and glinted on a small puddle pushing out from the threshold; Jacob clenched a fist and pushed open the door with his leading hand. Inside was mute darkness. Jacob found the cord and pulled on the light. She was lying beside the bath where he had left her. The moment detonated into severe reality once again. Jacob sparked into action searching the flat frantically. 'Something to wrap her in... towels...blankets? Oh dad where are you now when I need you the most?' Jacob stood impassively in the hallway attempting to get his mind to activate. *'Try on top of the wardrobe in the bedroom son.'* 'Thank god! I don't think I could go through with this alone.' *'You had better hope that god has better things to do tonight than help you J.J. Now come on, we don't have much time.'*

On top of Alison's wardrobe he came across a tattered sleeping bag. 'Perfect!'

Shouted Jacob and rushed back to the bathroom.

He found himself automatically flicking on the light switch whenever he entered a

room. An action which was usually complemented by the pithy phrase,

'Stupid cunt!'

On The Road Again

He saw her face everywhere.

'For fuck sake Jacob, keep it together…you've got to keep it together…focus!' The car headlights illuminated a solitary figure walking by the side of the road just ahead causing him to lower his head in an attempt to obscure his face from view, glancing fleetingly at the figure as he passed. It was Alison. 'What the fuck? But it can't be.' Gasped Jacob, and stood hard on the breaks.

He sat frozen, hyperventilating, eyes fixed forward, afraid to look round. 'Just fucking do it.' Jacob urged himself. 'Just turn round and take a fucking look.' He closed his eyes and listened to the steady drum of the engine; building up energy, courage, momentum…then in one motion, spun round on the faux leather seat and opened his eyes. The roadside was empty save for numerous great and imposing trees, lit up red and spectral by the tail-lights, their dark limbs searching out, receding and bleeding into the ink-black night.

He shouldered open the driver-side door, ran to the rear of the car and flung open the boot. The bundle lay motionless where he had left it. A viral compulsion to unwrap it and look inside seized Jacob's brain, but his outstretched hand was repelled by an invisible reverse magnetism. He turned from the bundle in exasperation and raked back his wet hair, hoping desperately that this external stimulation would spark his brain to act. A small tree-branch lay on the grass verge by the side of the road. "That should do the trick." Said Jacob like a scoutmaster and trotted over to retrieve it. Using the stick Jacob gingerly levered back the top of the sleeping bag to reveal the damp blonde mop of Alison's hair. She was, most definitely, still in there. A chill shudder ran up and down his spine and he quickly closed the boot using the branch then stared at it for a moment wondering why he hadn't used his hand. Unable to establish a rational answer, Jacob tossed the stick back onto the grass verge and resumed his journey.

*

It's was nearly four am and around five miles to Loch Lomond. Jacob was wondering whether to go all the way in by car, or if he should park and walk the last few hundred metres. On balance, he considered that it was probably better to risk driving all the way rather than chance walking around in the dark carrying a corpse. Another wave hit him. 'What the fuck have I done?' He shouted and struck the steering wheel violently with the heels of both palms. 'Maybe if I just go to the police... tell them it was all a big mistake... an accident?' Jacob contemplated the possibility briefly before throwing it out of the car window. 'Who the fuck am I kidding? I know what they do to people like me in prison! I wouldn't have a snowball's chance in hell.' He thought he heard a voice whisper his name from the behind and anxiously scanned the empty back seat in the rear-view mirror. 'Dad?' No reply, only the whirr and grind of the engine and the noise of hard rubber on tarmac. 'looks like you're going to have to do this one on your own J.J

Jacob was almost there and slowed down, afraid of missing the turn-off. The old access road was so overgrown that he nearly did! It looked as if no-one had been there since his father had brought him and his brother as young boys. He killed the lights and shortly after the engine. The car crunched over gravel and dirt before leaving the road for uneven grassland, finally coming to a halt some twenty-five feet or so from the edge of the loch. The air was bitter and suffocating as Jacob exited the vehicle, pausing to gaze towards the water and plot his route through the undergrowth. Peeking out fleetingly from behind a cloud, the moon illuminated the tops of the trees and the fine grey mist that hung just above the water's surface. All was silence save for the rhythmic swishing-lap of the loch waves.

*

Jacob tried hard not to think as he swung the boot lid up and open, reasoning that it was not really Alison that lay wrapped in the sleeping bag. She was gone and all that remained was the empty husk she had once inhabited. It wasn't a human being he was about to commit to the loch but simply a piece of cold, dead meat. The light in the boot made the green and yellow of the sleeping bag seem electric against the blue-dark of country night. He attempted to reach a hand forward to pull back the bag and have one last look at her, but his fingers again refused to obey, curling back into a fist of revulsion. Jacob lifted the hand to his eyes and it opened like a flower. *'Just get on with it man.'*

Her awkward weight seemed much heavier now than when he had lifted her in passion. The muscles in Jacob's shoulders and lower back burned with exertion; sweat rained down heavily on his face and body. The edge of the loch was barely fifteen feet away, but his lungs burned and begged for more oxygen. Jacob stumbled and went over on his left ankle. There was a sickening crunch and pain instantaneously ripped through his foot and lower leg, but he managed somehow to right himself without dropping his load. The water glinted appealingly just a few feet in front; he struggled on, legs now feeling as if filled with molten lead. 'Come on you bastard!' Jacob urged his aching body, 'Nearly there.'

But the edge had sneaked up on him; Jacob and his burden plunged chest deep into the freezing black of the loch, the arctic water punching the air from his body as it hit. Jacob gasped sharply, trying desperately to fill his lungs, the silt under his feet slipping away the more he struggled against it. The water was now at his neck - oxygen refused to remain in his chest expelling itself at every opportunity in involuntary screeches.

Alison's dead weight dragged Jacob further into the loch, the water now kissing his lips. His father had told him how the loch shores fall sharply away not far from the waters edge, that he should never swim there alone, of how a twelve-year-old boy he knew at school had dived down one day to explore the hidden

313

depths and had never been seen again. The image of the boy falling into dark oblivion haunted Jacob every time his father had taken him fishing on the loch. He remembered wondering if the boy was still down there somewhere, eyes staring wide, waiting for a saviour who would never arrive. But Jacob wasn't ready to meet him just yet. Far enough in, he dropped his shoulder and let the current take his load, watching the bag slip off into the deep like some massive green eel. 'I'm sorry Alison, goodbye my love…'

There was a tug on Jacob's leg. 'What the fu…' The sleeping-bag had snagged on his trousers and was gathering momentum as the loch shelf dropped away steeply to the edge into darkness. He kicked frantically at the bag trying to free himself the loch darkening ominously as they descended. Jacob desperately grabbed at the loch bank attempting to find an anchor. His hands were scratched and bleeding, nails ragged and torn.

The ledge was in clear sight now and Jacob was frantically pulling at his trouser buttons, pain shooting from his wasted fingers. They ripped apart and he pushed them off, his lungs about to explode, and kicked frenetically for the surface.

The night air made the loch water feel almost warm as Jacob's face emerged. The moon again looked out and into the loch. Jacob paused and directed his eyes down through the gloom, picking out the dark shape of the sleeping bag drifting into the abyss. Alison's face protruded, her eyes pained, appealing, her lips silently shouting Jacob's name. 'Alison…you're…but how? I have to go back! I have to go...' But Alison had gone to find the lost boy.

One of the coolest new things was the colour of sound. He saw the old man's voice from downstairs as a golden brown, the low muffled barking of his dog a heather-purple. The laughing excitement of young children shone out vibrant yellow, the music on his radio was an overwhelming rainbow. It was only her voice echoing somewhere in the near distance that did not luminesce. Instead it burrowed further into the ink-black nothing, threatening to pull him under.

I See Darkness

Head thumping, stomach cramped and sickly, cold sweat running down his face and back. Jacob was unsure how long he had lain there on his studio floor. He rubbed the stubble on his chin trying to calculate without success how long it had been since his last shave. It had been increasingly difficult to tell truth from illusion, conscious from unconscious and Jacob scanned the room for clues as to where, when and indeed, if he had woken up. He raked the greasy damp hair from his eyes, back over the crown of his head catching and tearing the scalp with a ragged nail as he did so. The pain was minor compared to the razor cuts and cigarette burns he had become accustomed to, using it in recent times, as a barometer of reality - but it was pain nonetheless. Jacob dropped his guard and tried to sit up.

His lungs went into spasm and chest contracted uncontrollably, pain shooting up and through, exploding in a fit of coughing and phlegm. Rolling onto his face Jacob pushed painfully up onto hands and knees before making a lunge for the cigarettes and lighter on his work-table, managing to knock them onto the floor. He stretched to retrieve one of the three remaining cigarettes that had spilled out. Lifting the lighter, Jacob shakily lit up and inhaled.

As the fit subsided to a *petit mal*, he dragged himself up off the floor and collapsed into a battered armchair. Empty bottles littered the floor of the room; he had been trying to un-focus the world since '*it*' happened. Alison was everywhere. On the few occasions he had allowed himself to sleep, she manifested in his dreams like a demon. It was her reflection Jacob saw when he looked in the mirror; she appeared in every television show and newspaper. Her dead eyes taunted him from the bottom of whisky glasses. Only here in this room, in his small studio – bare floorboards, naked ceiling light, flaking paint-work, torn-peeling wall-paper, stained curtains - she seemed unable to penetrate. There were no mirrors in his sanctuary, his haven.

Jacob scavenged the debris for whisky, his eyes momentarily drawn by the newspaper article describing Alison's apparent suicide – the Sunday glossy beside with a picture of Justin, Jacob and Quentin smiling saccharin from its' pages.

'But this is worse than any prison cell my love...' He lurched forward and grabbed a dirty glass from the floor, and began crawling round emptying the dregs from the various bottles into it. However, after about ten minutes of scavenging, Jacob had gathered barely enough alcohol to get a small flea slightly tipsy. He sat back down on the unclothed floor and tried to think.

Another few minutes passed in which all possibilities that involved moving more than ten feet or connecting with another human being were summarily dismissed; but then through the thick alcoholic haze Jacob saw the faint glimmer of a light-bulb flicker somewhere above his head. Struggling to his feet, he staggered over to the shelves beside the window, and there amongst the emaciated oil paints, ruined brushes and charcoal dust, sought out a tin of paint thinner. 'Well needs must!' he said flipping off the lid. 'I've probably drank worse.' He poured a good measure into the glass, swirling it round in a vain attempt to get the two liquids to mix. 'Fuck it!' He conceded, and threw back the rancid cocktail. It burned all the way as it descended, not entirely as unpleasant as he had expected, at least not to begin with. As the liquid filtered into his empty stomach Jacob felt it bite and tear at his guts like acid and glass. He tried to scream as the pain knocked him to the floor, but no scream came, only a sound like air escaping from a punctured inner tube.

He lay involuntary foetal on his side, unable to remove the knees from his chest. An invisible hand turned the dimmer switch slowly down and the world grew darker.

Jacob gagged trying hard to keep the alcohol inside of him, the taste of paint thinner, whisky and bile gargling at the back of his throat in an attempt to escape. The room was a confusing, spinning fuzz. Jacob closed his eyes tight and held on. *'Just got to ride this out'*

*

Eventually his insides stopped turning cartwheels and the room scraped to a slow grind - a stylus jumping on a scratch. The pain gradually melted to a dull ache and Jacob's body unfurled, arms flopping unconsciously out to the sides, a soothing warmth washing over as he lay prostrate-messiah. Jacob scratched open his eyes -

the ceiling was still there where it had always been. Slowly, painfully, he sat up, spitting out the remnant vomit and wiping his mouth on a crusted shirt-sleeve, before rising unsteadily, one foot at a time. The light in the room seemed different... strange. 'Everything's fucking green!' He rubbed his eyes... still green... then looked at the empty glass on the floor and cursed, 'Fucking stuff! Green? Fucking Green!'

Once he had finished checking the lights for possible malfunctions and found nothing, Jacob considered the possibility that some kind of contaminant may have inadvertently spilled into his eyes as he lay writhing in agony earlier. He turned to search for a mirror, but remembered quickly. 'Alison...' Jacob pulled things off shelves, out of boxes, drawers looking for a reflective surface. He tried wiping the surfaces of glasses, of whisky bottles, but nothing Jacob could find was any good. Another flash of inspiration detonated and Jacob grabbed the curtains and yanked hard.

A cracking noise preceded the curtains tumbling down, pulling the filthy, dusty nets with them as they fell to the floor, exposing the window. Jacob looked hard into the glass and there staring back at him were Alison's dead eyes. 'No, no, no! He screamed and attempted to lift the destroyed curtain pole back into place. It was no use - his earlier enthusiasm had gouged great holes in the wall where the fixings used to be. Jacob threw the tangled mess to the floor and turned his back on the window.

She was in front of him skin green and peeling, body bloated in putrefaction. 'How could I let you in?' Jacob made for the door trying desperately to escape. Alison stood dripping and naked in the hallway, hands outstretched. He flung the door shut and thrust the heels of his palms hard into his eyes until the pain bit and he saw stars. 'In darkness Alison! You can't touch me there!' Jacob concluded and ran to the work table, grabbed up the tin of paint thinner and poured it into his eyes.

'AAAAAAAAAAAAAAAARRRRRRRRRRRRRRGGGGGGGGGGG!!!!!!!!!!!!!!'

Pain stabbed like burning coals being pushed into his head. The world fell away studio, flat, tenement building, Glasgow, Scotland... All receding beneath him into the liquid black until he felt... nothing.

Alone at last in darkness.

Book 2

MOVING PICTURES

Burning crimson red soon deepened to ink black solidity. No shard of light under the doorway, no chink in any curtain, just...darkness.

In the beginning, the very beginning, flashes of lightning, blue green electric sparks would light up the outlines of faces, buildings, trees, his father towering miles above him. It had filled the doctors with hope and Jacob with foreboding. But the storm quickly passed, never to return. Memories, neuron-images, chemical photographs, unconscious thought made into three dimensional reality; not real vision at all -phantom sight, his brain adjusting to the loss as it would if Jacob had lost an arm or a leg.

The doctors had tried to console him by saying that his particular flavour of blindness was not always permanent, that there were things that could be done, procedures, transplants. But Jacob was having none of it, he liked his new home. No longer limited to the space he was in, Jacob could now visualise the world beyond, stretching off into infinity and time. In his mind were constant images, not visual, but of another substance, four-dimensional. He was inside his thoughts, tangibly experiencing them as quickly as they flowed through his consciousness, moving within the infinity of his introspection.

*

'It is no longer black since I discovered that my mind is not located within my head. I know how it feels to travel at the speed of light, to fly. These things have always been in my soul. I have been forced to discover this inner realm because the outer light has been extinguished. I always wanted to paint what was inside, but could never unlock the door. Now I live in my dreams and colourful emotions. I never think about what people look like anymore, I don't care about their faces because I recognise them in my soul. Sight had allowed me to become superficial; I thought that there was nothing outside my perception. But now I realise that the most fantastic of landscapes, the most exquisite beauties, are actually here on the inside.'

LEVIATHAN

'Bitter cold November. I sit on the shore and listen to your soul singing to me. My eyes have gone but my cold heart can still see across the waves. Your song ceases and the waters grow still and silent once more. Every day I come here and wait patiently for you to appear. Weeks have gone by. I sometimes feel like giving up, have you left me forever?

Wait.... Oh sweet angels voice again, is this a hand I see in the midst of the loch? How can I be certain? I plunge my head under the surface and glimpse the silver blue of your body, the swirling gold of your hair. Beautiful music surrounds me.

I awaken to cold darkness yet again.

*

Soon I will join you in the black, black depths. Down below where the light does not penetrate, down below where there is no sound. Deep into the bottomless void where I should have stayed with you before when I had the chance. But soon my love I will come to you and we will remain frozen forever in the unquestioning morality of silence.'

Sculpture Garden

I exit the bus and have the driver point me in the direction of the information office. The assistant there seems somewhat surprised to see me, but is only too happy, if a little over-enthusiastic for my liking, to lead me where I want to go. The bench is right by the waters-edge. He is guiding me lightly by my right elbow. I can hear the water getting closer as we stop and reverse slowly towards the seat.

'Okay here sir?'

I sit down and fold away my white cane.

'Aye son, this is fine.'

I hear the assistant take a step back and pause, and imagine him standing there with an inane smile slashed across his face.

'Now sir, there's a path directly in front of you - to the left leads right round to the other side of the loch, and if you take this one to the right, it'll lead you back towards the toilets, the shop and of course the information office. I'm afraid at this time of year the shop has restricted opening times, but I'll be in the office until four-thirty if you need anything or even if you just fancy a tea or a coffee. You'll probably need one later to heat you up!'

I wish that he would just shut up and leave, but I don't want to raise any suspicion. Just try to appear as anonymous as possible. Blend into the scenery.

' Thanks son, maybe pop in on my way back. I'll just sit here for a while and listen to the water...get some fresh air.'

'Well there's plenty of that today sir! Not many people make it up here this time of year so you'll get peace and quiet.'

I smile in the direction I think the assistant might be looking.

'Okay then sir, I'll say goodbye then.'

I begin to relax as the assistant's footsteps recede. But the steady crunch of gravel stops too soon. I hear the assistant spin round and immediately tense up.

'Oh sir, if you do need to go anywhere please be sure and stick to the path. The edge of the loch is just a few feet in front of you on the other side of the path. There's a sharp drop hidden in there, it's quite treacherous, even if you *can* see. Oh I am sorry sir... I didn't mean...'

I force my face into what feels like a smile.

'Don't worry about it. No offence taken.'

'It's just... well *we* wouldn't want you falling in sir, especially not in this weather.'

The assistant is stammering, clearly embarrassed and in a desperately attempt to backtrack. I try hard but I suspect, unsuccessfully to mask an ironic smile as I reply.

'Absolutely not, that would be a tragedy right enough.'

An uncomfortable silence follows. I'm worried I might have given the game away. I need to say something quickly.

'Don't worry about me son, I'll not be moving from this spot. Well not for an hour or so anyway, then I'll be down for that cup of tea.'

The assistant gives a short falsetto laugh.

'Right you are sir. I'll see you in a bit then.'

And with that he beats a hasty retreat. I wait until the assistant's footsteps have melted into the distance before standing up and walking towards the sound of lapping waves. A crisp breeze is whipping up off the water burning my nostrils with icy freshness. The crunching gravel of the path underfoot gives way to cold-wet-grass, short and managed at first, but very soon, longer, wild, natural, tangling and pulling at my feet and ankles. After a short trek my foot falls upon natural uneven stone. The water makes a different noise here - violent, boiling, crashing and dangerous. This is the spot, where the land has fallen away to reveal a deep v-shaped fracture in the naked bedrock. Sheer vertical slabs of rock smoothed by millennia of unrelenting waves, forming a lethal cell from where escape would be highly unlikely, if not impossible. I had almost fallen in here as a boy. Only the quick wits and strong hands of my father rescued me on that occasion. I stop for a second and listen, but my father is not here to save me this time. Almost unconsciously I step up on the ledge. My heart beats faster with every pounding wave. Oxygen races through his chest and into my brain, the same rush felt when looking over the edge from a great height, or when driving a car too fast through the blinding rain of a thunderstorm. Very strange; I've always associated this feeling with vision, with seeing exactly how far I might fall or how fast I was going, with seeing arise hazards in the road, possible dangers, what might happen. But this time is different. As the angry waters of the loch beat the rock below, I know exactly what is going to happen. I know exactly what I am going to do. Very soon now my love, very soon...'

'Hey mister! You're a bit close to the edge there! Don't you think you should come away back a bit before you fall in?'

A strange male voice brakes in somewhere in the near distance behind me. 'Are you ok?' The voice continues. I try hard to ignore it as I step my other foot up onto the ledge. The voice comes again, pleading this time.

'Mister, don't take another step... Please! Walk back over towards me, that bit you're standing on is really dangerous, I don't need another funeral on my hands right now.' The voice sounds youngish, early...mid twenties maybe? I step back from the ledge. Can't afford to involve anyone else. This has to be done properly. There can be no return. I resolve to wait it out, act dumb.

'Sorry son, I get a bit confused now and again. Haven't got used to this blind thing yet.'

I say turning in the direction of the boy's voice and making a show of un-pocketing and flicking out my white cane to full extension.

'Oh sorry mister, I didn't realise.'

The young man says apologetically. I hear footsteps moving quickly towards me.

'Here, let me help you.'

A strong but gentle hand grasps my arm just above the left elbow.

'Come over and have a seat next to me.'

He continues leading me back over towards the bench.

'Thanks very much son.'

I say, trying hard to sound thankful. I remember something the boy had said that puzzled me.

'So, what did you mean by *another funeral*? Not anyone close I hope.'

We reach the bench and sit down. Alison's face is trying to break through, but only patches make it. I hear the young man pause and take a breath. It's hard to tell whether he is uncomfortable with the subject or the weather conditions.

'I'm sorry son, it's none of my business. I shouldn't have asked.'

'No, honestly it's okay. It's just that, well the thing is, I haven't really spoken to anyone about it yet, even though I can't seem to think about anything else. And yes, she was pretty close or rather she was beginning to be. I didn't really get the chance to get to know her as well as I wanted to.'

'I know exactly how you feel.'

Alison tries to break through again. This time it is a struggle to block her out.

'Well I'm glad one of us does.'

Replies the boy. There is an echo of sad laughter in his voice. His reaction intrigues me so I probe further.

'What do you mean?'

There is a momentary gap in the conversation. I sense the boy's unease.

'It's okay son, you don't have to tell me. I know how hard these things can be.'

'No it's fine mister, really. I want to tell you. I need to tell someone. It's like, before the funeral, I didn't really feel anything much. I was in shock or something I think her death hadn't really sunk in. But when they came to bury her body, all these people I didn't even know kept coming up and telling me how sorry they were at my loss. My loss! They knew her better than I ever did, even though I am her brother.'

He pulls me further in.

'So you never really knew your sister? I don't mean to pry, but how did that happen?'

I hear the boy turn in his seat so he is facing towards me. His voice lowers.

'Our dad was killed in a car crash so mum was left on her own. She couldn't afford to bring both of us up so I was sent off to live with my aunt. She brought me up as her own and no one knew any different until my real mum got cancer and.... Oh sod it! I may as well tell you the real story; we'll probably never see each other again anyway. Oh, sorry mister, no offence.'

333

I give a conciliatory laugh and reach out to pat the boy on the shoulder but miss, brushing his cheek instead.

'Don't worry son, none taken. Carry on.'

'Well, mum got pregnant to a married man when she was only fifteen. She was sent off to live with my aunt Effie, in the country. When the baby was born, a little girl, Effie and her husband Frank, good, clean decent people, said they would bring the baby up as their own, to give my mum a second chance kind of thing. But as soon as she arrived back in Glasgow, she jumped straight back into bed with the married man. He got her up the duff, yet again, only this time the family disowned her.'

'That's harsh son. And the second child, that was you?'

'Got it in one...ermm? Shit, I don't even know your name.'

'Jacob... my name is Jacob, but call me Jake.'

I extend my hand into the darkness and feel the boy take it and shake firmly.

'I'm Daniel Addison... Dan. Pleased to meet you Jacob, sorry Jake.'

'Pleased to meet you too. Well now that we know each other...'

'Yeah, old friends eh! Where was I? Oh yeah, my so-called family! So they appeased themselves by claiming that they'd tried their best with mum, but that she was obviously a *little trollop* who couldn't keep her knickers on. As far as they were concerned she was beyond help. So that was that. Mum and me were left to get on with it. She had to work two jobs - her main one at a hosiery during the day and an extra little job behind the bar of a local hotel at night. She didn't get paid anything for the hotel job, but the owner, Mr McDonald, Eddy, used to let us live there rent free, meals thrown in as well. He was really good to us was old Eddy, more of a father to me than anyone.'

'And what about your biological father, did you ever see him?'

'My father, if you can call him that, very occasionally sent mum some money. He came to see us a couple of times, but I don't remember much about him; only smells really, tobacco on his fingers, whisky on his breath. Can't remember how old I was the last time I saw him - must've been only about five or six. Anyway, to cut a very long story a little bit shorter, mum eventually got married to Eddy. He must have been at least seventy at the time, but I don't blame mum; she'd had it hard all her life and when Eddy offered her the comfort and security of a roof over her head and a steady business, naturally she grabbed it with both hands and held on tight. Eddy only lasted another couple of years. I still really miss him. He didn't have any children of his own so he left everything to mum and me.'

'I'll bet a distraught relative or two crawled out of the woodwork when they heard that there was a hotel up for grabs?'

I interject cynically, immediately regretting that I have spoken.

'Sure, a couple of money grabbing, very distant relatives threatened to contest the will, claiming that mum had forced Eddy to change it so that she'd inherit everything. But the truth was that Eddy had his lawyer change the will long before he and mum got hitched. She didn't know anything about it! He just wanted to make sure that we would be okay, you know? That's the kind of man Eddy was. So nothing ever came of the protests and mum and me lived a relatively comfortable life from then on. I worked hard at school, helped mum around the hotel when I could, studied hard and eventually got accepted to art school.'

My spirit leaps! A fellow artist?

'Oh! So you're an artist? I used to be a painter, before this.'

I point to my eyes.

'Portraits mainly. Managed to scratch a living. And you Dan, what did you study?'

'Fine art, to begin with, started off painting the figure, but I felt so constrained. I needed to do more than just create two-dimensional images, they seemed so flat, distant…lifeless almost. So I switched to sculpture half way through my second year. I was bashing away quite unsuccessfully at a big hunk of clay in one of the studios, wondering if I had made the right decision when it just came to me… like an epiphany… a revelation. I saw myself as a child elbow deep in the school playing fields trying to make a man out of the mud. I think I had just heard or read the bit in the book of Genesis about god creating Adam from earth, and I was having a go myself. I had completely forgotten about it until then, but had always been obsessed with recreating the human form; I just didn't know why. From that moment on my work has taken on a whole new dimension. I find it a very spiritual thing, religious almost. It's still so amazing to me that I can take a pile of what is basically mud, and using my own hands, give it shape and form give it a personality and life of its own.'

I try hard to hide my frustration at this digression. It is all very interesting, but I want the boy to get back to the main event! I thus greet this dissection of his artistic origins with stony silence. The silence extends and becomes a little uncomfortable. I think about spouting some words of reciprocal appreciation, but I'm anxious for Dan to regain the thread and consequently offer nothing more than a knowing smile and a slight nod of the head. I hear the boy shifting uncomfortably before he continues. 'So there I was, nineteen years old, and I actually knew what I was going to be doing for the rest of my life. There was passion and purpose in my art. It was what I was born to do. By the time I was twenty-one my work was selling all over the country and I was building quite a healthy reputation. So I finished my degree and right away got the offer of a post-graduate scholarship to go and study in New York. I couldn't believe it. It was like all my birthdays and Christmases coming at once!'

I feel like giving the boy a shake and screaming at him to stop being such a bloody self-indulgent little shite and talk to me about heartbreak, depression and death, but manage to restrain myself and force another knowing smile instead.

'I would probably still be in the States right now if mum hadn't got the cancer.'

'That's more like it! I straighten myself up on the bench and try not to look too eager.

'Two and a half years she suffered with it; fought it all the way. It was towards the end that she told me about my sister. It took me nearly three months to track her down - she'd moved around quite a bit. By the time I found her, mum had already died. When I was sorting through her things I found some old photos of my father along with a couple of his letters - probably the only letters he ever sent her. It didn't take too long to find him though; I read his obituary in the newspaper the very next day! He had died of a massive stroke apparently. Can you believe that? The day after my mother! All of a sudden I was an orphan. Pretty weird eh?'

Recognition swoops like a hunting eagle, slashing at my breast, tearing into my heart. Dan continues.

'Then I found my sister. Aunt Effie had never told her the truth, you know that she wasn't her real mother, or who her real parents were. But now my sister's dead too. The police say they don't know if it was murder or suicide; she didn't leave a note.'

This time Alison breaks through. I see her surface at the centre of the loch, arms outstretched, eyes pleading.

'This is where they found her, washed up on the shore over there to the right.'

I watch as she emerges slowly from the water, her lips moving, speaking, but I can't make out the words.

'I didn't have her in my life for very long, but she was my sister. It felt as though I had known her all my life, like we'd never been apart. She would never have done herself in, it wasn't in her nature, she wasn't the type. She was so full of life, so vibrant, you know what I mean?'

'Oh yes Dan, I *know* exactly what you mean.'

Alison is almost on the shore now. I strain to hear her voice, but she is still too far off.

'I believe there's an invisible bond between siblings and no matter how far apart they are, that connection always holds them together, drawing them to each other.' She is on the shore walking towards me.

'I feel as though I should be a man about the whole thing and accept the inevitability of death and all that crap. But the truth is I don't want to be a man about it, I want to be a baby, I want to scream and roar and cry. I want my mother and my sister to come and give me a cuddle, tell me everything is going to be okay, that the bogie man has gone and the sun is coming out! But I don't have anyone; I'm all alone in this fucking world! It's just not fair!'

'You're not alone Daniel.'

Alison stands just a few feet in front of me now. She reaches out to touch my face and speaks once more. This time I can hear every word.

339

'I love you Jacob.'

'No, Alison would never have left me all alone like this. I told her that our father was dead, showed her his obituary. I even took her to his graveside! No, she would never have left me on my own, not after everything that we had been through. Some bastard's done this to her and I just hope to god that the police find him before I do!'

I reach out a hand to touch her, but she is already receding into the atmosphere.

'Alison… I love you too.'

My hand drops back to the bench the dull thud causing Daniel to turn his attention on me.

'Oh Jake, you're crying. I'm sorry mate, I didn't mean to upset you.'

I clear my throat and wipe away the tears with the sleeve of my coat.

'There's no need for you to feel sorry for me Dan, I'll be just fine. But I need you to listen to me, I have a confession to make.'

POSTSCRIPT

Look around you, wherever you are. People going about their business, many different expressions on the young and old and ancient faces. Some are smiling, some laughing, others scowling and angry.

But most showing no emotion all.

Trapped within their mortal shells, they create personal worlds within worlds. Here they are the centre of everything, here they can do anything, be anyone. In their private universes they have the power of creation, of life and death.

Look around you once again.

Do all these people still seem the same to you? All have an opinion, a story to tell.

In their minds they are the law.

The world begins and ends with them.